What's Blood Got To Do With It?

SCANLIFE

[Scan Barcode w/Mobile Device for more information]

What's Blood Got To Do With It?

Shelia E. Lipsey

NorthStar
www.BonitaAndHodgePublishing.com

What's Blood Got To Do With It?"
Copyright 2012 Shelia E. Lipsey

ISBN: 0983893519
ISBN-13: 978-0-9838935-1-6

First Edition October 2012
Printed in the United States of America

10 9 8 7 6 5 4 3 2 1

This is a work of fiction. Names, characters, places, and incidents either are products of the author's imagination or are used fictitiously. Any resemblance to actual events or locales or persons, living or dead, is entirely coincidental.

Library of Congress Control Number: 2012904894

Cover designed by HPP Designs

What's Blood Got To Do With It?

Shelia E. Lipsey

Other Books by Shelia E. Lipsey

BEAUTIFUL UGLY SERIES

(Book 1)
Beautiful Ugly

(Book 2)
True Beauty

MY SON'S WIFE SERIES

(Book 1)
My Son's Wife

(Book 2)
My Son's Ex Wife-The Aftermath

(Book 3)
My Son's Next Wife

(Book 4)
My Sister, My Momma, My Wife

STAND ALONE NOVELS
Always, Now and Forever Love Hurts
Into Each Life
Sinsatiable

BENDED KNEES ANTHOLOGY
Against the Grain

GROUP NOVEL
Show A Little Love

NON-FICTION
A Christian's Perspective – Journey Through Grief

"If you enter this world knowing you are loved and you leave this world knowing the same, then everything that happens in between can be dealt with." Michael Jackson

Acknowledgements

To every reader, book club, every person who has ever taken the time to read one of my books, I must tell you how deeply grateful I am. To everyone who ever thought that I could do the unthinkable, reach the unreachable, attain the unattainable, and live the dream that only a good God could place in my heart and within in my spirit – I cannot go without saying, thank you. To my mother, my late father, my sisters Sandy, Vette and Vonne, my sons Kevin and Jay, my grandsons Kevin, Jr., Leland, and Kaleb, I thank you for loving me, believing in me, and always thinking the best of me. To my goddaughter, Ladetria, who takes tremendously good care of me, and to my one and only bright, smart, beautiful, intelligent, kind, loving, and outstanding niece, Shante', I love you so much. To my family, my friends, and loved ones, I love you and praise God for feeding my spirit, for helping me become the person God already sees me as being.

God's Amazing Girl, Shelia

Prologue

"Blood is thicker than water."

November 1, 1989

Upon exiting the womb, the newborn uttered a barely audible cry. Was it born of prophetic significance? Everyone nearby heard it. Immediately, it was whisked away. A flurry of nurses preened, sucked, injected, and wiped this one so small, so fragile, and so precious. The difficult delivery had left the mother's braided hair a glowing, damp mess.

Tears slowly cascaded down the mother's pinkish cheeks as she whispered, "Adanya."

"Come again?" said a nurse nearby.

"Adanya." The teenage mother nodded and repeated the name. The hard delivery, coupled with a sedative, put the mother into a deep sleep.

1

"Pity is stronger than love." Unknown

2012

Tar black heels attached to shapely brown legs click-clacked across the cement floor. Self-assuredness marked each step. She was the personification of confidence. A black and white thigh-length dress typified her aura. A high-powered executive? She was not. A self-made millionaire? She was not. A well-kept mistress? She was not. A successful businessman's wife? Not that either. A high-priced call girl? Nope. Born with a silver spoon? Sort of.

Adanya Katherine Anniston lived in a world of her own. A world surrounded by lushness, where the sight of money and power was an everyday occurrence, but also a world that included love of God and family. She graduated from a prestigious all girls' preparatory school in Memphis at the age of sixteen and soon after entered Spelman College.

Adanya appeared to have everything a twenty-two year

old Communications and Cultural Master's graduate could imagine. She was raised by loving parents who were not severed by divorce like so many other families. The Anniston's were successful in their own right.

Adanya adored her naturally curly, coarse, brown hair, along with her pronounced Puerto Rican and African ancestral facial features. She was gorgeous in her own classification of how physical beauty is often defined.

Her Puerto Rican mother, born in the Bronx of New York; and her father, a black man from the heart of Memphis, the Bible Belt some called it, defined her in ways she would come to learn more about throughout life.

Her maternal grandparents, Eva and Maurice Kaplan, Sr., much like a storybook tale, met and fell in love while attending Lemoyne Owen College in Memphis, Tennessee. For years, the Kaplan's played a pivotal role in education as teachers, fought for civil rights as people of color; and stood boldly to proclaim their faith and belief in what was right. They were the proud parents of identical twin girls, Annalisse whose name carried on the Puerto Rican heritage of their family, and Anaya, the African side.

◊

Adanya strolled in the small classroom full of college students. Many were like her, from the affluent, society driven, upper class sector. She gracefully approached her desk, placed her phone on top of it, and set her laptop tote next to it.

"Good afternoon. I trust each of you had an adventurous and pleasant weekend." Adanya smiled slightly. Without further salutations, she began lecturing the class of fourteen students.

Adanya had initially considered teaching public high school, but quickly decided against it after she consulted with her dearest confidante, her father. He was glad she wanted to continue in the field of Education like her grandparents, but he also encouraged her to increase her vision and not settle for being a teacher.

Adanya and her father, Kenneth John Phillip Anniston, were definitely a close pair. He absolutely adored his only child and daughter. He loved her infectious smile, the innocence she portrayed, her gracefulness, and the love she had for him, which was immeasurable. Anything he could do for her, Kenneth was willing to do.

Adanya, after all, was a precious gift from God. Her name alone appeared to instill within him a sense of pride because of its Nigerian meaning - 'her father's daughter.'

The family background and how her name was derived was not a talked about subject, nor was it part of Kenneth's past that he chose to discuss. But true to his heritage, and much like his wife, his spiritual beliefs had brought him through the steep, tough rungs of the past.

Not only were the Annistons wealthy monetarily, but they were wealthy in the blessings of their relationship. A strong couple, Annalisse and Kenneth remained faithful to each other even in lieu of their successful lifestyle. Many times money and power ruined marriages but not the Annistons. They were known throughout their neighborhood and at their church for their philanthropic work and kind spirit.

Adanya was the type of child that soaked up everything her father told her. She was daddy's girl, one whom when she was little, loved to climb on his lap whether he was at work in his huge office overlooking the mid-south, or at home resting comfortably in the family library sitting in his pillow-soft, indigo recliner. Adanya may have been an adult, but she still relied heavily on her father's love, guidance, and direction.

◊

Adanya slowly strolled back and forth from one end of the classroom to the other as she lectured. "Gunther Kress in Communications and Culture states, 'Communication, the idea is a matter of great interest. Great jobs are linked to the skill level of communication. Promotion in a job depends on it...'"

Adanya's form of college lecturing seemed to have a magnetic effect on her students. If one searched around the state-of-the art class room at the faces of the students, all eyes were pointed in her direction with an uncanny type of magnetism. Adanya, after all, wasn't much older than most of them. Sometimes it was hard for her to make that distinction and to maintain professionalism after being approached by some handsome, smart, going somewhere young men, in not only her class but throughout the college campus. Being an assistant professor at such a young age was tough, but she wouldn't trade her job or position for anything in the world.

Her first lecture of the day ended right before noon, just in time to meet her friend, Nanette, at the coffee shop less than a block away from the college campus.

Nanette was a guidance counselor for a private all boys' school a few blocks away from where Adanya taught.

"On my way 2 the coffee shop," Adanya texted.

"Already here. Goin n now. Will get us a seat."

"K." texted Adanya, and continued walking toward the

coffee shop.

◊

"Hey, girl," said Nanette when Adanya approached the table. "I already ordered your turkey burger combo."

Adanya sat down in the chair across the table from Nanette. "Thanks. I appreciate it."

"No problem. So, how has your day been so far?"

"Umm, pretty calm. Nothing much going on. I have a couple of more lectures before I'm finished for the day. What about you?"

Nanette shrugged her shoulders. "Same old same old. But I'm not complaining. I'm blessed to have a job."

The server brought both of their lunch orders. Before eating, Nanette stretched out her hand and automatically Adanya grabbed hold of it. They bowed their heads and Nanette blessed their food.

"Amen," they said in unison after the short prayer.

"Hey, would you like to go to a Grizzlies game with me and daddy tonight? Daddy has an extra season ticket."

Nanette shook her head. "I wish I could but I have college entrance essays to read tonight. You mean your daddy isn't out of town at one of those tech conventions he frequents. I thought he rarely missed them."

"Believe it or not, lately he's been spending more time in the office rather than flying around the country like he usually does, unless it's absolutely necessary, of course. He has a good team of loyal employees in place that he hired from some of the cities he frequents, and it's decreased his workload tremendously.

"I know you're glad about that, because you act like you and your daddy are joined at the hip." Nanette giggled.

"Yeah, I'm more than glad. I don't like all of that

traveling he has to do and the IT business is so demanding. I don't want him to be heartbroken because I'm not enthralled with the IT business to the extent that he is. I mean, I have nothing against it, because it's provided us with the comfortable lifestyle that we enjoy," Adanya said between taking a bite and chewing her juicy grilled turkey burger.

"I'll probably become more involved a few years down the line, but not right now. Too hectic for me." Adanya smiled, and took a handful of fries and stuffed them into her round mouth.

"It's still good to know you have your father's business if you ever decide to go that route." Nanette sipped from her cup of iced decaf coffee, followed by a bite of her sandwich. "Hey, forget about work, maybe it's time we get a love life, girl." Nanette grinned. "Or should I say, maybe it's time you get one." Nanette pointed a finger at Adanya for emphasis.

Adanya giggled and wiped her mouth with her napkin. "Where did that come from? I don't need a man in my life, at least not right now. I do not have time, even if I wanted one. It'll only complicate matters. When it's time, he'll find me."

"Love is never complicated, dawling," Nanette said in an exaggerated southern drawl and with one hand flowing in the air.

Adanya waved her off. "You are too crazy for me. Anyway, my daddy says I have plenty of time for a relationship. He wants me to concentrate totally on me for now." Adanya placed her hand flat against her busty chest.

"Your daddy, your daddy. To listen to you talk, the only person in your life is your daddy. I never hear you say anything about Mrs. Anniston. We've been friends since college, and I can count on one hand the times you've talked about her. She's such a nice woman too. And talking about pretty, you've got her looks."

"I love my mommy. You know that, but you also know that she can go off on a tangent sometimes. She has select friends she deals with, and you know it. My mother is what I call a social diva. All of her time is spent working on some project or charity, so I do not interfere with that. Plus, I can't help it if I'm a daddy's girl. I have his blood running through these voluptuous veins," said Adanya without a hint of conceitedness. She ran her hand up and down the length of her arm and smiled.

Nanette shook her head. "You are so silly."

The two friends continued eating lunch. They commented in whispers about several cute guys that walked into the coffee shop. Some of them were total hotties, whom they tried to guess if they worked at the Executive Plaza a couple of blocks away, or on campus, or some of the other nearby businesses. A couple of them Adanya had seen before, eating lunch at the popular spot. Then there were one or two Adanya recognized as students she'd seen on campus.

A few minutes into their girly game, Adanya's eyes engaged with eyes that reminded her of the ocean and skin that reminded her of the sands of Siesta Key.

Nanette followed Adanya's eyes. "Who are you looking at?" Adanya didn't have time to respond because those ocean eyes were gazing into hers.

"Hello, how are you ladies doing this afternoon?"

Adanya shifted her gaze and locked eyes with Nanette.

Nanette, speechless, looked at the hunk standing before them and shrugged her shoulders.

"Are you talking to us?" Adanya glanced up.

"Of course," he answered. "Definitely you."

Nanette cleared her throat, then took her napkin and poised it over her mouth to shield the smile Adanya saw form on her face.

"I'm fine. Thank you."

"Me too," quipped Nanette and took a sip from her straw.

"I'm Bleak…Bleak Blessinger," he said and extended his hand toward Adanya.

Adanya hesitated then glanced over at Nanette like she was pleading for help. Nanette gave none so Adanya shook his hand.

"Hello," answered Adanya without giving up her name." Uh, how can we help you?"

"Well, you can help me out a lot if you would tell me your name," he said in a flirty manner.

"I don't think so." Adanya suddenly felt a light but swift kick on her shin from Nanette.

"Ouch," she said.

"Something wrong?"

"No, not at all. But if you'll excuse us, we only have a few minutes to finish our lunch and get back to work."

"Oh, of course. I'm sorry. I didn't mean to be rude. But I've seen you somewhere before. I can't quite remember where. I thought knowing your name might trigger my memory."

"Ohh, that's ashamed." Nanette continued to sip on her coffee, not mumbling a word. Adanya made a mental note to let Nanette have a mouth full as soon as she could get rid of Bleak.

"Well, Bleak, I'm not sure where you've seen me, but I really don't have the time for conversation right now."

"Sure. Understood. Maybe I'll run into you again."

"Yeah, maybe." Adanya then turned away. Bleak walked away and headed out of the crowded restaurant.

"Girl, he was fine. I can't believe you wouldn't tell him your name."

"Are you crazy? That was nothing more than a cheap pick up line. He's probably one of the college students on campus. Just being a flirt, that's all." Adanya took the last bite from her sandwich and washed it down with her remaining soda. "Let's get out of here."

They paid their checks and proceeded outside. Stopping on the side of the entrance to the coffee shop, they chatted some more.

"Since you're going to the game, I guess I won't be talking to you tonight." Nanette huddled herself inside her thick top coat to ward off the biting winter weather.

"Probably not. I'll be enjoying some daddy-daughter time while you spend your night, let's just say, reading." A glow spread across Adanya's face and she grinned.

"Don't rub it in. Anyway, we'll talk. Do you want to meet back here for lunch again tomorrow?"

"Sure. That sounds good." The two friends hugged each other tightly.

"Maybe you'll run into Bleak again. Wouldn't that be cool?"

"No, but if I do, I'll give him your name and phone number," Adanya teased."

"Come on, Adanya, you have to admit that he was a cutie. Those curly locks of blonde hair and those dashing greenish blue eyes, girl he had it going on."

"I won't deny that, but I'm not about to entertain the thought of getting involved with anyone from campus. Honestly, I'm not interested in being involved right now, and most definitely not with some white boy. I have too many other things on my mind. Having a boyfriend or dating would only complicate matters."

"First, you don't know whether he's from the college or not. Second, you need to stop shooting down men before you even give them a chance. And third, I know you are not trying to play the race card. You're the one that's always talking against prejudice. You are so green. It's time to have some fun, get a boyfriend, go on a few dates, and enjoy your life."

"Just because you like having a boyfriend and doing the dating thing, don't try to put that label on me. Anyway, I don't have time to stand here and indulge in useless banter. It's cold out here, and we both have to get back to work. I'll see you tomorrow," said Adanya. "Whatever." Nanette waved one hand in the air. "But one day you're going to be swept away and when it happens, I'm going to be bouncing off the ceilings with I told you so's." Nanette laughed and walked off."

2

"The trouble with the future is that it usually arrives before we're ready for it." A. Glasow

Adanya clung to her father's arm as they pushed through the crowd of Grizzlies fans and into the FedEx Forum.

"Daddy, I have a feeling we're going to win tonight."

Kenneth Anniston squeezed his daughter's forearm. "We better win after having to fight through traffic, not to mention this huge crowd. I don't think we've been to a game this season with as many people turning out tonight. But it's the first time in a while that we've been on a winning streak like this. It looks like we're going to be good contenders for a championship team this year."

"Whatever you say," agreed Adanya. "Do you think those two guys that call themselves

Grizzlies Super Fans will be here tonight?" Adanya laughed as they inched closer to the entrance of the FedEx Forum.

"They always are," Kenneth Anniston answered.

"I hope we're lucky enough to be sitting close to them. You know those guys are all over the Forum on game night."

"Yeah, I know and I'm like you, I hope our season tickets

pay off and they're sitting in our section. Wouldn't it be a riot?"

They finally made it inside the congested Forum and took off toward the direction of their seats.

Adanya relished the chance to hang out with her father. For her, as long as he was in her life there was no need for her to be involved with anyone.

The game ended with the Grizzlies winning again. To top it off, she and her father were lucky enough to have the two, well-loved notorious Super Fans sitting in their section. After the game ended, they were able to take several pictures with the famous duo. Adanya and her father moved aside so other fans who were in line could take pictures with the Super Fans.

"Honey, I'll be right back. I see one of my clients." Kenneth pointed to the left of him.

"Okay, I'll wait here," she said as he walked off.

Adanya's mouth opened when she saw the guy from lunch standing almost directly in front of her. He was laughing and talking with a group of people. She quickly turned her head and shuffled through the crowd toward her father, hoping that Bleak wouldn't see her. Unfortunately, it was too late. She felt a light tap on her shoulder.

"We meet again."

Adanya looked around. "Oh, hi."

"See, I told you that I've seen you before. Probably here."

"I don't think so. I don't attend these games that often."

"Is that right? Well, seeing you here makes it my lucky night."

"Excuse me." Adanya rolled her eyes and walked off.

A deep crease formed on Bleak's face as he watched her leave. He shrugged his shoulders and laughed. "We'll see each other again," he whispered to himself, before he turned and walked back to his friends.

◊

"Daddy, you all right? You've barely said a word since we left the Forum."

"I, uh was just thinking about the big win we pulled off. That was a great game."

"Yeah, it sure was. And we got pictures too. I can't wait to load them on my social media site." Adanya smiled.

Kenneth reached over and patted his daughter's hand. "Honey, where do you know that young man from?"

"Who?"

"The guy I saw you talking to."

"Oh, I really don't know him. I only saw him for the first time earlier today when me and Nanette went to lunch. He walked over to where we were seated and introduced himself; saying he thought he'd seen me somewhere before. He asked me my name."

"Did you tell him?"

"No. Of course I didn't. I don't know anything about him."

"That's my girl. You know I want you to meet a nice young man one day, but I don't think he should be a white guy. You should stay within your own race. Plus, I don't like the way he approached you. You have to learn how to discern a man's true motives."

"Don't worry. You've taught me well. And as far as considering dating outside my race, well, I'm not trying to be racist, but the man I one day hope sweeps me off my feet will definitely be a brother."

"Just be careful. You're a beautiful young lady, and I know how men operate. If you have any questions, you come to me. And if you see that guy again, I want you to let me know."

Adanya frowned. "Why? I don't think he's a psycho or anything. He didn't come across like that. I think he was just flirting."

"Still, I want you to keep your guard up. You never know what's on these guy's minds."

"Yes, sir."

On the drive home, Adanya nestled on the passenger's side of her father's luxury automobile. Her thoughts leaned toward Bleak. *Of all people to run into, why him? What kind of name is Bleak anyway? Why am I bothered about it? Stop it, Adanya. He's just another flirtatious man trying to get what he wants out of a woman.* She would definitely take into account what her father told her.

The closer they got to home, Adanya felt herself growing weary. Her eyelids fluttered and she positioned her head comfortably on the back of the head cushion. It had been a great day and a fantastic evening.

◊

"Pumpkin. We're home."

Adanya raised her head suddenly. "I didn't know I'd fallen asleep." She opened the door, stepped outside of the car, and the two of them went inside, and out of the cold garage.

"How was the game?" her mother asked when she walked inside.

"We won."

Kenneth gave a thumbs up sign. He walked up to his wife and kissed her on the forehead.

"Mom, Daddy, I'm going to my room. I'm exhausted."

"Okay, sweetheart," her mother told her.

"G'nite, Pumpkin."

Once in her bedroom, Adanya prepared for bed and then

decided to call Nanette.

"You saw him at the game? How did he look?" Nanette sounded more excited than Adanya ever had about a guy before.

"The same as when we saw him at lunch, except instead of dress slacks and a button down shirt he was in a pair of jeans and a Polo."

"Was he with a girl?"

"I couldn't really tell, but I don't think so. I saw him standing with a few people. I didn't see a girl next to him but that doesn't mean he wasn't with one. Anyway, who cares?"

"You care or you wouldn't have called me to tell me."

"Nanette, you get excited over the least bit of things. So what if I called to tell you? It doesn't mean a thing. I just wanted to tell you because I knew you would get a kick out of it."

"I'm glad you did. Did you tell him your name this time?"

"Nope."

"What did your daddy have to say about him?"

"Nothing, because he wasn't around, thank God. He saw somebody he knew so he was busy talking to them when Bleak stepped to me. Ugh, the nerve of some of these dudes. Girl, I tell you these guys will do anything to get into a girl's-well, I'm not even going there."

"You are judging the man without knowing anything about him. That's totally unfair. You wouldn't want someone doing you like that."

"I know and you're right. But I'm just being cautious. Most of these guys aren't serious. All they want is sex, and white boys are no exception. And you know me; I'm not about to entertain someone like him who walks up on me like he did. He doesn't know me from any other female out there."

"Maybe, he wants to get to know you."

"Look, I'm tired and I'm starting to feel bad, like I'm coming down with a bug. I'm going to lie down. I'll see you tomorrow."

"Okay."

"Bye." Adanya turned back the bedspread. Before climbing underneath the cover, she knelt on her knees and prayed. Afterward she pulled the sheet and comforter up close around her neck. The winter season should explain her chill, but it had been warm inside the Forum, the car, and it definitely was warm inside the house. She tossed and turned. During the night, she started to feel feverish and her chills increased. Her body ached with every turn.

After several hours of torment, she got up, took a couple of fever reducer caplets, and drank a glass of juice. She returned to bed and with the morning light, she felt somewhat better.

◊

"Good morning, sweetheart." Annalisse studied her daughter's face for a few moments. "Are you feeling all right? You look a little pale."

"I feel a little better than I did during the night. Right after I went to bed, I started having chills, and I felt feverish and achy. It's probably a twenty-four virus, or maybe I was just plain tired."

Like she was an infant, Adanya's mother approached her and placed the back of her hand lightly against her forehead. "Doesn't feel like you have a fever."

Adanya pulled away. "I know; I told you, I'm better. I'm leaving now. I've got to get to work."

"Okay, try to have a good day."

Adanya hurried out of the door with her cream colored, wool, ruffled coat buttoned to the top of her neck. She arrived at Rhodes Communications Building, parked, and in record time, jumped out and hurried out of the cold into the warmth of the building. Toward the end of her third lecture of the morning, Adanya was feeling worse than she had the night before.

She reported to the Communications Director and informed her that she was going home. She texted Nanette and cancelled their lunch date.

On the way home, Adanya felt her body temperature rise, and her throat had begun to ache. The weather outside was also turning brutal. The frigid air reached the inside of her car and disregarded the car's interior heat. She pushed the remote to open her side of the three-car garage when she approached her parents' massive 5,500 square foot house. Her mother's black BMW x6 looked like it had never moved.

Adanya envisioned her mother as one of the "Housewives of Whatever," and smiled slightly at the thought. She got out her car and turned the garage doorknob leading into the wide open foyer. She had no idea what caused her to ease inside the house rather than announce her presence. Maybe it was the fact that she felt more awful with each step she took.

She heard her mother's voice going a mile a minute. Annalisse did most of her business consulting from the confines of a huge home office. She was obviously on the phone, one of Annalisse's preferred past times when she wasn't entertaining.

"I don't know, Kaye. It's been twenty-two, going on twenty-three years. Imagine living with this for that long. I'm tired of hiding. I want to live my life. I want to be freed from the grips of the past." Her mother's voice sounded tear-filled.

Adanya remained in the entrance hall, too afraid to move. She was frozen in time. What was she talking about? Any other time she would have disregarded her mother's conversation and went up the back stairway to her room. She didn't mean to eavesdrop, but her feet held still like they were meshed in hardened stone. She continued to listen while she tipped inside the half-bath located right off of the foyer and tore a sheet of toilet tissue off its roll to wipe her running, crimson nose.

"Hold up. Adanya is grown. It's time she knows the truth. And what about me? I'm only thirty-eight years old. I've done more than my share to make a good life for her. I know God has His ways. But this has truly been one of those times when I have to constantly remind myself that I'm not supposed to lean to my own understanding."

What is she talking about? There was no retreating. She had to know what her mother was talking about, and what did she have to do with it. She took a careful position closer to the kitchen so she wouldn't miss a word.

"I hear what you're saying, but you know for yourself that some things that God allows are just too far-fetched. I can't help but wonder why He does the things He does. I mean, think about my autistic twin sister. Compare her to me. Here I am, a member of Mensa, married to a good man who loves me and God with all of his heart; but because I have a womb that doesn't ovulate, I haven't given my husband a child. Tell me how I should make sense of that?"

Adanya felt faint. But she couldn't stop listening.

"Yes, I hear what you're saying, Kaye. And I am thankful. I know that the circumstances back then could have turned out different. But on the other end, I feel like me and Kenneth are reminded of our past every single, solitary day when we see Adanya. And then, my sister. Poor Anaya; it's just hard to imagine what goes through her limited mind."

"Sure, I hear you," Annalisse said into the phone. "And yes, I'm appreciative that I had parents that were able to send me to college. I'm grateful that I had the chance to step up to the plate and at least try to make things easier when it came to my sister. I still can't imagine what Anaya had to go through."

Annalisse was silent for a few seconds on the phone, apparently listening to Kaye's rebuttal.

"Okay, so what's that got to do with any of this? Kenneth was blessed to start a lucrative tech business, and...so what? All of that is truly favor from God, I know. But, just try to listen to me for once. Understand where I'm coming from."

Adanya heard her mother's hand hit against what sounded like the granite kitchen island countertop. Her voice rose and the words that came out sounded laced with anger. "I didn't complain, well except to you, not one time. I accepted full responsibility of raising Adanya after I finished college and so did Kenneth. Don't get me wrong, I love her like my own. I thank God for her, but the fact remains, she's not my child. And she needs to know that, Kaye. She deserves to know the truth."

Adanya suddenly felt light headed. Everything around her grew dark before she collapsed. When she awakened, she was in her bed with a heavy quilt covering her body. She sat up suddenly, and surveyed her surroundings somewhat confused.

"Ahhh." Her mother rushed inside Adanya's bedroom while her father's familiar footsteps trailed behind Annalisse's. Adanya placed her head in her hands and shook from side to side.

"Adanya, baby, how are you feeling? You scared me to death. You really have it bad, don't you? I didn't know what to do when you passed out like that. Tomorrow, you are going to the doctor and get some antibiotics. The flu is nothing to play with."

Adanya looked past her mother and connected with the awkward stare on her father's face.

"Who am I?" Adanya cried. "Tell me right now." She jumped out of the bed, balled both fists staunchly to her side, and started screaming like a toddler having a tantrum.

"Settle down, Pumpkin." Her father walked closer to her and encircled her body in his arms, but Adanya pulled out of his hold. "What's wrong? Do we need to take you to the ER?" he asked.

"No, I don't need to see a doctor, and I'm not your pumpkin. I want to know what's going on. I heard you, mother, or whoever you are," Adanya continued to wail. She glared at Annalisse with eyes that looked like they were about to pop out of their sockets.

Annalisse peered at her husband with a look of fear mixed with concern on her face. "I don't know what you're talking about. What is it you heard, sweetheart?"

"Don't play with me, mother. You know darn well what I heard."

"Adanya, calm down, honey. Just tell us what on earth you're talking about?" Annalisse continued to look at her daughter with surprise.

"You think I'm like your sister? Well, I'm not Aunt Anaya. I have the capacity to think, and I know what I heard you telling Miss Kaye," yelled Adanya.

"What is she talking about, Annalisse? What were you and Kaye discussing?"

"Oh, you mean you haven't told Daddy how miserable you are?" Adanya feigned laughter.

"Wait, please don't do this," her mother said.

"No, don't you do this." She pointed at Annalisse with contempt plastered across her face.

"Look, will somebody tell me what this is all about?" Kenneth reached out both hands and walked toward Adanya to embrace her, but she quickly took a step backward.

"Don't you touch me. I bet you're just as much to blame as she is."

Kenneth searched his wife's eyes for answers.

"I was talking to Kaye on the phone earlier this afternoon." Annalisse looked ashamed. Her high yellow complexion turned a shade darker.

"So what does that have to do with anything? You're always talking to Kaye about one thing or the other."

"Oh, so you really didn't tell Daddy. How could you?" Adanya started crying. "How could you lie to me all of these years? I'm not your daughter?"

Kenneth stumbled. His left palm landed on the dresser, which steadied him somewhat. He looked at his wife of eighteen years with an unknowing expression.

"What...what is she talking about? He looked like he was desperately trying to pull himself together. "Where has all of this nonsense come from?"

With tears flowing from her eyes, she answered in a broken voice, "Kenneth, she knows."

"What did you say?"

"Kenneth, honey, I didn't mean for any of this to happen. I was just having one of those days, and, well, I felt like I was about to explode. I've, we've been keeping this hidden for so long that I needed to vent, and so, so I–"

Kenneth waved her off with his hand. Anger was

apparent in his voice. "You…Annalisse. How could you?" He transferred his gaze toward his daughter, and the angry looking expression on his face turned to one that looked like sorrow.

"Baby, I know this has to be hard. But you have to know that we love you. We always have. And we always will. I don't know how much you know, or what all was said, but please believe me." He shifted his eyes over at Annalisse. "We are your parents. We always will be," Kenneth tried to assure Adanya in a loving manner.

"You think I'm crazy. That I'm supposed to act like I didn't hear what I heard?"

Adanya dashed pass the frightened looking couple and started opening drawers and throwing her clothes out on the floor. Next, she swiftly opened the door to her walk-in closet and grabbed a huge piece of luggage from off the top shelf. Taking the clothes by handfuls, Adanya started throwing them in the suitcase.

"Adanya." Her father followed her and tried to hold her in his arms.

"Don't touch me," Adanya hollered, sending a mist of her saliva in the air.

"Come on, Pumpkin." Her father pleaded and reached out toward Adanya a second time.

"I said, don't touch me."

Kenneth stepped away with hands upraised.

Next, Annalisse walked over to where Adanya stood. Adanya was practically ripping her clothes off their hangers.

"Adanya, listen. Let me explain. I don't know what you think you heard; but I *am* your mother." She grabbed hold of Adanya's feverish arm.

Adanya broke loose again. Her face was cherry red, her body felt weak. She started to feel lightheaded again. As she walked out of the closet, she staggered.

"Annalisse, get her some water and a couple of acetaminophen caplets," Kenneth ordered as he caught his daughter's fall, and led her to sit down on the end of her bed.

Annalisse turned and ran out of the room and down the stairs.

"Pumpkin, I want you to settle down and try to rest. This whole thing is a misunderstanding."

Adanya leaned backward, and tilted her head to the side. "Don't try to insult my intelligence." Her hands went up over her head, and she pounced up from off the bed. "And for your information, a misunderstanding is when you thought momma told you to buy a stick of margarine but she told you to by a stick of butter. Or, or, when you have a disagreement with someone. That's what I think about a misunderstanding. Or, or" her hands were all over the place as she stood back up and went back to the closet where she started yanking clothes off hangers again, "when you thought you had an appointment on Tuesday," she rambled. "But you misunderstood and the appointment was on Thursday. Anyway, this is not a misunderstanding, so don't even try to make light of it."

Annalisse reappeared moments later with a glass of water in one hand and a bottle of acetaminophen caplets in the other.

She pointed at Annalisse. "You're no better than her. You're a liar, and I don't want to hear anything you have to say."

"Don't you talk to your father like that," Annalisse scolded. "This is not his fault. Since you're so determined to blame somebody, blame me." Annalisse walked further into the bedroom.

"Why? If the shoe fits, I say he should wear it. Especially

since he's so busy trying to make you out to be some innocent victim, when both of you have been lying to me all of this time," she said in a weakened voice. "Please, just leave. Both of you. All I want you to do is get out of my room."

In silence, Annalisse set the bottle of caplets and the glass of water on the round table near Adanya's bed. "Please, settle down and take the pills. I'll make you a bowl of hot tomato soup. It'll help you feel better."

"Just get out," Adanya insisted.

Adanya didn't so much as flinch until after she heard her bedroom door close behind the two of them. She sat up, opened the bottle, and tapped out two red and white caplets. In the blink of an eye, she popped them in her mouth followed by swallows of water. The ice cold water did little to soothe her aching, sore throat. She kept sobbing, which only added to making her feel worse.

Everything had changed in a flash. All because of a stupid case of the flu, or a bad cold, Adanya had walked into a life-altering experience.

She lay in the bed and continued to sob. When her mother knocked on the door and called her name some time later, Adanya refused to acknowledge her.

Annalisse came inside the room anyway, carrying a dinner tray. "Adanya, sit up. Eat this while it's hot." Annalisse sat the tray on the table next to Adanya's bed. "You'll feel better."

Adanya didn't move or say a word.

With shoulders slumped, Annalisse turned and left.

Adanya sat up and reached for her cell phone that was lying next to her on the bed. The aroma of the piping hot bowl of tomato soup wafted underneath her nose, but she had no desire to eat. She called Nanette.

"Come on, answer the phone." Adanya pulled the

bedcovers over her body and hovered underneath them with her legs gathered up to her chest.

"Hello."

"Nanette." Adanya's tears spilled over again. Droplets penetrated inside the cell phone.

"Girl, what's wrong? I got your message saying you were feeling bad, but I didn't think you had it that bad. You sound horrible."

"Everything is messed up." Her cell phone crackled. "My whole life is a lie." Adanya sobbed.

"What? What did you say? Your phone is breaking up."

"Let me hang up and call you from the house phone."

"K." Adanya reached over the dinner tray, retrieved the cordless phone, and dialed Nanette again.

"Hey."

"Hey. That's better. So what were you saying?"

"I said my whole life is a lie."

"What are you talking about? What's going on?"

"That's it. I don't know where to start."

"From the beginning," replied Nanette.

"I left work early because I was feeling awful. I guess between yelling during last night's basketball game and being around a crowd, I don't know; I guess I caught a flu bug. But that's not what's wrong."

"I hear you, so tell me what's going on," Nanette urged.

"When I got home today, I overheard my mother on the phone. She was talking to her best friend, Kaye."

"Uh, and," said Nanette.

"And, she was telling her that she was tired of playing mother to me."

"So you were eavesdropping on your mother? Girl, you so crazy."

"This is no time for your antics, Nanette. I have a serious problem."

"Sorry, but come on now; you are a grown woman. Your mother is probably wondering when you're going to get your own spot so she and your daddy can have some time to themselves. I had barely turned in my cap and gown before I was saying adios to my parents." Nanette laughed.

"I wish it was that cut and dried for me, but it's not."

"Well, tell me. What did you overhear?"

"She was going on about being only thirty-eight years old, and she'd basically given up her life to raise a child that isn't even hers."

"What did she mean?" Nanette sounded alarmed on the other end of the phone.

Adanya wanted to holler but her aching throat wouldn't allow her. "Can't you connect dots? Dang, Nanette, I'm not her daughter."

"Not her daughter?"

"She was talking about my Aunt Anaya like she's my mother, but that doesn't make sense but even if by some outrageous chance that was the case, who is my daddy? This is like some kind of television drama, a nightmare unfolding before my eyes. I don't know what's going on."

"Did you ask her?"

"Of course I asked her."

"What did she tell you?"

"What she didn't tell me was the truth. All she said was I didn't hear what I thought I heard. Like I'm some kind of an idiot." Desperation filtered through Adanya's voice.

"I can't explain why she said that. Maybe she's stressing out about something. You know how we get sometimes. Look, I'm leaving Harbor Town. I'll stop by your house on my way home."

"What are you doing in Harbor Town?"

"Gerald."

"Oh," Adanya mumbled.

"When did Gerald move to Harbor Town, and why couldn't he have come to see you instead of you going over there?"

"He and two of his friends moved in together."

Gerald and Nanette had been in a relationship for nearly four months. Nanette really liked him and he seemed to like her just as much. But in Adanya's opinion, Nanette made herself too available to Gerald. She was like that with most of the guys she'd dated in the past.

On numerous occasions, Adanya told her that she acted clingy and possessive whenever she was involved with someone. Nanette either didn't care what others thought or she was just plain naïve.

"Look, it may take me a minute to get there. It just started sleeting," Nanette explained.

"No, don't come. Concentrate on getting home safely. I'm in the bed anyway. I don't know what happened to me, but I passed out earlier today."

"Hold up. You mean as in like you went unconscious?"

"Yes, Nanette. That's the 'I passed out' I'm talking about." Adanya's words dripped cynicism. She shook her head and pursed her lips. "Anyway, all I remember is coming home, walking into the foyer, and hearing my mother saying all of those terrible things. She sounded like she hated me, like all these years I've been nothing but an imposition in her life."

"Now you know that is not true. Your mother loves you."

"Yeah, right; sure she does."

"I'm not going to get into that because you're talking crazy. Anything else you remember?"

"Not really. I recall opening my eyes and feeling confused; I couldn't remember how I got in my bedroom, let alone in my bed." Adanya peeked outside of her window and saw plum size pieces of sleet falling.

"Adanya," Nanette gasped. "Girl, that sleet is coming down hard."

"Yea, I just looked out my window. You need to get home before it gets bad. From looking through my window, there might be the makings of an ice rink outside. Be careful driving."

"But I don't want you by yourself feeling the way you do."

"You're my best friend, Nanette. I know I can count on you, but I want you to go home and get out of this weather. You know these Memphis drivers. When a few sprinkles of white stuff, especially sleet, comes down, all chaos breaks out on the streets and highways."

"You're right. I'm going to head home then, but only if you're sure you're going to be all right."

"I'll be fine. Haven't you heard the saying what doesn't kill you will make you stronger? Guess I'm about to find out."

"Look, I'll call or text you when I make it home."

"Okay. I'm going to try to sort some things out. I can't think clearly right now. I'm too dumbfounded," Adanya said in a choked voice.

"Hang in there. Try to get some rest so you can feel better. There has to be some sense to this madness."

"Yeah, I hope you're right. I'll talk to you later."

Adanya put the phone back on its charging base. Snoopy whined at the foot of the bed. It was the first time she noticed that he was in the room with her, but it was no surprise. Adanya adored her eleven-year old English bull dog. She'd had Snoopy since he was eight weeks old. He was what her daddy called a just because gift.

When she first saw the short, chubby puppy, with the flabby jaws, she fell in love with him right away. He had indeed proved that he was not only man's best friend, but hers as well.

"Come here, Snoopy. I need a friend."

Snoopy took two small pounces and was in Adanya's arms. She held on to him while her wet tears fell on his white coat. Snoopy didn't budge. It was as if he sensed that something wasn't quite right. He lifted his head and licked the salty tears from off the side of Adanya's face as she rocked back and forth in the bed.

"Why now?" she whispered, followed by, "Who am I, and what happened to my life, Lord?"

3

"Betrayal can only happen if you love." J. Le Carre

Adanya stretched and moved around slightly in her bed. Snoopy was at the foot, but as soon as Adanya moved, he propped up his big head and began to whine.

"I know," she dragged her words in slow tune with her body.

She looked around and realized it was morning. Memories of yesterday's horrific events rushed to her mind. She still felt achy and her throat was dry. She could barely swallow without it throbbing. The tray with soup and crackers was gone. The luggage and the clothes she'd thrown around the room were nowhere in sight either. She felt the need to resume crying, but told herself she didn't have time; she had to find out the truth.

She adorned herself in her thick, white terry cloth, hooded robe. Snoopy jumped down off the bed. Adanya placed her feet inside of her slippers that were always parked somewhere close to her bedside, while Snoopy wagged his tail with excitement.

"Good morning, big boy." She leaned down and patted him on top of his head. With caution, Adanya turned the doorknob to her bedroom door like she was an intruder.

Snoopy took off up the hallway, stopping momentarily to look back and make sure Adanya was close by.

Adanya listened for sounds of the people who she once trusted more than anyone else in the world. Now the same people had quickly become strangers to her. She tiptoed into the hallway, down the stairs, and began to follow the aroma of fresh coffee coming from the kitchen. The house was quiet. Almost eerily quiet.

Ummm. She inhaled the sweet aroma of caffeine as she made her way to the kitchen. *Must be after six. The coffee pot is timed for six o'clock every morning, seven days a week.* No one was in the kitchen. Adanya walked over to the kitchen sink, stood and peered out of the window backdrop. A light snow covered the ground, and ice layered the black top. More than likely, classes were dismissed for the day. It took barely an inch of snow for everything to shut down in and around Memphis.

Arf Arf.

"Okay, Snoopy. I'm sorry. Mommy doesn't mean to neglect you." Adanya turned completely around and headed toward the door leading out to the massive back yard. Snoopy bolted past her and jetted through the doggie door just as soon as Adanya unlocked it. He ran around the yard several times and then went to the extreme back area of the yard, where he relieved himself, before he raced back toward her, and she let him back inside.

The two of them zeroed back to the direction of her room. She was going to call in to be sure that classes were indeed cancelled for the day. Just as she turned around to leave from out the kitchen, Adanya met her mother's uncertain stare.

Annalisse's eyes were swollen, like she'd been crying all night long. She had each arm tucked inside the other, hugging herself.

Adanya ignored her mother's harried look. "Where's Daddy?" She asked before she answered her own question. "Work?"

"Yes, you know your father. Not even the apocalypse could keep that man from going into the office. He said to tell you that he hopes you feel better, and he wants you to get some rest today."

Adanya released an audible breath. "Look, let's not do this."

"Do what?" Annalisse bit her bottom lip and half-rolled her eyes.

"Tell me everything." Adanya waved her hand in a fit of anger. "Now."

"Not if you don't calm down. I'm still your mother, and you're going to treat me like it too, young lady." Annalisse kept hugging herself. "Now, sit down. Oh, and in case you don't already know, Rhodes is closed."

"Thanks," Adanya responded barely above a whisper. She poured herself a cup of coffee and mixed in two teaspoons of cane sugar. She sombered over to the table, set her coffee down then pulled a chair out and sat at the table. Snoopy stationed himself beside her chair when she sat down. He looked up at her and cocked his head. "I'm sorry, Snoopy. Mommy forgot." Adanya got back up, went to the pantry, and removed a bag of dog food. She poured some into his feeding bowl and made him a bowl of ice water, which he simply loved and immediately began to lap. She returned to the table and her waiting cup of coffee.

Annalisse was not a coffee drinker. It was Kenneth and Adanya who indulged in the caffeine brew. She went to the refrigerator instead, removed the pitcher of grape juice, poured herself a glass, and then sat down at the table across from Adanya. "I don't even know where to begin."

"From the beginning would be perfect, don't you think?" Adanya answered without pity, or even empathy, in her voice. "Or maybe we should start with the part where you told Miss Kaye that you're still young and you have your own life to live. All I want is the truth."

Annalisse twisted the fingers of both hands together, nervously. "Okay, here it is. What you heard is true. I am not your biological mother. But I am your mother, Adanya. I'll always be your mother."

Adanya gasped. She felt like her world was spinning out of control. She grabbed hold of the kitchen table to keep from falling off the chair.

"Adanya." Annalisse jumped up. "Are you okay"

"I'm fine." She swiped her forehead. "When did you all adopt me?"

"We didn't exactly adopt you." Annalisse's head slowly dropped.

"What do you mean?"

"We didn't have to."

"What? I'm really confused. Who is my biological mother? Where is she? Why did she give me away?" Adanya shot off one question after another.

Annalisse slowly raised her bowed down head and looked at Adanya. "I think you know. Your Aunt..."

"Don't you say it." Adanya slammed her hand on the table and made hot coffee and grape juice splatter.

Annalisse's body jerked. "Anaya is your mother."

Adanya placed both hands over each of her ears and shook her head. "Nooooo." Her left hand flew up and grabbed hold of her throbbing throat. "You're telling me that my aunt, your sister, your twin sister to be exact, the woman that Gram and Gramps have to care for like some kid..."

Adanya pointed a finger toward Annalisse. "You're saying she's my mother? You're sitting over there telling me that she gave birth to me and not you?" Adanya's tears spilled over, droplets landed in her coffee and on her robe. "How? How can that be possible? What? Just tell me. Give me the answers," she demanded.

Adanya stood up. Rigid arms ending with clinched fists were stretched out at her sides. A steady stream of tears cascaded down her face like a waterfall. She had never felt so angry before in her life. It frightened her. Somehow, she could relate to how people must feel before they do harm to someone. She didn't want to think like that, but an untamable force toyed in her mind, one that wanted Annalisse to feel the torment she felt at that moment.

Annalisse cried too. Snoopy, totally ignored, lay on the kitchen floor, and probably in his dog mind, realized there was going to be some real mess about to go on.

Sucking in her breath, and twisting her hands, Adanya composed herself. "Who hurt Aunt Anaya?" Adanya sat back down. "Who took advantage of her? Whoever it is, I know he has to be rotting away somewhere in a jail cell." Adanya grew upset at the thought of someone sexually assaulting her Aunt Anaya.

Annalisse resumed talking. "We were sixteen years old. It was all a horrible mistake."

"You aren't making any sense. Just tell me, Momma, tell me who and where he is."

Annalisse's chest rose and fell. She pursed her lips and lowered her read. It was several seconds before she slowly looked back up. "My boyfriend. He…," she paused, "mistook Anaya for me."

Adanya's eyebrows spoke volumes as they formed a thick black lower case M across her forehead. "Thought

Anaya was you?" Adanya's mouth popped open and stayed open. Her pupils grew large. The brightness of the streaks of sun pouring through the kitchen window reflected off them. "You'll say anything, won't you? I don't even know who you are anymore, and why you're doing this. Why are you telling me all of these lies? You're really a piece of work. You know that?"

"Look," Annalisse's voice revealed frustration. "If you want me to tell you what happened I will, but I will not listen to you insult me. Which is it going to be?"

Adanya rolled her eyes. "Go on."

"It was downright hard, if not impossible for people to tell me and Anaya apart. It wasn't until we were almost two years old, when Mama and Daddy said they began to notice that me and Anaya may have been identical but we were totally different mentally and emotionally. You're a grown woman now, so you already know without me having to tell you, that Anaya couldn't take care of herself, let alone a baby. And there was no way that Mama and Daddy were going to consider an abortion."

Adanya remained silent.

"I believe everything happens for a reason."

"I don't understand any of this. You're telling me everything except what I need to hear; what I have to know."

"It was all a big mix-up.

"So you're saying I'm a mix-up?"

"I didn't mean it that way, and you know it."

"I don't know anything anymore." Adanya's nostrils flared and a terrible nauseated feeling formed in the pit of her belly. "How can you take up for somebody who raped your own sister? What is wrong with you?"

"He didn't rape her. He thought–"

"Momma, please." Adanya showed her the hand. Don't

come to me with some he thought she was you garbage."

Annalisse stared at her daughter with blank eyes.

"Anyway..." Adanya stopped like she'd suddenly been mean mugged in the face. She pushed herself away from the kitchen table. Her hand flew up to her open mouth. "But, you, you're always telling anybody who'll listen about Daddy being your first and only boyfriend. You said you were teenagers when you had me, but I was still conceived in love. Please. Don't you even try it. You better not try to blame this on my daddy!"

"I told you," Annalisse yelled back. "It was a mistake. Something that never should have happened, but it did. He really did think Anaya was me. And it was my fault."

Adanya's eyes bucked. She moved her lips but no words came out.

Annalisse bowed her head. She kept struggling, like she really did not want to rehash her past. "You see, some nights I left me and Anaya's bedroom window unlocked so Kenneth could sneak inside."

"You were sneaking daddy inside the house? You, the both of you, who preached to me day in and day out about saving myself for my husband, telling me not to let some boy con me out of my virginity; all of that from you and Daddy. Y'all are so fake, two phonies, hypocrites. It's people like you that make people stay away from the church." Adanya snarled as she unleashed her venomous, verbal assault.

Annalisse slapped her across her mouth so hard that Adanya's head snapped back and forth like a rubber band.

Tears gushed. Adanya rubbed the side of her cherry red cheek. Her speech was cut off. Her cheek stung like someone had doused her with acid.

"Don't think I'm about to say I'm sorry for slapping the

taste out of your mouth either. This is not some soap opera. This is real life. And in real life, I will not allow you to talk to me any old kind of way. I don't care if you're grown or not. You are out of line, and I won't hesitate to pop you in your mouth again. I am your mother, whether biologically or not. Nothing is going to change that. So you better recognize, girl. And, I know what we taught you, and I'm not going to renege on any of it. You have standards to live by. Before you judge me, let me admit to you that I was young and I was in love. I know we shouldn't have been having sex, but still Kenneth is the only man I've ever been intimate with."

"And that's supposed to make it better? Too bad he can't say the same." Adanya spoke with anger while rubbing her cheek. "What else have you and Daddy kept from me?"

"I need to tell you what happened while I can. I'm afraid if I stop now, I won't be able to relive my past again."

Adanya waved her hand carelessly.

"Sometimes at night," Annalisse paused, "after Anaya was asleep, yes, it's true, I would let him come over."

Adanya couldn't picture it. Her mother, sneaking her father in the house? It was almost funny, but there was no time for humor. She listened as Annalisse continued.

"It wasn't that many times. And, me and Anaya had twin beds. So she never knew he was there because I made sure she was sleep."

Annalisse sniffled as tiny dribbles of snot escaped from her nostrils. She stood up and walked over to the counter top. A half roll of paper towels hung on its holder. Annalisse yanked off a couple of sheets. Hands shaking, she wiped her nose and mouth and returned to sit down. She used the remaining sheets to nervously wipe up the pool of coffee and juice.

"The night it happened, Anaya and I had been lying in

my bed together. I was reading The Terrible Tickler story to her. She used to be afraid monsters were underneath her bed, so after she started crying, I told her she could get in bed with me and I would tell her a story to make her laugh instead of scared. The Terrible Tickler was her most loved story. Well, she fell asleep while I was reading. I didn't bother moving her. I climbed in her bed instead, and started to think about the bad news Kenneth had gotten earlier about college."

"So what does all of this have to do with me?" Adanya sighed. Annalisse ignored Adanya a second time. "I tossed and turned. I couldn't sleep. I decided that I was hungry so I got up, went to the kitchen, and made a sandwich and got a warm soda from one of the many cases daddy kept in the pantry. You know how much he loves those clear, zero calorie drinks."

Adanya rolled her eyes up in her head. *Come on, stop all of the theatrics*, she wanted so badly to tell her mother.

"I wasn't gone that long. At least I didn't think that I was, but obviously, I was gone long enough. And Kenneth wasn't supposed to be coming over, so there was no reason to put Anaya in her own bed.

"Sure he wasn't," Adanya smarted off again.

"Look, forget this." Annalisse slammed the palm of her hand on the table while her other hand flew up in the air as she got up. "No more. I'm not going to sit here and listen to you and your insults and back talk, I told you."

"My insults? Back talk?" Adanya released a breath of air and bit her bottom lip. "I'm not going to go there."

"I tell you what, when you're ready to listen like an adult, and act like one, then come see me. Maybe I'll tell you the rest. But as for now, I'm finished. You'll have me catching a charge because I'm about to beat you down."

"This didn't happen to you," Adanya yelled. "It happened to Aunt Anaya. And it's affecting my life. I would think you would understand.

"And you should understand that this is the most difficult thing I've had to do? I'm a victim too."

Adanya rolled her eyes. "Okay, I hear you. Just tell me the rest."

Annalisse sighed and then resumed her story. "Like I said, I kept the window unlocked a lot. He came in like always, and got into my bed. Of course, it was dark in our bedroom; and he had no reason to think that it wasn't me. No reason at all. But it wasn't me. It was Anaya. Don't you see, Adanya? It was all a terrible mistake. Kenneth didn't mean to do what he did. He'd had a lot on his mind that whole week. After he didn't get accepted into Howard like he thought he would, he got really depressed. He told me on the phone earlier that same evening that he felt like he was a disappointment to his parents, and to his whole family."

Adanya screamed, "My daddy is not a rapist. He would have known that she wasn't you. You're lying." Adanya jumped up from the table. Tears flowed. "You probably have all along. Why are you doing this? Do you hate me and Aunt Anaya that much?" She screamed.

Like a lion, Annalisse pounced up, inhaled, and screamed back at her daughter. "No, I don't hate you. I hate what was done. But I loved Kenneth back then, and I love him now. I love you too, and so I raised you as my own daughter. Anaya barely showed being pregnant too. Mama and Daddy never told anyone our family secret, not even their closest friends. Everybody assumed that I had gotten pregnant and that I was the one that had the baby.

"And when they questioned me after you were born, I

told them I didn't show during my pregnancy. I guess folks bought it because no one said anything after I gave them that explanation."

"But you said I was born in Nashville because that's where y'all lived at the time. So that was a lie too?"

"Yes and no. We used to go there most holidays. Mama and Daddy had a cabin up there. You remember the cabin. We used to take you up there until you were four or five, and then some years later they sold it."

"I don't know if I can take any more of this. It's all too far-fetched to believe. I must be dreaming." Adanya pinched herself on the arm like that would make her wake up from the nightmare she was living.

"You're not dreaming, Adanya. Do you need some time?"

Silence infiltrated the thick tension in the airy kitchen. Snoopy lay fast asleep next to his food bowl.

Annalisse exhaled. "As soon as Anaya gave birth to you, I stood in as your mother, and Kenneth adored you. We finished our senior year and then went off to Fisk University. Mama, Daddy, and Mr. and Mrs. Anniston took care of you, and after we graduated, we became your full time parents.

"It wasn't hard for people to believe that you were mine and Kenneth's baby. We were so in love with each other back then even though we were young. We called you our daughter from the beginning. We came home from college to see you as often as we could. Sometimes Kenneth's parents would bring you to see us too. When we graduated from college, we got married and the three of us moved into our first home. We never discussed what happened again. Outside of me and Kenneth's parents, Anaya's doctor was the only other person who knew."

"How is that when you were talking to Kaye about me? And how can you be so sure Aunt Anaya doesn't know that I'm her daughter. Maybe she knows but she just can't express it. " Adanya looked like she could draw blood from Annalisse.

"I don't think so. Just because she gave you your name, Mama said the doctor still says she probably has no recollection whatsoever about what happened. She's never reacted in a way that would make us believe otherwise.

"She gave me my name? How can a person with the mind of a five or six year old, give me a name that fits in with our family? All of this is absurd."

"Mama said that after Anaya had you, she started saying 'Pretty Adanya.' Maybe it was because she used to call her baby doll Pretty Adanya, so Mama said that's what they were going to name you, and they did.

She might be autistic and mentally challenged but she is still capable of love. We all love you. It's why we did it. We did it to protect you and Anaya."

Adanya shook her head. "So to save yourselves, you and Daddy never told me she was my real mother?"

"When would have been a good time to tell you? Look at how you're taking it now."

"I can't listen to any more of this." Adanya jetted around and ran down the hallway, to the stairs, and back upstairs to her bedroom, with Snoopy right on her heels. She slammed her bedroom door so hard it sounded like it popped off its hinges. She pulled out her suitcase again, and began a repeat performance of the night before. She looked in her closet and pulled out a pair of deep blue leggings and a wide-mouth, long-sleeved sweater. She disrobed from her night clothes, groomed her body, then began to dress while Snoopy sat on the bed quietly watching her every move. After Adanya put on a pair of leather boots, she picked up her purse on the nearby night stand and hurried back down to the kitchen, past her mother and outside to the garage. She kissed Snoopy on the top of his nose.

"Where are you going? Adanya, please don't go." Annalisse begged.

Adanya ignored her mother's cries and got inside of her car, hit the remote, and the garage door flew open. Without giving the car time to warm up even a little, she backed it into the street, and proceeded in the direction of her father's Collierville office.

What was usually a seventeen minute drive took a little over thirty- five minutes due to the weather. Thoughts of the things Annalisse said caused Adanya to become physically ill to the point where she couldn't hold back the sick feeling flooding her stomach any longer. She pulled off on a side street, opened her car door, and threw up. When she finished, she pulled a tissue from the console and wiped her mouth along with the tears that had started to form again. She continued the rest of the way with the sick feeling still present. But nothing was going to keep her from confronting her father.

Her father's office building finally came into view. The sign read Anniston Digital Technology Corporation. She wrapped herself in her coat, parked, and dashed inside and out of the cold.

"Why, hello, Adanya," the receptionist said. "I can't believe you're out in this weather."

"Hi, Sherri," Adanya responded minus the smile that was usually plastered on her adorable face. "Is my father in his office?"

"Yes, let me tell him that—"

Adanya didn't wait on Sherri to finish. She walked past

her and headed straight down the hall to the elevator and up to her father's fourth floor executive suite overlooking a broad area of the Memphis skyline. She didn't bother to knock. She burst inside, and luckily, he was in his office alone.

"Tell me that everything that woman said is a lie. Tell me," Adanya insisted and rushed into her father's arms as soon as he got up and walked from behind his oversized desk.

He gently rubbed her hair back from her face and held her chilled body next to him. This time, Adanya didn't push him away. She needed him to tell her that Annalisse was a liar and was crazy.

"Shhh, Pumpkin. Don't cry."

Adanya raised her head and met his eyes. "Why did she lie to me? Why did she say that you, you did something terrible to Aunt Anaya?"

"Pumpkin." Tears gathered in his eyes. "Listen to me. It was a terrible thing that happened. I was young, stupid, and sloppy drunk. Believe me, I didn't know it was Anaya."

Adanya jumped back like she'd been popped in the face-again. Her father walked up on her and reached one hand out for her.

Adanya didn't respond. "We didn't tell you because we wanted to protect you." He kissed her on her forehead tenderly.

Adanya cringed and stepped back.

"Baby, listen. I love you. Your mother loves you. God blessed us with you."

Adanya looked broken. "Don't you even try to put this on God. You raped Aunt Anaya."

He took hold of her elbow and led her to the boardroom style, five-seat sofa in his office, and waited until she sat down before he sat next to her.

"Hear me." As he talked, he shift from one leg to the other. "I have loved your mother since the very first day I laid eyes on her back in seventh grade. We were middle school and high school sweethearts; she was the love of my life. I've always told you that. And she still is." He cleared his throat; and lowered his head.

Adanya continued to listen, but it was hard for her to comprehend what he was talking about.

"We had great plans for a future together. I wanted to go to Howard so bad back then. It was going to be Howard or nothing. But when I got the letter telling me that I wasn't accepted, I was torn to pieces. I felt like I was a total loser. I had other college scholarships, including one at Fisk, but for me it was Howard or bust. I didn't know how to accept the rejection."

Adanya looked at him like he was a stranger.

Kenneth didn't let up. He acted like he needed to talk, had to talk about it all. He was talking so fast. He got up and started moving around in his office like a mad man, hands flailing and his voice was strained.

"I thought I was going to go crazy. I felt like I was a disappointment to my parents, to my teachers, to Annalisse, to everybody who looked up to me." He grabbed hold of the sides of his temples with both hands. "I didn't think I would be able to get an education that would help me realize my dreams. I couldn't think. I couldn't eat. I became so angry."

Lord, please wake me up. Wake me up.

"When I got that rejection letter, I did something really stupid. I sneaked out and met up with a couple of my homeboys. One of them had an older brother who thought it was cool for us to drink. He used to do it, so he didn't see the harm in it.

"I had never indulged in alcohol before that night. It never appealed to me. But that night, man—I just didn't care.

I got wasted. I mean stupid, out of my mind wasted.

"Anyway, after I got drunk, I wanted to see Annalisse so I went over to the house. Next thing I remember is seeing Anaya walk into the bedroom, only it wasn't Anaya. It, well you can figure out the rest."

Kenneth sobbed, bending over like he hoped for solace from his child. There was none. He wiped tears with the back of one hand and looked back up toward Adanya."

Adanya cried loudly. She wanted him to stop talking, but then again she didn't want him to stop. She had to know and she hated that she wanted to know.

"Annalisse lunged at me and started pounding me off of Anaya. I was out of my head; out of my mind. I didn't know what was happening. I quieted Annalisse by putting my hand over her mouth until I could be sure she was really Annalisse and not the other way around, and, I didn't want her parents waking up, at least not until I had a chance to tell her what had happened. But it was too late, because Mr. Kaplan stormed in the room. I thought he was going to kill me. It took Annalisse and Mrs. Kaplan to keep him from beating the brakes off me.

"It was an ugly scene. One that I'll always remember." Kenneth swiped his hand across his mouth. "Trying to explain to them what happened was the hardest thing I had to do, but I did it. If I had to go to jail for making the worst decision of my life that night, I deserved it. It wasn't easy. I didn't know if the Kaplan's were going to press charges against me or not. But they didn't. I don't know how they ever forgave me, but they did."

Adanya couldn't move. She listened to the horrid truth, the sad truth, the life changing truth.

Kenneth continued. "It wasn't until weeks later, after Anaya started having morning sickness, lying around, and not feeling well that Annalisse told me she overheard her mother and daddy talking about how Anaya had missed her period and they were scared that she might be pregnant. I was crazy out of my mind with worry. My folks were so upset with me. I had shown that even if I had been accepted at Howard, I probably wouldn't have lasted up there. I definitely messed up." Kenneth paused. "Do you want me to keep on?" he asked as he used his thumb to wipe away the tears.

Adanya nodded.

"Annalisse didn't want anything else to do with me. I couldn't blame her. For weeks, I begged her to forgive me. I begged Mr. and Mrs. K; I begged my parents; I begged God to forgive me. I prayed hard. I loved Annalisse so much; I couldn't see living my life without her by my side.

"She finally gave in, and took me back. We finished college, got married and started raising you.

"The bottom line is you raped Aunt Anaya." Adanya's voice was laced with contempt. "And you didn't spend a day in jail? You got a slap on the wrist and went off to college? Went on about your merry little life? You and Annalisse?" Adanya's hands flailed. "You're sorry, that's for sure, but not the way you think."

"Don't you realize the hurt Annalisse went through after she learned what had happened? It took her a really long time to forgive herself."

"Whooptie do. Is that supposed to make me feel sorry for her? Well, I don't. She should feel the way she's feeling." Adanya began to walk away.

"Honey, wait."

"What?"

"I know I really screwed things up, but I didn't mess up

when it came to you. If I had the power to make that night where it never happened, then I'm telling you if it meant I wouldn't have you, then I'm not ashamed to tell you that I wouldn't change a thing. You're my baby. You're my blood."

"But think about what you did, the crime you committed, and then hid for all these years. Then answer this one question. Adanya stared at him, and without so much as a grimace she asked, "What's blood got to do with it?" Before he could answer, Adanya whisked out of his office.

4

"In the book of life, the answers aren't in the back."
Charlie Brown

Adanya rushed out of the office building, blinded by a truth she didn't want to accept. She didn't know how she would face her life with what she'd come to learn in such a short time span. Two times, she almost wrecked her pearl white Audi Roadster, once going into a tailspin on the slick covered street leading her in the direction of her grandparents' house. They would tell her that this whole thing was a mistake.

She drove as fast as she could, without causing an accident, until she arrived at their one story, three bedroom brick house, tucked behind the signature white brick walls of Schilling Farms community. A patch of ice caused the Audi to slide but thankfully, it stopped a few yards short of hitting her grandparents' garage.

She got out of the car and hurried to the front door, placing her gloved finger on the buzzer and didn't let up off it until she saw the oak door open. It was her grandfather.

"Child, what are you doing out here in all this bad weather?' Maurice Kaplan looked around outside like someone could have been chasing his granddaughter. He opened the door wider so she could come inside. She walked into the living room and rubbed her hands together. Her grandmother, planted in front of the television, stood up from her seated position.

Adanya scanned her surroundings.

"Where's Aunt Anaya?"

"In her sitting room. Why? Did she call you? I tell you that girl will get a hold of a number and once she has it in her address book, she'll call people all day long, and night, if we let her," Mrs. Kaplan commented, and then chuckled.

"No, she didn't call me."

"'Danya," her grandmother said and stared. "Go over there and sit by the fireplace and warm up. What's going on?" she asked. "Girl, you're acting like you just witnessed a murder or something."

Without saying a word, Adanya did as she was told. She removed her coat and then took a seat in the chair closest to the fireplace but it did nothing to warm her. She shivered from the coldness, from her sickness, and from the ice, that was quickly forming around her heart.

"You have me worried," he said.

Mrs. Kaplan retreated to the same chair where Adanya had parked her body. Her slim, petite silhouette easily found space next to Adanya. Bewilderment attached itself to her face and uncertainty overtook her voice. "Talk to us, 'Danya," she urged. "What is it, baby?"

A slight hesitation appeared in Adanya's eyes. She felt like she was being tormented by confusing emotions and thoughts of what was real and what wasn't. The phone started ringing.

Mr. Kaplan walked over to the phone lying on the end of

the sofa where Mrs. Kaplan had previously sat. He viewed the caller ID.

"It's Annalisse."

"Don't answer it," Adanya shouted. Her outburst startled both of her grandparents.

Mrs. Kaplan nodded at her husband and he let the phone continue to ring. When it stopped, Adanya's phone started ringing, but she refused to answer it too.

"Why don't you want us to talk to your mother?" Eva Kaplan asked her granddaughter.

"Look, whatever is going on, you can talk to us," her grandfather said."

"Is Aunt Anaya my mother?"

Mr. and Mrs. Kaplan seemed to turn a shade darker at the same time.

Mrs. Kaplan's hand flew against her mouth. "Oh, Lord, have mercy."

Immediately, Maurice Kaplan started wandering aimlessly around the perimeter of the spacious family room. "Where did you hear that?"

Mrs. Kaplan took hold of Adanya with both arms and rocked her from side to side like she was an infant. "Yes, who told you such a thing?"

"I heard Mother…Annalisse yesterday." Adanya spoke softly. "She was talking on the phone about it to Miss Kaye." Adanya proceeded to tell her grandparents what had occurred. When she finished pouring her soul out to them about everything that had transpired, Adanya felt totally exhausted. "All I need for you to do is tell me the truth. I want somebody to tell me the truth."

"Hi, Pretty Adanya." Anaya quietly appeared at the entrance to the family room. A smile as wide as a moon pie filled Anaya's face when she saw Adanya.

Mrs. Kaplan got up from the sofa and walked over to her daughter, placed one arm around her lovingly, and kissed her on the side of her neck that was shielded by her shoulder-length braided hair.

Adanya looked away. She couldn't digest the fact that this woman who talked and acted like a child was actually her mother. She couldn't face her or look at her the same. She felt like she wanted to scream.

Anaya looked hurt and started crying. "Pretty Adanya, mad at me?"

Adanya jumped up, zipped past Anaya and ran to the bathroom, with Gram trailing behind. She didn't have time to close the door because her grandmother blocked it. Gram walked into the bathroom and then closed the door behind. "I know this is hard for you. God only knows what you're going through, baby. But Anaya loves you, so do not take it out on her. Everything that happened may have been wrong, but out of all of the bad that did happen, still, the goodness of God came out of it because we were blessed with you. We have a beautiful, smart, loving, young woman in you, Adanya. I know it has to hurt like hell, and yes, I said 'hell', but it's the only way I can show you that I recognize your despair.

"I don't know how much you know, but obviously you know that Annalisse isn't your biological mother. But the woman on the other side of that door," she said pointing at the bathroom door, "has a child's mind, but an open heart, and she loves you. And so does Annalisse and Kenneth. We all love you, honey. What we decided to do back then has come back to haunt us. Maybe we should have told you, but how? How could we explain it to you? Now there's a rift in this family that only God can bridge."

Adanya sat on the toilet and covered her face in her hands.

"I'm sorry you had to find out like you did. But I can tell you this; if for one minute, me or your gramps thought he intentionally hurt Anaya, he would have been locked up without so much as a heartbeat. But he was young. He made a cruel mistake and he was sorry for it."

Adanya remained silent, and her head remained buried in her hands.

Her grandfather knocked on the door.

"I'm coming in. I have something to say too."

Grams spoke up. "Come on in."

He walked into the large bathroom and planted himself on the side of the Jacuzzi style tub across from where Adanya sat.

"'Danya, I've known your daddy since he was a youngster. I remember when he used to come by here to see Annalisse, called himself wanting to court my baby. His parents, your paternal grandparents, were and still are some of our closest friends, but you know that. Only thing between us is distance and that's because after they retired and decided to move to Tucson we don't get to see them too often. But like I said, I'm not telling you something you don't already know. As for Kenneth, I believed him back then; I smelled the alcohol on his breath that God awful night. He smelled like the stuff had been poured all over his body.

Tears swelled in Maurice Kaplan's eyes as he relived the events of that fateful night. "My first thought was I wanted to kill him, but it was the hand of God that held me back. Your Gram has been by my side forty-seven years; she and Annalisse kept me from choking the life out of him. It took them a while to get me to stop and listen. The boy was sorry and hurt. God knows that he didn't realize what he had done. That's why it's dangerous for young people to venture into drugs and alcohol, thinking it'll make things better."

Adanya turned and faced her grandmother. With sad eyes, she spoke. "Gram, what about me? Who thought about my hurt? Who thought about the day that I would find out about all of this? Everyone seems to have been thinking about Annalisse and Kenneth, and about how to turn something foul into something good. Nobody seems to have thought about what Anaya went through. For God's sake, Gram, my mother was raped by my father. Nothing can ever change that."

Mrs. Kaplan placed her hand on Adanya's shoulder. "Nothing is going to change the past. But I do know that we had to learn how to forgive. Holding on and feeling bitter toward Kenneth was not going to change the fact that you were brought into this world. And as bad as it was, we do not believe he raped her like you keep accusing him of. Maybe we made the wrong decisions back then; I don't know. But what I do know is that Annalisse has been a good mother to you. Not once has she complained about that."

"Why would she complain? It was her and my daddy's fault for what happened to Aunt Anaya, and now everybody expects me to be fine like nothing ever happened. Well, I'm not. And you and no one else can make me feel better," Adanya yelled. "And if she couldn't give him her consent to have sex with her, then he raped her," she added.

"Hold on," Mr. Kaplan stated with firmness. "Don't you ever raise your voice to me or your grandmother, young lady. Now, I know this is hard for you, but I will not tolerate your disrespect. Do you understand me?"

"Yes, sir." Adanya dropped her head.

"And I'm sure when Annalisse was talking to Kaye she was talking out of frustration. It's not been easy for her to keep the truth from you. It hasn't been easy to come to terms with the fact that she could never give Kenneth what her own sister gave him. It has to be times when she wonders if Anaya understands that you're her birth daughter. Anaya gave you your name. She lights up when she sees you. What do you think that does to Annalisse? She's constantly badgered with memories of what happened. But what can be done about it now? Nothing. As for Kenneth, he loves you. For heaven's sake, you're his child. You're his blood. If I didn't believe that with everything in me, I wouldn't be here defending him."

"Don't you get it? That's the problem. Why didn't someone tell me when I was old enough to understand? Maybe then, things wouldn't be so bad. I can't look at Anaya as my mother. When I see her, when she came in the living room and called me Pretty Adanya, I saw a little girl. A little girl in a grown woman's body. Not a mother, not even a full grown woman, although she's both. But she can never be a mother to me. Never." Adanya cried. She felt weak and sick again.

"Shhh, baby. It's all right. Cry, sweetheart. Let it out." And Adanya did. She sobbed until Anaya knocked on the door.

The phone started ringing again. "I'll get it." Gramps left, closing the door behind him.

"I want you to stay here tonight. It's getting pretty bad out there and you've been through enough drama. Have you eaten anything?" her gram asked.

Adanya shook her head.

"Let me fix you something to eat." A knock on the bathroom door interrupted their conversation. "Yes?" Eva said.

"It's Annalisse on the phone. She said she's not hanging up until she talks to Adanya."

"I'm not talking to her," Adanya told her gram.

Without opening the bathroom door, Eva responded. "Tell her she'll talk to her later and not to worry. She's staying here for the night."

"Okay." Gramps shuffled away from the bathroom.

"Maurice," is Anaya okay out there?"

"Yea, I put the TV on the Gospel Channel," he replied.

"Now, you listen to me, 'Danya. I believe that everything, and I do mean everything, happens for a reason. I didn't say that it's always good, but what I am saying is that we have a lot to be thankful for. Look at you." She got the hand mirror from out of the vanity and placed it in front of Adanya.

Though her face was red and her eyes were swollen, Adanya studied her reflection.

"You are beautiful. You have been a blessing to this family. Yes, I know it was through unfortunate circumstances. But had it not been for what the devil was planning to use to destroy this family, we wouldn't have the precious woman you're looking at."

"Gram, I'm sorry, but I don't see it. I can't help if. I feel betrayed, lost, and empty." She cried in the bosom of her grandma. "Everyone has lied to me. Everything that I've been taught about who I am, about growing up, being an Anniston, I'm now questioning it all. And how stupid am I?"

"You are not stupid, and I do not want to hear any such thing coming out of your mouth ever again. As for questioning who you are, you are an Anniston. Annalisse is your mother; she's done what Anaya will never be capable of doing.

"I should have known something wasn't right about me and my life. I was blinded by my wonderful, oh so perfect life. But the joke's on me."

"You stop that kind of talk now, child. Maybe you didn't come from Annalisse's womb, but she has loved you, raised you, and cared for you. You are her daughter."

"Gram, you weren't upset to find out that she was going behind you and Gramps' back sneaking my father inside the house?"

"Oh, you better believe I was upset. I was absolutely heartbroken. I felt like everything me and Maurice taught her was for nothing. We raised both your mother and Anaya up in the church. We read the Bible to them and had family Bible studies at home almost every Friday night. Poor Anaya, though she's mentally challenged, she loved for us to read the Bible to her, and she still does to this day. You know for yourself how much she loves her gospel music."

Adanya smiled slightly. "That's true. I bet she knows the title of every CD she has in her room, and she has tons."

"Yes, she does," Mrs. Kaplan said and smiled. "Listen, I don't want to downplay anything that happened. It was hard to deal with what Kenneth did, but then for Anaya to turn up pregnant; Lord knows that was another trial. I was so angry. I fussed at God and blamed everybody. It took me a long time to forgive Kenneth and Annalisse. I felt like they were selfish and that they disregarded everything they had been taught.

"Kenneth's parents were just as messed up about everything too. But God had to show me, really all of us, how to forgive. It was a tough lesson, but we had to learn it, nevertheless. So I'm telling you that I've lived long enough to know that everything will work out in time. You'll see."

5

"An ounce of blood is worth more than a pound of
friendship." ~Spanish Proverb~

Adanya found it difficult to sleep because Anaya
wandered in and out of the guest room at least four times
during the night. She stood next to Adanya's bed and rubbed
Adanya's hair while singing her name, Pretty, Adanya.
Pretty Adanya."

It was close to one in the morning when Adanya
received her last visit. Adanya drifted into a twilight sleep;
she felt herself tossing and turning. By the time morning
came, she still felt wiped out and achy. The chattering of her
grandparents, along with Anaya, roused her from her sleep
so she got up. She was somewhat confused by the days.
After a minute or two, she was glad to remember that it was
Friday and she had no class lectures. Plus, the university
remained closed because of the biting winter weather. Maybe
she would have time to get over the flu, cold, whatever it was
and make a solid decision about what she was going to do
with the facts she'd learned

Adanya stretched and yawned. "Good morning," she said
as she sauntered into the kitchen. Her grandma immediately
stood.

Anaya ran up and hugged her. "G'morning, Pretty Adanya."

"Good morning, Aunt Anaya."

"I laid out towels and some toiletries in the back bathroom. I washed and dried the clothes you had on too, so you can put them back on after you get yourself cleaned up," Mrs. Kaplan told Adanya.

"I don't know what I was thinking last night, because I have clothes in my car."

"Don't worry about it. Maurice is outside. He can get 'em. You know that you can stay here as long as you need to."

"Thanks, Gram. I'll see. What's Gramps doing outside in the cold?"

"Clearing ice off the front porch and walkway."

"Oh."

"After you get dressed, come in here and put some of this hot food on your stomach. It'll make you feel better." She raised one hand up to stop Adanya from saying anything, whether she intended to or not. "It won't be anything heavy. Just a slice of toasted sour dough bread and a bowl of oatmeal. I have some hot apple cider tea too. You have to keep your energy up so you can fight off that nasty cold, flu, or whatever it is."

Adanya didn't put up a fuss. She went into the bathroom and took a hot bath. Thirty minutes later, she was sitting at the kitchen table alone, eating the breakfast Gram had prepared.

Gramps entered.

"Gramps, thank you and Gram for last night. I didn't know what I was going to do or where I was going to go. I still haven't processed everything that's happened, but I'm praying that God will show me what to do, because if he doesn't, I don't know how I'll get through this."

Gramps walked over to Adanya. "He took hold of her hand, guiding her to her feet, he hugged her.

Adanya felt his hot tears landing on her left shoulder. To discover all of the lies and deceit caused an emotional turmoil to play like a marching band in her mind.

"Gramps?"

"Yes, sweetie."

"Gram wants me to stay, but I can't." She tilted her head upward and looked into his red eyes.

Gram appeared. "Where are you going to go? Back home I hope."

"It won't be home, and it can't be here."

Adanya walked swiftly past her grandparents, and went to retrieve her bag of luggage and her coat. After putting on her coat, she prepared to leave, but stopped dead in her tracks. Mr. and Mrs. Kaplan were right behind her. She struggled to maintain an even tone to ward off the sense of rage that had started boiling inside. "I want to say goodbye to my mother."

Her grandparents stepped aside and gave her clearance to go toward Anaya's sitting room.

Knock. Knock.

Adanya turned the door knob gently and slightly pushed the door open. "Aunt Anaya." She peered inside and saw Anaya with an intense stare directed at the flat screen posted on the wall. The male and female hosts on the screen were engaged in what looked like amusing conversation. Anaya appeared hypnotized by their laughter and dialogue because she didn't budge or bother to look up. Adanya took cautious liberty to go and sit down next to her.

"Aunt Anaya."

As if coming out of a trance, Anaya turned her head to

face Adanya. She smiled and then turned her attention back to the television.

Adanya fought back the tears as she looked at Anaya for the first time as her biological mother. She thought back to the night that the sweet innocence of her mother was stolen; whether it was by accident, or rape, or God's will; whatever the politically correct term, it had happened and Adanya felt sickened by it.

Adanya watched Anaya while her mind flashed a screen of questions. How would she ever be able to make sense of any of this madness? How could what happen be chalked up to a mistake? How could Annalisse marry the man who impregnated her own twin sister? How? What other secrets might they be keeping from her?

"Aunt Anaya, I'm getting ready to leave. I wanted to tell you goodbye."

Anaya's eyes remained glued to the television screen.

Adanya slowly got up. She kissed her on the cheek and rubbed her hair. "Bye, Pretty Anaya." She walked out of Anaya's bedroom. "Gramps. Gram," she called out as she made her way into the front of the house. They were sitting quietly in the family room. "I'm leaving."

They both got up and followed Adanya to the door.

"'Danya, I wish you would stay. We need to work through this as a family,"

"Gram, I don't mean to be disrespectful. I promise I don't, but look what happened the last time everybody worked things out as a family." Adanya scurried out of the house before she allowed their hurt to make her change her mind.

Adanya sat in her car and hoped the heater would start warming up the ice cold interior. She was glad to see that the sleet and ice had started melting. The sun was trying to push itself from behind the clouds. She texted Nanette. "can I come ovr?

Nanette texted right back. "Sure c u soon b careful."

The drive didn't take as long as it would have had the streets still been iced over. She arrived at Nanette's townhome in twenty minutes. Almost instantaneously, after she used the door knocker, Nanette opened the door.

"Don't you look a hot mess?" Nanette said, in her jammies, with a multi-colored quilt hanging off her shoulders.

"I feel like a hot mess. How could my life become so screwed up in a matter of twenty-four hours."

"Girl, puhleeze. After I thought about what you told me last night, I started tripping really hard. I figured you were trying to pull some kind of prank on me or something." Nanette pulled the quilt tighter around her narrow shoulders.

"I wish," remarked Adanya.

"Sit down." Nanette's demeanor turned serious. "I'm sorry if I came off like I'm insensitive. This is just some wild stuff; the made for TV kind of drama."

"Yeah, tell me about it." Adanya clenched her jaw, and tried to stifle her cry. "What am I going to do? I cannot go back there. It's no longer home."

Nanette sat with her legs propped on the couch, her arms clasped around them. Tears appeared in her eyes like she was experiencing firsthand the hurt and disbelief of her best friend.

"Tell me what to do." Adanya pressed. Her cell phone rang while she searched for answers in Nanette's hazel eyes. She ignored it.

For an instant, Nanette's piercing glance sharpened. "Why didn't you answer?"

"That was my father. And my mother keeps calling too,

but I can't talk to either of them right now."

"Well, I'm here for you. But I'm going to be honest, I have no idea what to tell you. This is too much like a soap opera. Why don't you just chill for now, we can talk it out later

Adanya exhaled and gave in. She pulled off her boots and laid back on the tangerine oversized chair. Within minutes, she had drifted off to sleep.

◊

Nanette shook Adanya and aroused her from her sleep. It was late afternoon. Her eyes slowly opened and Adanya sat upright in the chair.

"What is it?" she asked.

"Wake up and listen. I've been thinking. Why don't you call your parents." Her hands flew up in the air.

Still groggy, Adanya sat up. "I don't know. The last thing I want to do is have another confrontation with them. I can't take any more of their excuses."

"Think about it at least. If you want, I'll go pick up Snoopy and bring him over here. That way you can have some alone time. Maybe that way you can begin to think things out before you go back."

"That would be great. You sure you don't mind?"

"That dog loves me. I have a few errands to run first, then after that, I'll go get him. In the meantime, you know how to make yourself at home."

"Thanks, Nanette. I love you, girl."

"I love me too." They chuckled.

"Call me if your plans change and you can't pick him up. I know how you can get lost when it comes to Gerald."

"If you had given that handsome hunk, Blake, Bleak, Block, whatever his name, a chance, you'd probably be doing the same thing."

"Humph, I don't think so. You got the wrong one." The two friends laughed some more and for a while the past twenty-four hours were just that – the past.

"You don't think you'd consider going out with him?"

"Who? Bleak?"

"Duh, yeah. Who else would I be talking about?"

"I don't know. Could be one of the number of eligible men I have hanging around. I don't tell you everything." Adanya laughed at her own made up words.

"Girl, please." Nanette paused. "Hey, what about I introduce you to one of Gerald's friends?"

Adanya picked up one of the sofa pillows and threw it at her. "You better not."

"But you need a distraction." She chunked the pillow back. "Let me get up and get ready to get out of here. I want to do what I need to do and get back."

"I think I'll do some online apartment searching."

"You know you're welcome to stay here."

"Yea, I know but I need to get a feel of what's available out there. Plus it'll keep my mind busy."

"Sure, understood."

Nanette left Adanya alone in the living room while she retreated to her bedroom to change. Adanya flipped channels. The ringing of her cell phone barged into her channel surfing. It was Annalisse.

"Why do you keep calling me?" Adanya blasted her as soon as she answered the call.

"Where are you? Mama said you got up and left without telling them where you were going. And you've had your phone turned off or on silent or something. Honey, please, tell me that you're okay. We're worried about you." Her voice sounded high pitched and tired.

"Is Daddy there?" Adanya asked coldly and ignored her mother's questions.

"Yes. Please, come home. We need to talk, sweetheart."

Adanya sighed heavily. "Seems like that's something that should have been done years ago."

"Honey," we need to talk. For the sake of our family."

Adanya hesitated. "I can't. I've heard more than enough." She ended the call without allowing her mother the chance to respond.

Nanette entered the room, prepared to leave for her errands.

"Nanette, I am so tired already."

"What happened now?"

"Uggg, my mother, uh Annalisse, I should say, just called."

"Hold up." Nanette jogged out of sight and returned seconds later with a key. "Take my spare door key just in case you feel the need to get out and get some air."

Nanette placed the multicolored key into Adanya's hand.

"Thanks."

A serious expression replaced Nanette's usually relaxed, carefree look. But this was not a laughing matter. Trouble was on the horizon and no one could tell how much more things were about to explode.

◊

Adanya drove with no particular destination in mind. She had tried to take the time alone to evaluate her true feelings but sitting alone in Nanette's apartment hadn't worked. Without thinking, she made a right onto Park Avenue then called Nanette. "Have you picked up Snoopy yet?"

"No, I was about to head over there. Why? What's up?"

"You were right. I needed to get out and get some air. And I also need to act like the grown woman I am, and handle my own business."

"Are you talking about going to talk to your parents?"

"Not necessarily. I'm talking about I can go and pick up Snoopy myself."

"I told you I was on my way."

"I know, but really, I'll get him. I don't plan on hanging around there. I need to get some more of my clothes."

"Okay, but call if you need me."

"I will. "

Adanya turned on the street she'd lived on since the age of twelve. She swallowed the knot that had formed in the base of her throat. She didn't use her remote to open the garage, but chose to pull up and park in the front driveway.

Adanya got out of the car and knocked on the front door. Annalisse answered.

A smile revealed itself when she saw her daughter. "Why didn't you use your key? Never mind, I'm just glad you came home." She reached out to hug her, but Adanya brushed aside and escaped Annalisse's reach.

She stopped just a hair past the entrance. Adanya looked at Annalisse. "Home? This can never be home again. I just came by to get some of my things." Snoopy came running toward her and almost jumped in her arms. "And to get Snoopy, of course." Adanya leaned down and picked up the excited dog. He gave her sloppy kisses and she returned his affection with pats and hugs.

Once she was fully inside the house, Adanya looked to her left in the open area, and with surprise met the solemn stares of her father and grandparents, all sitting in the hearth room. She didn't know how to react, respond, or relate to any of them at this moment. The harsh memories invaded her mind like a tidal wave. She stopped and returned their stares with one of her own. Only hers was far less sympathetic, and if anything, revealed Adanya's mounting anger.

Annalisse nervously stepped in front of Adanya. "Sweetheart, let me get your coat. You look a little weak. You're still fighting that cold, aren't you."

Adanya jerked away before her mother could help her take off her coat. She put Snoopy back down on the floor. "Don't bother. I can do for myself. I'm not a baby. But it seems that's something you all have forgotten." She took off her coat, turned, and hung it up in the coat closet in the hall. Adanya strolled into the hearth room, then stopped.

"What is this? Another one of your secret meetings to decide my poor mother's future…or mine?"

"You should be ashamed of yourself," her father said.

She looked around at everyone present and said with a bite in her voice. "Me? Ashamed? Why? Because I'm speaking the truth?"

Her father looked away.

Her grandmother offered advice. "Honey, I want to let you know that you're entitled to feel the way you do. You should take all the time you need to get through this. Talk to us one on one. Get counseling. Spend more time with Anaya. Whatever it takes, we're going to support you."

"Speaking of Aunt Anaya, where is she?" Adanya scanned the room.

Annalisse spoke up. "With Kaye."

Adanya began with a spiel of her own. "You all handled me and Aunt Anaya in a totally disrespectful, unkind, not to mention careless manner. Now my mother is almost forty years old, and what does she have? Nothing but a bedroom full of stuff, a phone so she can call me, you, Annalisse and Kenneth, maybe some friends from church, but even that's monitored. Outside of that, she has no life."

"You can't say that. That is her life. She lives in her world, and she's quite happy in it," Annalisse retorted.

"Who made you a mind reader?" Adanya snapped. "Plus, I don't care what any of you say, it's not fair that my mother grew up never knowing me as her daughter." Adanya pointed at herself. "You all made that determination for her, and for me." Adanya crossed her arms and faced Annalisse head on. "Guess you're supposed to be the perfect twin. Too bad you happen not to have kids of your own." Adanya's face was a glowering mask of red. "Walking around frontin', talking all your God talk, telling folks' how good God is to you."

"Listen, here, 'Danya. I know a lot has happened, but it's still no reason for you to come parading all up in here like you're going to whip somebody's behind or something. We are your elders, at least most of us will admit that," her grandmother said sternly and looked around the room.

"Gram is right," Gramps added. "Everything that we decided back then was done after much prayer and fasting. You forget that your mother was a minor, a child back then. She had no real say so about what we did."

Adanya rolled her eyes.

Kenneth stood up and started talking. "I know I stayed on my knees many nights asking God to forgive me and work things out. I was worried about Annalisse. I was worried about Anaya. I was having a baby by my girlfriend's sister."

Kenneth walked up to Adanya. "I'm so sorry." His shoulders shook as he spoke and his sobs gave way like a dam bursting. He reached out and clung to Adanya like he would never see her again.

Adanya wiggled out of his grasp. and stared at him for several seconds, then said, "There is nothing, absolutely nothing you can say that will rid me of the disgust I feel for you."

Before he turned and walked away, Kenneth wiped his eyes with the back of his hand like he was trying to keep the tears from escaping.

Gramps stood. "Look, everybody, I suggest we gather around the table, eat, drink, laugh, and talk like we usually reserve for Sunday afternoon. Adanya, your mother invited us to come over for lunch. I wish you would take a little time, sit down, eat, and we'll talk things out."

Kenneth leaned in and reached toward Annalisse. She stepped into the crook of his arms.

Annalisse cleared her throat. "You all can go in the dining room. Kenneth and I will bring out the food."

Adanya folded her arms in defiance "I didn't come here to eat."

"Adanya, this isn't going to work out overnight. This is one that God has to step in and clean up after His foolish children," said Gramps.

Kenneth looked at his father-in-law. "I hope you're right."

Adanya stood in the middle of the room like an ice sculpture. "Enough said already. I have to get out of here."

"Be reasonable, Adanya. You don't have to leave. There are five bedrooms in this house. You can sleep in any one you choose if you don't want to sleep in your own room. This house is large enough for you to be here and we'd never know you were here. You know that. Just stay at home where you belong." Annalisse's eyes shifted.

Kenneth spoke up. "You can have all the time, space, and whatever else you need to work through this," Kenneth begged.

"What is it going to take for you to understand?" Adanya turned around and headed up the stairs toward her bedroom.

Annalisse made a move toward her. Kenneth, who looked like he'd aged ten years overnight, held his wife back. "Let her go."

Adanya packed as much as she thought she'd be able to take in one trip. She strutted to the front door but came to a halting stop when she almost tripped over Snoopy.

"Snoopy, don't look at me with those big, black, sad, puppy dog eyes." She knelt down and cuffed his chin. "Mommy's not leaving you." She put his doggie sweater and leash on, then got her coat out of the closet and put it on. With pieces of luggage in her hand, and Snoopy trailing next to her, the cold outside meshed with the coldness forming around her heart.

◊

"I think I got most of my winter clothes, at least."

"I don't think so. You have a ton of stuff. I don't know where we can put it all."

"I hope I won't have to inconvenience you for too long. I can afford to be on my own. To be honest, I should have moved out from my parents' house a long time ago."

"Whatever you say, but you know you're welcome to stay here."

The girls gathered the luggage and headed toward the small room Nanette had designated as her office. The futon would be Adanya's bed for the time being. While they unpacked and rearranged things, they talked.

Nanette placed some items in the office closet. "What did they have to say?"

"Gram was trying to tell me why everything went down like it did. As far as I'm concerned, all they're doing is trying to justify their deceit."

"I can't imagine what I would do if I was in your shoes."

"It's caused me to think about a lot of things." Adanya cleared her throat.

"A lot of things like what?" Nanette closed the closet door and took a seat in her office chair.

"Listening to how everyone has maintained a family secret that hurt me to the core is really no longer the problem. It's the need they had to feed the deception."

Nanette embraced her torso with both of her arms. "All I can say is that most people do the best they know to do when trouble arises. I know that what has happened makes you look at your life and your family in a whole other manner. I would be totally bombed if something like this happened to me. But the fact remains that you are here. You have a special needs mother, but you also have Mrs. Anniston who has dedicated her life to loving you, providing the best for you, and flourishing you with love just like a mother. As for Mr. Anniston, I know that man must deal with a lot. To think that he slept with your mother's twin sister. Oh my, gosh. That's nasty." Nanette wrinkled her pointy nose and pulled back her dyed, honey blonde locs from off her face.

"That's what I'm talking about. Things should have been handled better. I'm so confused. Do I call Annalisse my mother? Do I call Aunt Anaya, mother too?" Adanya broke down in tears again, and fell in the chest of Nanette.

Nanette rubbed back her hair. "Shhh. It's got to work out. I don't know how, or when, but it will. Remember, God's way is perfect, Adanya. The battle is not yours. It belongs to Him."

"Yeah." Adanya sighed before she addressed another subject. "Maybe I need to think about some other options.

Instead of getting a place here, maybe I need to relocate; find a teaching position at another college."

"Please, I am not about to let my best friend leave me. You are going to get through this. Just pray and put this situation in God's hands."

Adanya whirled around and stopped. "How do you suppose I do that, Nanette? How do I let go and let God, as people say?"

"I wish I knew, I really do. All I can offer you is my shoulder to cry on."

"That'll do."

6

"To be a Christian means to forgive the inexcusable, because God has forgiven the inexcusable in you." ~C.S. Lewis~

Adanya turned into the liquor store. It was time for her to step out and do whatever it took to ease her pain. She walked into the store and felt like all eyes were on her. She was practically lost, not knowing what to ask for. She thought about some of the commercials she'd seen and looked around the store baffled and confused.

"May I help you?"

Adanya jumped as she turned to face the man who stood next to her with a friendly smile on his face.

"Anything in particular?"

Adanya stuttered. "Uh, not really."

"Are you looking for wine or something like vodka, brandy, rum?"

"Give me a minute, please." The man nodded and walked away. Adanya peered at the numerous posters. Her eyes stopped when she saw a poster with Sean 'Diddy' Combs holding a bottle of liquor. Adanya approached the man who had gone behind the glassed- in counter. She pointed to the poster. "I'd like a bottle of that."

"All right, Miss." He showed her a bottle and told her the price. Adanya nodded. He waited. He must have seen the look of unfamiliarity on Adanya's face because he instructed her where to place her money.

She put a twenty dollar bill on the slider. He pushed the bottle of vodka through the chute along with her change. Adanya jumped back, slightly startled.

She quickly placed the alcohol in her oversized designer purse and dashed out the store. Once she got inside of her vehicle, she backed up and drove off with lightning speed. If only her parents could see her now. She dismissed the thought and tears flooded from her eyes.

Adanya drove to Nanette's house. She was glad that Nanette wasn't there. She petted Snoopy who greeted her by almost jumping right into her welcoming arms. He kissed her all over her face.

She held him in her arms and went to her room where she placed her purse on the bed. "Come on, let me take you for a walk." She looked inside of her purse and pulled out the vodka and studied it. How much should she drink? Enough to take the pain away, but how much was that? She opened the bottle and didn't bother going to the kitchen to get a glass. She took a giant swallow right from the bottle and gagged as the disgusting, burning liquid as it went down her throat.

Ughh. How do people drink this stuff? She tucked the bottle inside of her coat pocket, got Snoopy's leash, and they went down the street toward the nearby pet friendly park.

Snoopy sniffed the grass, eyed a few dogs that passed, and finally found a spot to relieve himself. Adanya began to feel lightheaded. But not enough to keep her from retrieving the alcohol from her coat pocket and taking another swig. This time it wasn't as big of a gulp as the first one, and it didn't burn her throat as much either. She felt her head spinning. But her nerves seemed to calm down. She allowed Snoopy to walk around another five minutes or so before she turned around and headed out the park.

She stumbled. Was she wobbling? Is this how drunk people feel? Snoopy walked in front of her on his leash. "Snoopy, you are such a beautiful dog. She giggled.

Inside the apartment, Adanya unleashed Snoopy and went to the bathroom as a wave of nausea came over her. She leaned over the toilet but nothing came up. For several minutes, she remained in the bathroom but there was no reaction. She giggled and then staggered to her bedroom and plopped down on the bed without so much as removing her coat.

"I'm home." No answer. "Adanya?" Nanette walked up the hall until she arrived in front of Adanya's room. The door was partially open. "Knock, knock. May I come in?"

"Help yourself. You're my best friend."

Nanette walked into the room. "You sound better."

Adanya jumped up off of the bed.

"Why are you jumping? And why are you in here with your coat on? You sick again?"

"I feel grayyy-eight," Adanya's voice boomed.

"Ew, you stink." Nanette looked swiftly around the room. "You've been drinking? Are you crazy?"

"No, I'm not crazy. I feel good, good, good like a woman should." Adanya laughed and spread her arms. "Absolutely nothing is wrong with me." She swiveled around a couple of times and then fell backward, landing squarely on the futon.

Nanette walked over to Adanya. "How much have you had?" She sat on the side of the bed and helped Adanya remove her coat.

"Nanette, my best friend in the entire world." Adanya sat

up and then immediately fell back on the bed again. "Oops, my head is spinning. Am I on a merry go round, Nanette?"

"Where is it, Adanya? Give it to me right now."

"You want some? Sure," she slurred. Adanya reached over on the side of the bed where Nanette had laid her coat. She clumsily fumbled inside of her coat pocket until she pulled the bottle of vodka out and pushed it in Nanette's face. "Here you go, best friend. Take a sip of this. It might taste a little bit, a little bit, uh not so good at first, but it'll past." She laughed and kicked her legs up in the air.

Nanette jerked the bottle of alcohol out of Adanya's hand. "I'm going to make you a pot of black coffee. I'll be right back."

Adanya suddenly screamed. "Don't leave me."

Nanette didn't move. "Adanya, you can't let what happened make you do this to yourself. You weren't raised to go out and get drunk. You know this isn't right."

"I don't know what's right any more. I don't know who's right. Can you help me, Nannie? Hey, that's a good nickname for you. Nannie. Nannie. Nannie," she said in a drunken state.

"Hold up. I'll be right back. Okay?"

"'K, but you better hurry up or I'm leaving."

"You are not going anywhere. Now wait here." Nanette left the room, rushed to the kitchen and made a strong cup of instant coffee.

She returned with the hot brew only to find Adanya snoring loudly, legs hung over the bed, and Snoopy sitting on the floor looking up at his master like he understood her pain.

Nanette sighed. "Lord, help me to help my friend." She turned and went back to the kitchen, and poured the cup of coffee down the sink, then took a seat at the kitchen table. She looked down when she heard Snoopy whining at her heels. "It's going to be okay, boy."

◊

Adanya woke up with a splitting headache and a pasty, dry mouth. When she sat up her head started spinning and her stomach churned. She got up and ambled to the bathroom with. barely enough time to make it to the toilet before she started throwing up.

"Nanette, are you here?" She ventured out into the hall. "Snoopy," she called, but she didn't see him either.

She went back to the bathroom and turned on the faucets so she could take a bath. While the bathtub filled, she went into the kitchen and saw food Nanette had cooked. She turned up her nose. It was too much for her to consider eating. She opted for a can of chicken noodle soup she found in the pantry. "I'll eat this when I get out of the tub."

Adanya relaxed in the soothing hot tub of water. With her head back against the tub, she thought of how disgusting the alcohol made her feel. But at least it made her forget about her problems, if only for a little while. While she bathed, she heard the familiar sound of Snoopy's bark as he approached her room.

"Adanya."

"I'm in the bathroom." She heard Snoopy's cute whine. "Snoopy, chill out. Mommy will be out in a minute."

"Are you all right in there?"

"Yeah, I'm fine."

"Have you eaten?" Nanette asked from the other side of the bathroom door.

"I took out a can of soup. I saw the food you cooked, but I couldn't eat it. Sorry."

"No problem. We'll talk when you come out."

"Okay."

◊

The friends sat in the front room on the couch.

"Adanya, what were you thinking? Drinking is not the way to solve anything. It's what got your family into trouble in the first place."

"I know, but you aren't in my shoes. Your family life isn't messed up. I don't know if I can believe anything Annalisse and Kenneth have told me, or my grandparents for that matter."

"You have to give this problem to God. He's the only one who can give you the proper guidance and direction."

"How could He let this happen? Don't you understand the magnitude of what they did? My mother was sexually molested by the man I call father, and nothing; absolutely nothing was done to punish him. It's like my family swept everything under the rug. Was it because they knew Anaya couldn't defend herself so they just pushed it all to the side and came up with this elaborate tale of deceit?"

"We don't know always how things happen or why they happen, but I believe it's all for a reason."

"I know the whole spiel about God's ways are not our ways, and frankly that's not good enough for me."

"Adanya." Nanette's voice rose in utter surprise. "How can you say something like that? That's not like you at all. You're always the one to tell me when I've gotten down and out or worried about a situation that God is in control. Now you want to sit here and act like you don't have a relationship with God?"

"All I'm saying is that I'm fed up with everything and everybody, including God." Tears gushed. She got up from the sofa. "Of all people, I thought you would understand. But you're acting like I shouldn't feel the way that I feel. Like I'm supposed to smile and go on like nothing has happened. Well, my whole life has changed, Nanette. Don't you get it?"

"Yes, I get it. But sulking and throwing a fit against God isn't going to solve anything."

"I need some fresh air." Adanya ran to her room and returned with her coat on.

"Where are you going? It's almost eight o'clock."

"I'm a grown woman. I don't answer to you."

Adanya patted Snoopy on the top of his head when he appeared at the door next to her. "Not this time. Mommy will be back soon." She left out the door, got in her car, and drove off.

Adanya had no idea where she was going as she drove through the city. Without rhyme or reason, she drove to the university. After driving up and down the streets of the university, she parked close to the building where she taught her communications class. Adanya sat in the car. Her ringing cell phone startled her but she refused to answer. She put it on Silent and then laid her head against the car's headrest. Another boat load of fresh tears cascaded down her face. "God, what am I supposed to do?"

The silence yielded no answers. She was devastated and torn inside. She left the university and drove to the deli. Once there, she went inside and asked to be seated at a table in the back.

The server asked, "How can I help you?"

"A cup of decaf and a turkey sandwich with the trimmings."

"Okay, I'll be back shortly with your order."

With her head lowered, Adanya fought off the beginnings of an unwelcomed headache. She used her hand to massage her forehead.

"Are you all right?"

Caught off guard, Adanya's head jerked slightly. She was surprised to see Bleak.

"What are you doing here?"

"I could ask you the same thing? I wouldn't imagine a pretty lady like you would be dining alone, and at this time of night."

"Who says I'm alone?"

"I ordered takeout," he said with a bag of food in his hand. "While I was waiting on my order, I noticed you sitting here in the corner. I never saw anyone join you. So I assume…"

"You know what they say about assuming, don't you?"

Bleak chuckled. "I'm afraid so."

"So what are you doing? Spying on me?"

"You look like you've been crying. Are you okay?" he asked without making reference to her question.

"I'm fine."

"Good, believe me, I am not trying to invade your privacy. I asked out of concern." He showcased one opened palm. "Anyway, sorry if I disturbed you." He turned to walk away.

"Hold up."

Bleak complied.

"I'm sorry. I have no reason to bite your head off. It's just that I, well anyway I didn't mean to be rude."

"No problem," Bleak answered.

"Uh, would you like to join me?'

Bleak looked surprised. "Are you sure?"

"Yes."

Bleak sat down across from her.

The server returned with her coffee and food. "Would you like a cup?" the server asked Bleak while he poured a cup for Adanya.

"No, thanks."

The server nodded and walked away.

"Do you want to tell me why you're out here alone with a face that looks like the whole world has turned against you?"

"It's really that noticeable?" Adanya cracked a half smile.

"I'm afraid it is."

Adanya turned the interrogation on him. "Why don't you tell me why you happen to be here at this time of night, and why do I keep running into you?"

"To answer your first question, I live nearby and I don't take to eating my own cooking. Especially since I can barely boil water, so I thought I'd grab something and take it home." He laughed. 'And this place has great food."

"And question number two," said Adanya.

"I can't say why you keep running into me. Maybe it's divine intervention."

Bleak flashed a radiant smile, and Adanya's eyes connected with his. She quickly averted her attention away from him. She took a sip of the steaming, hot brew and used her free hand to smooth back her frazzled hair.

"You want to talk about it?"

"Talk about what?"

"What made a pretty lady like you cry? Or should I ask who?"

"Nothing that I care to share," Adanya replied. "I don't air my personal business to strangers."

"Seeing that we keep running into each other, maybe it's a sign that we need to get to know more about each other, so we won't be strangers."

"Listen, I need to get out of here." She gathered her purse and coat and prepared to stand up.

"Don't let me run you off. I need to get home myself. I have a long night ahead of me and an even busier day tomorrow." Bleak picked up his carryout from off the table and stood up before Adanya. "Have a good night. Be safe." Bleak turned and walked away just as quickly as he had first appeared.

◊

Bleak pulled the collar of his jacket up around his neck to ward off the light chill.

Seeing Adanya again piqued his interest in her that much more. She said she hadn't been crying, but he knew better. Her eyes told the truth, but why was she upset?

He wanted to get to know her, but he believed the task that lay before him would be tough. She had an impenetrable wall built around her like Fort Knox. The question he had to ask himself was, did he want to find the key to unlock the mystery behind her sad eyes.

Bleak walked the two and half blocks until he reached his two bedroom, tastefully furnished flat. His job as a freelance graphic designer afforded him a comfortable income and the added opportunity to work a flexible schedule. That meant working sometimes through the night. During the day, when he wasn't soliciting potential clients or meeting with established ones, he spent time working out at the YMCA and tutoring youth in the afternoon at his church's after school program.

As for dating, he made little time for it, preferring rather to focus unspent energy on doing things that were far less tempting than a beautiful woman. Until he saw Adanya, he had no problems saying no to the many women who aggressively approached him, including some who were as grounded as he was in the church.

He worked on several projects after he finished eating,

but his mind kept reflecting on Adanya. *I hope she's all right. Maybe I shouldn't have left her alone.* When he made an almost irretrievable error on his project, he shook his head and told himself that it was time for him to get his mind together and concentrate on his work. This was no time to be taken in by the wiles of a woman, especially one that made it clear that she had no interest in getting to know him.

7

"The angry people are those people who are most afraid."
Robert Anthony

On her way back to Nanette's, Adanya stopped at the liquor store again. The hangover she suffered the week before didn't deter her from attempting to drown her sorrow in the liquid poison a second time. Her life was already in shambles. Things certainly couldn't get any worse.

Upon her arrival, she placed her key into the front door. Nanette opened it before Adanya had time to turn the lock.

"I've been worried about you," Nanette chastised her best friend. "You wouldn't answer your cell phone or respond to my text messages."

"I had to get away; try to get clear my mind."

"Running away from your problems isn't going to solve a thing."

"Look, how many times do I have to say it," she yelled. "I'm not a child. I am grown. I can do as I please. If you have a problem with that, then all I ask is that you give me a couple of more weeks until I can move into my own apartment."

"Don't get an attitude with me. I'm just trying to help."

"The only way you can help is by letting me and Snoopy

stay here until I can move. That's it."

"Whatever." Nanette closed the front door and turned to walk up the hallway. "Goodnight. I'm going to bed."

"Nanette."

"What?" Nanette answered in a perturbed tone.

"I don't mean to shut you out."

Nanette walked back toward Adanya and hugged her. She heard a thud. "What was that?" she asked and looked down on the floor at the brown paper bag. Before Adanya could bend down and pick it up, Nanette beat her to it. She looked inside the bag. "What are you doing this for? Drinking is not going to help. Why don't you get that through your head? You need to go before God, Adanya. You will not find the solution to your problem in this."

Nanette walked into the kitchen and stopped when she got to the kitchen sink.

Adanya hurried behind her. "Don't you pour that out. It's none of your business how I deal with my problems."

Nanette paid no attention.

Adanya reached for the bottle but Nanette used her elbow to push her aside. She opened the liquor and started pouring the pungent smelling liquid down the drain.

"You and Snoopy are welcome to stay here as long as you need to, but there will be no drinking here. Not in my house. Save that for when you have your own place." Nanette threw the empty bottle into the wastebasket and pounced off, leaving a shocked Adanya standing alone in the kitchen with Snoopy sitting beneath her feet.

Adanya picked up Snoopy and went to her room. She sat him on the bed, threw off her coat, slung her purse on the nearby chair, and started peeling off her clothes. "Mommy's going to take a shower. Maybe I can wash away some of the pain I'm feeling." After she got out of the shower, Adanya put on her pajamas, went to her room and kneeled down on her knees out of habit. "Since I'm down here I might as well tell you how I feel. I don't like what's happened. How could you allow my life to be turned upside down? How can you possibly use this to work out for my good? I need to know." She finished her prayers and laid on the futon.

Bleak Blessinger entered her thoughts while she tossed and turned on the uncomfortable futon. Bleak had sounded sincere, like he was concerned about her wellbeing. But why? He didn't know her any more than she knew him. She had no idea what he did for a living or where he lived. And the fact that she was attracted to him was also beyond her comprehension. If she were to date a man, he wouldn't be outside of her race. She turned and opened the drawer to the computer desk. There was still some liquor left in the bottle she had from last night. She opened it and swallowed the burning liquid.

"Ugh." The sense of calm that flooded over her outweighed the nasty taste.

◊

Knock. Knock.

Adanya turned in the bed.

Knock. Knock.

"Adanya, are you going to work?"

Adanya sat up. "Yeah," she answered slowly. Snoopy began to yelp. Adanya glanced at the clock. For some reason, her alarm had failed to go off. "Hold on, Snoopy. Give me a minute and I'll take you outside."

"If you want me to take Snoopy for his morning walk, I have time," Nanette said like she could read Adanya's mind.

"Okay. Come on in."

Nanette opened the door, walked in, and saw Adanya still in the bed.

"You're going to be late if you don't hurry."

"I know. I had my alarm set, but it didn't go off, or at least I didn't hear it. I'm glad it's hump day."

"Me too."

"Thanks for offering to take Snoopy out for me."

"Sure. Come on, boy."

Adanya got up and started getting ready for work.

When Nanette returned, Adanya was dressed and doing finishing touches on her hair.

"You want to meet for lunch?"

"I don't know." Adanya shrugged. "I'll text you."

"Okay. See ya and have a good day."

"You too." She went into the kitchen and had a cup of juice and a bagel and took an acetaminophen capsule to ward off another oncoming headache.

On her drive to work, her cell phone rang. The ringtone signaled it was her father. She ignored the call. Minutes later it rang again. It was Annalisse this time. Adanya ignored her call too. Let them stew in their own mess. I've had enough.

The day presented no unusual occurrences. Adanya noticed that most of the class appeared attentive. She surmised it was because of today's film outlining argumentation and debate. The day moved swiftly. After a faculty luncheon meeting, she had one additional lecture before she could call it a day. She hastened outside to a clear afternoon. She stopped momentarily and sucked in the air and then walked to her car.

"Have a good evening, Professor Anniston," someone said. Adanya turned around. She recognized the young man from her morning class. "Thank you." She smiled. When she sat in her car, she texted Nanette to see if she had special plans for dinner.

Having dinner w/Gerald. be there soon. Nanette texted.

Once home, with Snoopy content and lying down on the rug in the kitchen, she prepared an acorn squash and mixed vegetables. She recalled a lullaby her daddy used to sing to her when she was a little girl. "Michael row the boat ashore, hallelujah," she sang. She wiped tears that formed in her eyes. She missed her daddy.

"I'm home." Snoopy jumped up and raced to the door leading from the garage. Nanette came into the kitchen. "Smells good in here."

"Hi, girl."

"Hey. How was dinner?"

"Good. Gerald and I met up at Neely's and shared a plate of barbeque nachos. They were so good."

"I know they were. That place has some of the best barbeque. I'm cooking an acorn squash. You're welcome to some."

Nanette rubbed her tummy in a circular motion. "I can't eat another bite. I'm going to go and get out of my clothes and take a shower. You knock yourself out. We'll talk later." Nanette left the kitchen with Snoopy at her heels.

"Oh, so that's how you do, huh, Snoopy," said Adanya. "You leave me as soon as another woman walks in the door." Adanya and Nanette laughed.

Adanya sat at the table and ate her food in silence. She heard Nanette in the back singing while Snoopy barked. Adanya giggled between bites of food.

When she finished eating, she cleaned up her mess, and then went to her room and got her things together for the next day. Afterward, she called and talked to Anaya for a while before she met up with Nanette in the living room.

Nanette was curled up in her oversized chair with her feet

tucked beneath her. "So, have you talked to your family lately?" Nanette asked when Adanya sat down on the sofa.

"I talked to Anaya. And whenever I talk to her, I say hello to my grandparents. I don't know when I'll be ready to talk to Annalisse and Kenneth. Right now, I want to be somewhere else. I'm thinking about taking a trip to Atlanta."

Nanette furrowed her brows. "What's in Atlanta?"

"It's not what's in Atlanta. It's more like who's in Atlanta. I was invited for a nonprofessional interview dinner with the Dean of the Communications Department—part pleasure but mostly business. She has an opening for a professor. She contacted me, personally, to see if I'd be interested, especially since I'm an alumnus. And Atlanta is way cool, so I would have lots of fun and the chance to connect with a lot of people. You could move there too. I bet you wouldn't have a problem getting a job at a school down there."

Nanette shrugged. "Maybe, since I am a free spirit. As long as I'm doing well, being successful, and walking the straight and narrow the best that I can, then my parents are cool. But then there's my hunny, Gerald."

"How serious are you about him?"

"We're in love. I think that's as serious as it gets."

"Wow, I didn't know. I'm glad for you."

"Hey, you brought something to wear to church right? Nanette asked out of nowhere.

"I don't plan on going. I don't want to see my family sitting up in there with fake, happy expressions plastered on their faces like nothing's happened."

"I was talking about going with me and Gerald. We dress casual, and you have plenty in that bag of clothes in your room, Miss Fashionista, that you can put together. So Sunday morning, church it is." Nanette pointed at her friend and picked up Snoopy who had waddled in the room. "Oh, look at him, will you. If you decide to go to Atlanta, I'll have to dog sit. You know that every time Snoopy comes over here, he demands all of my attention." Nanette laughed and gave him a sloppy kiss on his nose. "I guess I'll be a good friend to you by walking my best little buddy again tonight. You take it easy. I'll be back later."

"Thanks. You're a doll."

Nanette went to the closet and combed through the diaper pouch sized doggie bag. "You are the first and only person I know that packs a doggie bag for her dog. Clothes, foods, snacks, bottled water, leash, meds, what is it you don't have in here? Snoopy has it made."

"Always be prepared. Nanette, seriously, why don't you consider riding to Atlanta with me? It will be fun. We can hang out and just do our thing after my meeting. And you can scout for jobs," suggested Adanya.

"I wish I could, but I have plans of my own. I'll be leaving out next week. I'll be gone ten days."

"What are you and Gerald doing? Eloping?" teased Adanya.

"No, this has nothing to do with Gerald. I talked to my parents the other day. They want me to fly up there for a visit since I missed Christmas, so I'm leaving for Denver next Thursday morning. Since you'll be in and out, that'll put me at ease about being gone and leaving my apartment empty. I wish you'd give some serious thought to moving in with me permanently. I could use the roommate or should I say roommates." She put the sweater on Snoopy and attached his blue leash around his neck.

"I don't know." Adanya was still too uncertain about what she was going to do with her life. Would it be a major move to Atlanta, or would she remain in Memphis and face the fire head on. "I'll think about it," said Adanya, "but first things first."

"For sure. Tell your mommy you'll see her in a little bit."

Snoopy barked twice.

Adanya spent time on the internet looking over the layout of Spelman's Communications Department but her mind was elsewhere. Thoughts of family, the possibility of starting over in a new city, with a new job, and leaving Anaya behind caused anxiety. She clicked off the internet, got up and went and lay down.

With surprise and totally unexpected, she thought about Bleak again. What was it about the guy that got her rattled every time she saw him? Why did she keep thinking about him? What was his reason for targeting her?

8

"What greater thing is there for human souls than to feel that they are joined for life - to be with each other in silent unspeakable memories." George Eliot

Nanette left for Denver, leaving Adanya alone with nothing but her thoughts. Spending time alone, away from family, away from her best friend, and away from God, caused her to pause and think about her life.

She had to find a way to move forward, leave the past behind. She reasoned with herself. People make mistakes, and maybe her daddy was telling the truth. Maybe the fact that he was intoxicated that night, maybe he really did think Anaya was Annalisse "Naw," she said, shaking her head, "I don't see it." And my mother? Annalisse? What's up with her? I can't believe she stayed with him after she practically saw what he did to Aunt Anaya. And Gramps and Gram, Paw and Maw Anniston, what was up with them that they overlooked what he did, talking about it was the best decision at the time. Seems like he never suffered any consequences for his actions. Lord, I don't understand."

Adanya felt like she was on a Ferris wheel. She shook her head briskly, like she was trying to escape from the confines of the walls that seemed to be closing in on her.

It was time to set her mind on something other than her family.

She couldn't quite remember the last time she'd eaten, but the growling sound coming from her belly, told her it had been awhile.

Adanya got in her car and drove around until she spotted a Danver's Restaurant. With quickness, she looked over her shoulder and saw that the traffic was clear. She jumped into the left hand lane, then farther left into the turn lane. Making a swift turn, she drove on the Danver's lot and proceeded to the drive-thru.

"May I help you?" the man blared through the intercom.

"I'll have a turkey burger with mustard, pickle, onion, and ketchup, a side of onion straws, and a medium lemonade."

Adanya sipped on the tart lemonade while she waited patiently for the rest of her order. The smiling drive-thru host was smacking gum and talking to someone else while he passed the combo meal to her. Adanya quickly studied the contents of her order to make sure everything was correct before she moved ahead.

While driving, she scanned her mind for things she could do to past the time. Normally, when she wasn't at work, she would be at home spending time with family or hanging around church. But church was a far cry from her mind. Not only could she not see herself going to the church she'd practically grown up in, she would never be able to stay in the same house with her parents again. As for living with Nanette, she already knew that was a temporary fix too. Nanette had her own life. They were best friends and Adanya wanted to keep it that way. Moving in permanently would only put a cramp in Nanette's life. The fact that Nanette had a boyfriend and a host of other friends who sometimes visited, and that was cool, but not all of Nanette's friends were Adanya's friends.

She resolved that the sooner she got her own spot, the sooner she could get on with revamping her own life and maybe reaching out to establish a closer relationship with Anaya.

Adanya ate while she drove in the direction of the college. There were several apartment complexes in and around the area. If she moved close to the college campus she could walk or sometimes bike to work. Adanya released a giggle at the thought of seeing herself all suited, booted, and riding a bike. She slowed her pace and turned into a complex that looked appealing.

Umm, these look nice, and new too. Even better than the ones I saw the other day. Adanya drove farther into the complex until she saw the leasing office. Outside of the office was a box that held brochures. She got out of her car and retrieved one. She pulled into a parking space, but kept the engine going, while she studied the different floor plans the complex offered.

Adanya concentrated on looking at apartments and townhomes with at least two bedrooms. She wanted to have space for Anaya to come on some weekends. That way she could spend time getting to really know the person that lived inside Anaya's world. It was not going to be an easy feat, Adanya believed, but she was determined that she was not going to turn her back on her real mother, whether Anaya understood their connection or not. It was time for a change in her life. Maybe what Gram said was partially true. Maybe God could turn around what had happened, and miraculously work it out for good.

Adanya was about to end her apartment search but was intrigued by a set of duplex flats she saw tucked on the corner of a side street. They were a little farther away from the college, but she could still make it to work by car in less than ten minutes. Her drive through the complex revealed a small complex of duplex flats with well-manicured lawns, private garages, a small convenience store on site, along with several other quaint businesses. She felt like she hit gold when she saw someone walking their dog. It had to be divine intervention for her to see the For Lease sign in front of one of the flats. Adanya stopped in front of the sign and wrote down the information.

I'm going to call. No sense in putting off later what I can do now. No one answered, but a pleasant voice invited her to leave her information. Adanya did. Her phone rang moments after she ended the call.

"Yes, I just called," she explained to the agent on the other end of the line. "I left a message about the flat you have for lease on Central Avenue." Adanya listened to the man as he told her about the twelve hundred and ninety-five square foot duplex flat. The private community was less than three years old. The duplex came furnished, had two bedrooms, a den, two bathrooms, an eat in kitchen, a private patio, and it was pet friendly. Adanya sucked in a deep breath. It sounded like everything she wanted. She released a welcoming sigh when he told her the monthly rate. It was well within her budget. She never had to worry about money before, but now she was determined that she was no longer going to expect or rely on her parents' hefty income to give her the lifestyle she had grown accustomed to. If she had to start from scratch that was what she was going to do.

Adanya made an appointment to meet with the leasing manager in an hour to tour the place. She remained in the area, checking out the rows of businesses located inside the community. There was a high end store stocked with bedding items, kitchen accessories, and decorative pieces that she could purchase to fix up the flat. She became giddy with excitement at the thought.

Time flew by a lot more quickly after she started imagining all the things she could do with a place of her own. She pulled up in front of the flat and waited. She didn't have to wait long because a car pulled up and parked next to her. A portly looking man got out and looked in her direction. She let down her window.

"Are you the leasing manager?"

"Yes, ma'am." The man walked over to her car and quickly passed Adanya one of his business cards. "Roy Mathis."

"Adanya Anniston," she responded, as she opened her door and stepped out of her car.

They talked while the two of them walked toward the unit. As soon as he opened the door, Adanya's eyes grew big.

"Ahhh, this is really nice."

"I'm glad you like it."

After the tour she decided to apply for it. Mr. Mathis informed her that if she were approved for the duplex, the move-in date would be the first of the month, just three weeks away.

Divine intervention or making a move without thinking: Adanya didn't know which it was, but she did know that it felt good to be taking some control over her life – everyone else had managed to ruin it.

9

"At the end of the day, a loving family should find everything forgivable." M. V. Olsen and W. Sheffer

Adanya pulled up to the curbside at the Memphis Airport baggage terminal. She had barely enough time for the traffic cop to blow the deafening whistle ordering her to move, when Nanette came running up to the car.

Nanette opened the car door while Adanya popped the trunk for her so she could place her two pieces of luggage inside. Nanette rushed into the passenger's side and hugged Adanya.

"How was Denver?"

"Girl, I had a good time. I think there may have been one sibling argument. But that made it all worthwhile. There's nothing better than being with your family and having that all important silly, family argument where everybody screams, hollers, and then gathers around the table to eat dinner like nothing ever occurred." Nanette giggled, so did Adanya.

"I figured you were enjoying yourself, which is why I didn't bother calling or texting you."

"I didn't talk to Gerald that much either."

"You," Adanya pointed jokingly, "did not talk to Gerald? Now that's a shock."

Nanette laughed. "I said we didn't talk that much. Hey, hold up, where's Snoopy?" Nanette looked in the back seat as if he would pop up like Jack-In-The-Box.

"I left him sprawled out on the rug, snoring like a little old man."

"You spoiled him," Nanette commented.

"He'll be all right, especially when he sees you. How was the weather in Denver?"

"Other than what Coloradans consider to be nothing special, it hovered around thirty degrees, but what can I say? Being back at home felt absolutely beautiful. I call it God's country."

"That's good."

"I wish you'd been there to witness it for yourself. The snow was simply a picture that God painted. No painter in the world could replicate it." Nanette exhaled. "Anyway, what happened while I was gone? I hope you have some good news to share about you and your family, or better still, Bleak."

"Hold up, hold up, let me dispel any preconceived notions you have right now. There is nothing to tell about me and Bleak because there is no me and Bleak. And as for my family, things haven't changed their either." Adanya drove out of the airport terminal and onto the busy street. "Anyway, you act like you've been gone since forever. If something had changed, you know I would have called or texted you."

"I know." Nanette leaned her head back against the headrest. "I'm beat. I can't wait to get home and flop across my bed."

"I hear you," said Adanya. She stopped at the traffic light. "I will tell you this."

"What?" Nanette rolled her head to the left and looked at Adanya's profile.

"House sitting, or should I say apartment sitting," she laughed, "allowed my mind to rest. It was like a sense of healing for me, you know. It alerted me to some changes I need to make."

"I hope this means you're going to hang around in Memphis and keep being my best friend and roommate."

"Yes." She paused. "And no."

Nanette's head popped up, her eyes bucked. "What do you mean by yes and no?"

"I put in an application for a duplex flat a couple of blocks from the college."

"I still don't know why you insist on moving. I told you, we could be roommates. We could rent a larger place and each have our own space."

"It's time for me to be on my own. Look at you. You have your own spot. You don't have to answer to anyone but yourself. I got a taste of that while you were gone. It felt good being on my own. I imagined having a place for me and Snoopy, and a place to bring Anaya. She could have her own room. And it's not like I can't afford it."

Nanette nodded. "True."

"Up until all of this family drama, I never had a reason to move out. I've heard Gram say that God works in mysterious ways. This may be one of those times. And she also said that every grown person needs their own place."

"I understand where you're coming from. It does feel good having my own spot. What about Spelman? Sounds like relocating is a thing of the past, huh?"

Adanya didn't hesitate. "Actually, I thought it and it

would have been a good career move, but when I got honest with myself, I thought, hey I already have a great job, one that I love. And if I relocate, then I won't have time to get to know Anaya as my mother. I can't do anything about the years we lost being mother and daughter, but I can't ever look at her as being anything less than that. I want to spend as much time with her as possible."

"I guess that's that on that." Nanette shrugged before she rolled her head to the right.

Minutes later, Adanya and Nanette were close to home. "Do you need to stop somewhere? Get something to eat?" offered Adanya

"No, I'm good. I'll make a sandwich or something when we get home. Unless you and Snoopy have cleared out the refrigerator."

"Ha, ha. We did throw this huge house party. Everybody in the neighborhood, including Snoopy's friends were invited," joked Adanya.

"As long as I can't tell when I get home," commented Nanette, followed by a chuckle. "Still haven't talked to your parents?

"Nope. Daddy is still calling, and I still keep hitting Ignore, hoping he'll get the message. I've talked to Gram and Gramps, but that's mostly to ask about Anaya and check on how she's doing."

When they arrived at Nanette's apartment, they removed her luggage and quickly opened the side door leading into the apartment. Snoopy rushed to the door with a wagging tale, and whining for his share of love. Nanette stooped down and kissed him on his black, cold nose, before he immediately turned to his owner. Adanya picked him up and kissed the top of his head. "You are such a brat, you know that, Snoopy. Such a brat," she repeated and kissed him again.

"I'm tired, so I'm going to hit the shower, then take me a nap. I feel like I've been up for two weeks."

"You aren't going to eat?"

"Nahhh, I changed my mind. Maybe later. After I get up."

"I might be gone when you wake up I'm going to call my grandparents and see about going to spend a little time with Anaya."

"Cool, be careful. I'm out." Nanette carried her luggage to her bedroom and disappeared.

Adanya called her grandparents.

"Hello."

"Gram, it's Adanya."

"How are you, 'Danya?"

"I'm good, Gram. I was calling to see what Aunt Anaya was doing this afternoon. I want to come by and pick her up, maybe take her for a ride, grab something to eat."

Silence was on the other end of the phone. Adanya thought she heard a deep inhale and then a slow exhale. "I guess it'll be all right. What time will you be here?"

"As soon as I see if Aunt Anaya wants me to pick her up. She may not feel comfortable. I mean how many times have I actually picked her up and taken her somewhere? Once, maybe twice—that I can recall."

Gram Kaplan answered back. "Anaya loves to go. She's what I call, car happy. All you have to do is mention the word 'go' and she's sitting on ready." Gram Kaplan giggled into the phone.

Adanya giggled too. "After I talk to her, I can be there in less than an hour. Will that be too soon because I can make it a little later. It's just a little after one o'clock."

"No, that's plenty of time. Call and tell her you're coming. You're going to make her day. She loves when somebody calls her."

"Yes, ma'am." Adanya heard her Gram's infectious laughter for the first time since the family secret had bought an ugly, gaping, dark hole of division. Maybe things could somehow work out—not today; but maybe one day.

Adanya dialed Anaya's phone.

"Hello." Anaya spoke loudly into the phone. "This is Anaya. Who is this?" she asked. Her voice was definitely high pitched and sounded excited.

"Hi, Aunt Anaya. It's Adanya.

"Pretty Adanya?" she seemed to ask and sounded like she couldn't believe Adanya had called her. "You coming to see me?"

"Me and Snoopy are coming to see you. Would you like to go riding with us and get something to eat?"

Anaya adored Snoopy. Gram and Gramps had been thinking about getting her a small dog or cat for a companion. Mrs. Kaplan understood how soothing an animal could be for the elderly, people who live alone, and mentally and physically challenged individuals.

"I want to go with you, Pretty Adanya."

Adanya heard Anaya clapping her hands. "Listen, Aunt Anaya. Gram is going to help you get ready."

"I'm already ready. Come soon, Pretty Adanya."

"Okay, I'll be there in a few minutes."

Adanya put on her coat, grabbed her keys and clutch bag and Snoopy's leash. "Yes, you're coming with me," she told him. He jumped and wagged his tail nonstop. She scooped him up into her arms and they got in the car.

When she arrived at her grandparents, Anaya was standing in the living room window with her apple red jacket on. Before Adanya could get out of the car, Anaya opened the front door and dashed outside.

"Pretty Adanya and Snoopy." Adanya opened the

passenger door and Snoopy jumped up and dashed off toward Anaya. She bent down and let him lick her face all over, while Adanya got out of the car and went inside to let her grandparents know that she was there. Her grandmother came to the front door, wiping her hands on a dish towel.

"What time are you bringing her back?"

"In a couple of hours."

"Okay, be careful."

"Yes, Gram."

Adanya and Anaya went to one of Anaya's favorite restaurants. Adanya wanted to give her a special surprise treat. It worked because it took almost all of the time they spent waiting on their orders before Adanya finally convinced Anaya that she had said thank you more than enough times. Moments like this. *How many more have I missed being denied the right of knowing my real mother?* Anger formed and rested at the base of her throat until she felt her breath quicken. She shook her head and forced herself to think about the present, and how happy she felt. This was time to start forming good memories. Adanya smiled.

Anaya stepped forward on the heels of Adanya when the number was called for them to pick up their orders. They carried their trays of food to the booth by the window that Anaya chose. She told Anaya she could keep an eye on Snoopy. Anaya watched Snoopy looking out the back window of the car as people passed by. "Snoopy wants to come inside, Pretty Adanya."

"Snoopy is fine. He's watching all of the people going back and forth." Adanya cuffed both hands underneath her chin. She looked at her mother who was chomping on fries and waving at Snoopy. *Why can't life be just as pure and simple as the picture of unconditional love that's showing on my mother's face?* Adanya had questions; plenty of them.

10

The thought of leaving home wasn't something I wanted to
think about, nor was it something I figured
I would ever have to do. Unknown

It had been three weeks since Adanya's move into her
new, spacious flat. She enjoyed her short commute to work.
Now that the weather was warming up, and Spring was
approaching, there were some days she chose to walk rather
than drive. She figured the extra exercise was good for
her.

Snoopy also liked the apartment. The enclosed patio
provided a place for him to lounge outside without causing
worry for Adanya. But all in all, she had to get adjusted to
living in a small, more confining space, as compared to living
with her parents.

The fact that she was fully responsible for paying her
own way had a positive impact on her life. She learned
how to budget her finances. Living solely off of her
instructor's salary, without the aid of her parents' generosity,
wasn't as tough as she had expected. Her father had taught
her how to handle her finances wisely, about investments
and savings. Each day, when she arrived home from work,
she loved the feeling of being on her own.

The past two Saturdays, Adanya had picked Anaya up

and carried her along to shop for things for the new place. She used her need to furnish and decorate her apartment as an opportunity to spend time getting to learn more about Anaya.

Adanya enjoyed spending time with Anaya, and Anaya always acted excited each time Adanya appeared at the door to get her. The two of them laughed and joked around. Adanya discovered that her mother had really good taste when it came to choosing items to decorate her first place.

Anaya had a knack of finding some of the most interesting pieces. When Adanya first moved to the apartment and showed it to Anaya, she explained that one of the bedrooms was going to be hers. Adanya told her that she could decorate it anyway she wanted. Anaya had great taste in color coordination. It showed off in the coordinating home accessories she chose. The mother and daughter duo shopped until they dropped. It turned out they both enjoyed shopping at T. J. Maxx. Adanya promised Anaya that she was going to be able to spend the night with her sometimes. When Adanya told Anaya this, Anaya could barely contain herself. She bounced around in the car like a small school child. As soon as Adanya pulled into the driveway of her grandparent's and turned off the car, Anaya rushed opened the door, got of the car and left Adanya following.

"Mommy. Pretty Adanya said I could spend the night at her house one day."

Mrs. Kaplan hugged her daughter. "That's nice." Mrs. Kaplan looked up at Adanya standing inside the doorway, surveying the touching scene. "Anaya, go to your room and change out of your clothes, honey."

Anaya turned around and rushed into Adanya's arms and squeezed her before she turned and dashed off to her room.

"'Danya, I'm glad you're spending as much time as you are with Anaya. She talks about you constantly. You're really making a difference in her life."

"Knowing she's my mother, how can I not want to be around her? I need to know her as my mother and not my aunt. And I want her to know me; really get to know me as her daughter one day. I will never deprive her of my love. Gram, she's amazing. I'm learning a lot from her. I thought I would be the one to teach her new things, but she's bringing so much joy into my life."

Gram laid her hand on Adanya's shoulder. "'Danya, you don't know how grateful I am to hear you say that."

"It's the truth. Well, I've got to get going. I'll see y'all next weekend." Adanya turned and walked outside toward her car.

"Are you coming to church tomorrow? Anaya would love that."

"I think you already know the answer to that. Buh-bye, Gram."

◊

Adanya and Snoopy walked around the tastefully landscaped grounds of her new home. She felt such an unbelievable sense of freedom.

"What's his name?"

Adanya jumped, and whirled around at the sound of the male voice.

"Snoopy," she instantly replied. It was Bleak, and he was standing next to her. Where had he come from and what was he doing in her complex?

Bleak snapped his fingers and spoke in a soothing voice. "Snoopy, how ya doing, boy?" Snoopy turned around and around on his leash. He jumped up on Bleak's leg.

"Calm down, Snoopy."

"Tell me the truth," Bleak said.

Adanya forced herself to settle down. "Tell you the truth about what?"

"Are you stalking me?"

Adanya stopped suddenly and looked up into Bleak's eyes. "Me? Stalking you? Don't flatter yourself. The question is, why are you here? This isn't funny. And it's not a coincidence that you keep popping up wherever I am. Did my parents hire you to keep tabs on me? I should have guessed by now that they had something to do with this," she rattled. "As if they haven't done enough already to ruin my life." She glared at him with burning, reproachful eyes.

"Look, I don't know what you're talking about. But I could be just as concerned about you. Why do you keep showing up in my life?"

"I do not. Adanya was both excited and aggravated at the same time. "I live here. What's your excuse?"

"You," he pointed a finger and looked around the grounds. "Live here?"

"Yes," Adanya bit back with words that flew from her lips like stones.

Bleak chuckled. "God does have a sense of humor."

"I don't see the humor."

"I do, because it just so happens I live here too." He chuckled again.

Adanya gasped. "What?"

"Building E, right over there." He pointed to the left of them. Adanya saw the large block-styled E on the side of the building. She lived in Building C.

"You must have known I lived here. Admit it. My parents are paying you, aren't they?"

"Who are your parents? Some rich people who want to keep track of their little princess?"

"None of your business. Come on, Snoopy."

"Hold up." Bleak reached out toward her without touching her.

"What is it?"

"How long have you lived here?"

"Why? You want to move next door to me so you can hear me breathe?" She shot him a cold, callous look.

"Come on, now. Have I ever been mean to you like you are to me? So give a guy a break, will ya?"

Adanya thought about what he said. He had been nothing but polite to her every time she ran into him. She had no reason to treat him so mean. "I moved here a couple of weeks ago."

"See now, was that so hard?"

Nervously, Adanya chewed on her bottom lip.

"Welcome to the neighborhood."

"Thanks." She looked away hastily to avoid his hypnotic eyes. "Maybe I could bring you and Snoopy a house warming gift after I come from church tomorrow?"

Her mouth dropped open. She stammered. "You go to church?"

"Is that strange or something?" He stretched both hands showing his palms.

"No, of course not."

"You?"

"What?"

"Do you go to church?" Bleak stooped down to pet Snoopy.

"Yes. But I haven't been lately."

"So what about tomorrow after church? I promise not to wear out my welcome. I'll bring you and Snoopy your gift, and I'll be out of your hair." The tenderness in his expression amazed her. She stared wordlessly. "I guess your silence means no."

"No." She shook her head. "I mean yes, but I don't have everything together. I haven't been over here that long."

"No problem. I can help you get things sorted out. If you want me to. So how does four o'clock sound?"

"Four is good."

"Are you going to let me get your number so I can call before I come?"

Adanya hesitated slightly. "I guess." Adanya repeated her number and watched as he put it in his cell phone.

"Well, I'll let you and Snoopy get back to your walk." Bleak flashed a smile.

Adanya was tongue tied. The words, "See you tomorrow," finally spilled out.

"I can't wait," he said and walked away in the direction of his building, leaving her with her breath caught in her lungs.

She and Snoopy finished their walk. Adanya stepped inside her apartment. A new and unexpected warmth came over her. "Of all people, he lives in this complex? How crazy is that, Snoopy?"

Adanya spent the remainder of the afternoon putting away some of the things she'd pulled from unpacked boxes. One of the pluses about her flat was that it had a detached garage, so she had plenty of storage space.

Nanette and Anaya had been a huge help with getting stuff unpacked and put away, but there were still clothes, books, and boxes that Adanya needed to sort through. Now that she was expecting her first official guest, she took extra precautions to make sure the space was as neat as possible. She thought about calling Nanette to come over and help her hang some of the pictures that she and Anaya had purchased earlier, but remembered that Nanette and Gerald were going on an outing with some friends.

◊

The following morning, streaks of sunlight filtered through her blinds and spilled into the bedroom, waking Adanya. Her usual, customary morning of getting ready for church caused her to reflect on the past seven weeks. She moseyed into the kitchen, looked inside her refrigerator, and basically the first thing her eyes zeroed in on was a bottle of vodka she had purchased the first night she moved into her new place. "Uh, uh." She shook her head. "No more of you." Without hesitation, she took it out of the refrigerator, opened it, and poured its contents down the sink.

"It's time to get myself together and move on with my new life." She hadn't admitted it to anyone but Snoopy that she really did miss her church. After she walked Snoopy, fed him, and then fixed herself a blueberry bagel, she sat on the sofa in her den and turned on her television. There were a bevy of televangelists she had her pick of choosing to listen to, but she zoomed past all of them. Her relationship with God and the church had faltered, and Adanya felt somewhat guilty. She blamed God for her problems, but the more she thought about what she had experienced lately, the more she missed her one on one time with God.

Gram had told her that people at church had been asking about her. One of the ministers at the church had called her a couple of times too, but Adanya had brushed him off as well.

Adanya began to think about the relationship she and her father shared. Why things had to be different now, was beyond her comprehension. Even if she wanted to go to church, she wouldn't be comfortable going to her home church. It was a small congregation where everybody knew everything about everybody else. She didn't want to sit in church with family who had taken part in deceiving and betraying her.

She turned off the television, and went outside and stood on her patio. She carried her phone outside with her and texted Nanette. "Where are you?"

"At church. Will call when service ends" Adanya laughed. "This girl is texting me in church. Snoopy, what do you think about that?" Snoopy lay out on the patio on his doggie rug, popped up his head and then plopped it back down. "Some help you are." Adanya continued laughing.

Forty minutes later, Nanette texted, "Out of church. What's up?

"Guess who's comin ovr?

"Parents?"

"Girl, naw." Adanya texted. "Bleak."

Adanya's cell phone rang. "I knew you would call after reading that one." Adanya laughed into the phone.

"Bleak, the mysterious, reappearing, he-so-fine, I-don't-care-what- color-he-is, hunk from the deli, Bleak? How did he pull that off?" Nanette asked with excitement resounding in her voice.

"You are one crazy chick. You have me busting my sides over here. But, yes, that's the right Bleak. Girl, he lives over here. Can you believe it?"

"Oh my gosh," squealed Nanette.

"He's coming over at four to bring me and Snoopy a house warming gift."

"What? A house warming gift? I can't believe this. I go to church, come back, and all this has happened? You must be kidding."

"No, I'm not, girl. See, I didn't talk to you yesterday, but anyway, I was outside walking Snoopy and lo and behold, he pops up. I mean it's sort of freaky that I keep bumping into this guy. But anyway, we talked for a while and then he asked if he could come over today after he got out of church."

"He's a church man too? See, Adanya, you're going to have to get yourself together and get back in church."

"Hold up, don't start."

"I'm not. I'm just saying that he might be a cool guy, and if he goes to church, he probably isn't that bad."

"It's not like I'm in this for a love connection. He may be all right, and if he is, I'll find out soon enough."

"I hear what you're saying. Look, Gerald and I are on our way to get something to eat. I sure wish you had come to church with us. Service was amazing. Anyway, call or text me later."

"All right. Have fun."

"Thanks, talk to you later."

Adanya did a once over of her apartment. Everything looked pretty much together. She passed the remainder of the afternoon grading essays. When her phone started ringing, Adanya's heart skipped a beat. She sighed deeply then answered.

"Hello."

"Hi."

"Hi," she answered.

"It's Bleak."

"I know."

"You haven't changed your mind about me coming over have you?"

"No, I'm a woman of my word."

"I like that. Well, I just made it home. What's your apartment number?"

"201."

"Got it. I'll see you in a few. Is that cool?"

"Yeah, that's cool. See you."

No sooner than Adanya finished changing into a fresh outfit, she heard a knock at the front door. Snoopy started barking.

"It's okay, Snoopy. Adanya went to the door and looked through the peephole. "Sit, Snoopy." She opened the door and welcomed Bleak inside.

In his hands, he held a box and a brown paper bag. "Good afternoon."

"Hi, come in." Adanya stepped to the side.

Bleak walked inside. He looked around the space. "Nice."

"Thank you. What's that?" she asked and pointed to the items in his hand.

"I told you I was going to bring you and Snoopy a housewarming gift. Right?"

"Yeah," answered Adanya. "May I sit?" he asked.

"Oh, I'm sorry. Sure." Adanya led him into the living room. "Sit wherever you'd like." She pointed. Snoopy trailed.

He pat Snoopy on the head. "Hi, Snoopy," Bleak said and sat the box on the table in front of him.

"How was church?" She twisted her hands in a nervous fashion and sat down in the chair caddy corner from Bleak.

"Good. And you?"

"You what?" asked Adanya.

"How was church for you today?"

"Uh, I didn't make it."

"Oh, I see, but you do go, right? At least I think you said that you did."

"I wasn't aware that you came here to discuss my religious preferences," she retorted.

"No, not really." He watched as Snoopy spread out on the floor next to Adanya. He opened the brown paper bag first. Snoopy's head popped up. "I hope you give Snoopy the okay to have these." Bleak laughed and then took out a plastic bag that held various sizes and colors of dog cookies.

"Oh my. Snoopy's going to have to go on a doggy diet if he eats all of those. What kind are they?"

"Peanut butter. Does he do peanut butter?"

"Sure, he loves all flavors, don't you, Snoopy."

Bleak called Snoopy and the dog hurried and sat in front of him. He opened the bag of treats and gave one to the canine. Snoopy snapped his mouth around the jumbo treat and headed to the patio door.

Adanya stood up and walked to the door to let him out. "He's going to nurse that cookie forever." She stood at the door and watched him find a nice spot on the patio for himself and his cookie.

Adanya turned around. She stopped suddenly when she saw Bleak holding something in his outstretched hands.

"For me?" she asked and pointed to herself.

"Unless you want to trade with Snoopy," he teased. "Of course it's for you."

She walked closer to him and he passed the box to her. Adanya opened it and a gasp escaped from her lips. "A Hope Chest. I haven't seen one of these since I was about seven or eight years old."

"I don't know if that's a good thing or a not so good thing," commented Bleak in an uncertain tone. "If you don't like it, I won't be offended. I can take it back and get you something else."

"No, you'll do no such thing." Adanya carefully inspected the square, gray, ceramic box with the word Hope imprinted in large letters on all sides, including the removable top. The chest had several Bible scriptures about hope engraved on it. She read one of the scriptures out loud.

"But those that hope in the Lord will renew their strength…they will soar on wings like eagles, they will run and not grow weary, they will walk and not be faint. Isaiah 40:31." Adanya paused and locked eyes with Bleak. "Thank you."

Adanya studied the box for several more seconds before she looked around her living room. "I think for now I'll sit it on, let's see, I'll sit it right here on my coffee table." She smiled.

"I'm glad you like it. So, tell me do you have sisters or brothers?"

"No." Adanya popped back. "And you?"

"Two little sisters. And…um, a twin sister. She's married and lives in Cali."

"A twin? My mother is an identical twin."

"Seems like we have a few things in common. I like that," said Bleak.

"I don't know if we have that much in common."

"Think about it. We live in the same complex. We frequent the same deli. I'm a twin." Bleak pointed at himself. "And your mother is a twin. We love dogs. We both seem to be rather private people. Need I go on?"

"No. I get the message." The conversation stalled. Adanya got up and went to the patio to check on Snoopy. It would give her time to regain her self-composure. There was something about Bleak that made her jittery. Not a bad jittery, just jittery.

"How's he doing out there?" Bleak asked. He stood behind her. So close that Adanya could feel the warmth of his breath on the back of her neck as he spoke.

"I don't see the cookie." She hoped he didn't detect the nervousness in her voice. "I told you he would like it."

"That you did." Bleak stepped back. "I don't want to wear

out my welcome, so I think I'm going to bid you and Snoopy farewell."

Adanya slowly turned. Bleak wasn't as close but he was still within her personal space. She cleared her throat and zipped past him.

"Oh. Uh, if you have to."

"I do. I have some work I need to finish."

"What kind of work?"

"I'm a freelance graphics designer."

"Nice."

"And you. What's your profession?" Bleak inquired.

Adanya smiled. "I'm an assistant professor of communications at Rhodes."

"Ahhh, I can just see you. Standing rigid in front of your class room full of young men who can't take their eyes off of you. Jealous girls that hate you because you're stealing the attention away from them."

That funny feeling began to form in her tummy again. Bleak's eyes were glued on her. "Anyway," she swiftly changed the direction of their conversation, "it was nice having you over. And the housewarming gifts, well, I love mine."

Snoopy waddled back inside the house. He licked his lips several times. "Guess that's his way of saying he likes his gift too."

"Cool." Bleak took a step closer to the door.

She moved ahead of him slightly and opened it. "Thank you again." She stretched out her hand and he reciprocated. He completely caught her off guard when he held on to it, and leaned over and kissed her on the cheek.

She blushed. "Goodbye, and don't work too hard."

He stepped outside and onto the porch. "Hey, would you mind if I call you sometime? I mean since we are neighbors, we can at least be civil to one another. If you need anything you can give me a call too."

"Need anything like what?" She became curious.

"Like, like," Bleak rubbed his chin. "dog sitting," he blurted.

Adanya laughed. "I won't fight you on that. I think you won him over as soon as he smelled the aroma of dog cookies."

"Good. Well, I'm out of here. Have a great week."

"You too."

Bleak nodded and proceeded to walk away.

Adanya closed the door, and leaned against it while Snoopy sat on his hind parts and watched with bulging eyes and a hanging pink tongue.

"Snoopy, Mr. Bleak Blessinger seems like a pretty cool guy."

Adanya kneeled and massaged Snoopy underneath his chin, an act he loved. He plopped his body down on the tiled floor. "You're such a softie." She massaged him a few more seconds before she stood and went to look at the Hope Chest.

Adanya looked around her new home and suddenly a bout of loneliness flooded her spirit. She was so used to being with her family. Most Sundays, after church she and her parents would have dinner at her grandparents' house, or they'd all go out to a restaurant. Things were a far cry from how they used to be. She made sure the doors were locked and went to her bedroom and started putting more unpacked items away. For the next few hours, she eased her loneliness by trying to make her house look like a home.

When she went into the room that was going to double as her office and Anaya's room, sadness forced a rush of tears to fall along the contours of her face. She imagined the pain and confusion her birth mother must have experienced at the hands of her father. Anaya was such a sweet, innocent woman and for her father to do what he did was an unforgiveable act as far as Adanya was concerned. Adanya went into the bathroom and got some tissue to wipe away her tears. She finished making Anaya's bed and placed some of the knick knacks around the room. When she finished, she allowed a slight smile to take the place of tears before she turned and went into her own bedroom.

◊

Monday morning, Adanya awoke to the sound of rain pellets pounding down on top of the roof. She sat up, yawned and slowly climbed out of bed. Adanya took her morning shower and then dressed in rain gear so she could take Snoopy out for his morning walk. Snoopy handled his business quickly, something he often did when it was raining outside.

For most of the day, the rain refused to let up. When Nanette texted her about lunch, she texted back and told her she was going to eat in the 'The Rat'. No one could ever explain why they called the dining hall, The Rat, but everybody did, including the faculty. They agreed to talk after work.

Two o'clock came quickly and Adanya left for her short drive home. She barely stepped inside of her apartment when she was met by Snoopy. "Come on, boy. Let's get this done so we can get back inside before this storm worsens. When she made it back inside and got out of her drenched clothing, she got a towel from the linen closet and used it to dry his wet fur. "I need to get you a rain jacket, don't I," she said to him as he patiently sat and allowed her to rub him down.

In the past, when she came home from work she would be met by her mother, and sometimes her daddy would be home. Either way, she would have talked to them more than once during the day. She missed that ritual.

After she changed out of her clothes and put on a pair of jogging bottoms and a tee, she went into the kitchen and stuck a breaded chicken patty in her toaster and warmed up some left over tomato soup she had in the fridge. Her cell phone rang. "Hello."

"Pretty Adanya."

"Hi, Anaya."

"It's raining."

"Yes, I know. Are you okay?"

"I'm scared."

"Moth…," Adanya stopped and then corrected herself. "Anaya, there's no reason to be scared. Remember, God is cleaning the earth and watering the flowers and trees."

"But why does He have to be so loud?" Anaya asked.

Adanya smiled. Because it takes a lot of water to clean the earth, and the thunder and lightning are God's angels helping him. You don't have to be afraid. Where are Gram and Gramps?"

"In the front," Anaya answered.

"Are you in your bedroom?"

"Yes."

"Well, I want you to get one of the books we bought at the store. Do you remember the book I bought you, the one about Jonah and the big fish?"

"Uh, huh," answered Anaya.

"Good, well I want you to get it, then climb in your bed, get underneath the covers and then look at all of the pictures inside. Don't think about what's going on outside. God's angels are all around you, even if you can't see them. If you look at your picture book, then I bet before you know it, you won't be frightened anymore. Okay?"

"I want to come to your house, Pretty Adanya."

"I'll come to get you in four days, and you can come over here with me and Snoopy. You can sleep in your brand new bed with the red bed covers you picked out."

"Okay, Pretty Adanya. Four days."

Adanya's phone beeped. "That's right. Now go on and get in the bed with your book. I'll call you back later."

"Okay, Pretty Adanya." Before Adanya could tell Anaya bye, Adanya heard the dial tone in her ear. She clicked over to the other line. "Hey, what's up? Are you out in that storm?" Adanya asked Nanette.

"I'm getting ready to leave work. We had a college fair today. Girl, this rain is coming down hard. There's a severe thunderstorm warning until six this evening."

"I hadn't heard. I was on the phone with Anaya, and I hadn't turned on my television."

"Is she all right?"

"Yea, she's just a little frightened because of the storm. But I think I got her calmed down."

"You're already a good daughter," complimented Nanette. "I've missed out on so much with her, Nanette."

"The past is done. There's no way you can turn back the hands of time. All you can do is take one day at a time and make the most of what you have now."

"Yeah, I know, but it still makes me angry every time I think about what my family did."

"You're going to have to get over it. In order for you to move forward, you're going to have to let go of what you do not have the power to change."

"Um, hmm, I know." Adanya flipped the subject. "Are you going straight home?"

"Yeah. But right now, I'm standing inside the doorway waiting for the rain to let up enough for me to run to my car without getting soaked to the bone."

"Be careful out there."

"I will. Oh, have you heard from Bleak?"

"No, and I'm not expecting to. He just came over here yesterday, Nanette. It's not like the man is going to start ringing my number off the hook. He made a friendly, neighborly gesture and that's that on that. So don't start making something out of nothing."

"Gosh, I was just asking. Oh, good, the rain is letting up. I think I better make a dash for it while I can. I'll talk to you later."

"Okay, bye." Adanya reached for the remote and turned on the television. Tickers were on the bottom of the television announcing flash floods and thunderstorm warnings just like Nanette said. A bolt of lightning caused Adanya to jump and she turned the television off and curled up in the fetal position on her sofa.

11

"Family is not an important thing, it's everything."
Michael Fox

It was Friday, the day for Anaya to sleep over at Adanya's place. After Adanya picked her up, the mother-daughter team set out to Target where they spent some fun time sifting through DVDs.

Anaya insisted on paying for the Shrek 3D movie she chose with a portion of the allowance Mr. and Mrs. Kaplan dispensed to her monthly from the SSI check Anaya received. Afterward, they stopped at McDonalds and carried their meal and movies home. When they arrived at Adanya's flat, they ate their food after taking Snoopy for his walk.

"Would you like to go back outside before it starts getting dark? We have a park here. I can take you there. They have a walking trail. They even have swings."

Anaya clapped her hands in joy. "I want to go."

"Great. Get Snoopy's leash again while I tidy up the kitchen and get the trash together."

"Come on, Snoopy. Let me put your leash on so I can take you to the park." Snoopy turned around and around and barked once.

"Are you ready?" asked Adanya.

"Yes, Snoopy and Anaya are ready for the park."

"Let's go, then." Adanya picked up the trash bag. "I'll put this in the trash bin when we get outside."

"Okay. Lock your door, Pretty Adanya. Mommy says you should always lock the doors so strangers won't hide inside to get you."

"She's right. Always lock the door when you're in the house and lock the door when you leave the house."

"I always remember to do that."

"Good for you. Real good," commented Adanya.

They reached the giant blue garbage bin and Adanya chunked the bag of trash inside and then wiped her hands, one inside the other. She haphazardly glanced at the building next to the garbage bin. Building E. Bleak's unit. For a moment, she stood frozen in place. That funny sensation filtered through her belly.

Anaya infiltrated her thoughts. "Come on, Pretty Adanya. Let's go."

Adanya shook her head slightly to clear her mind. She jogged a few steps until she reached Anaya. "We have a swimming pool near the park."

"For real?" Anaya's eyes opened wide. "I can swim like a fish."

"You can? Who taught you how to swim?"

"The swimming school. I can swim like a fish."

Adanya giggled. "Then when it gets warmer, we can go swimming. Would you like that?"

"Yep. I like to swim. I swim like a fish," she said again. "Mommy and Pops said it."

"Well, if Mommy and Pops said it, then I'm sure it's true." They reached the park and Anaya took off running with Snoopy keeping up with her. The park was deserted, all accept for a teenage couple who were cuddled on one of the benches. Adanya watched Anaya get on the swing. She continued to hold on to Snoopy.

Adanya followed and stopped behind Anaya. "Why don't I hold on to Snoopy while you swing?"

"Thank you, Pretty Adanya." Anaya pushed back against the swing until her feet left the ground, and she sailed forward then backward. With each movement, she swung higher and higher. Shrill screams of joy pursed her lips.

Adanya's phone signaled that she had a text message. She reached inside pocket of her pea coat jacket.

"Hope u had a good week."

"Bleak?" Adanya smiled. She had not seen or heard from him since his visit. She pretended that it hadn't affected her one way or the other, but the truth of the matter was she had truly enjoyed his company and hoped he that she might see him again. Before all the family drama, she had her father to spend time with. Now there were no more father-daughter outings, no more deep conversations around the fireplace in the winter, or long walks at Tom Lee Park where she and her daddy talked about her future, and engaged in father-daughter conversation. She missed her father's companionship.

Kenneth Anniston knew her like no one else, including her mother. Of everything that had happened over the past few months, the wound couldn't quite seem to heal. The wedge the family secret caused between Adanya and her father was far too deep.

Adanya pulled herself from her thoughts and looked at Anaya who was singing and swinging. Adanya felt her hands begin to tremble. "Girl, what's wrong with you?" she whispered. "The man only sent you a text. Don't read anything into it," she chastised herself. "Should I respond? I mean, why wouldn't I?" She felt Snoopy's tug. "Anaya, honey, will you be all right if I walk Snoopy to the doggie area? It's right over there," Adanya pointed to the front of where she stood, not far from the swing area.

"I'm having fun, Pretty Adanya."

"Okay, I'll be right over there where you can see me. Don't go anywhere."

"I won't."

Adanya walked Snoopy around the special doggie area. When he stopped at a nearby tree, she used the time to text Bleak. "Thank u. I did. hope u had 1 2."

Beep.

Adanya read his reply. "Plans 2nite?"

Adanya looked over her shoulder. Anaya was still swinging. Snoopy pulled her by his leash. Adanya stroked her brow. "Umm." She texted, "Yes plans with my mom And u?" she sent the text.

"@ home working."

"Pretty Adanya."

Adanya jumped, and Snoopy immediately started barking when he felt his master jump. "Ew, you scared me." Adanya placed one hand over her heart. "I didn't hear you come up."

"I'm sorry." Anaya looked sad.

"It's all right." Adanya patted her mother on the back of her shoulder.

"I want to go home."

"Anaya, I'm sorry. I didn't mean anything by what I said."

"I want to go," she repeated.

"But I thought you wanted to spend the night with me and Snoopy." Adanya felt disappointment form inside. "Don't you want to sleep in your new bed?"

"I want to watch my movie; the one I bought with my own money." Anaya pointed at her chest. "Snoopy is ready too."

"Oh, that's what you mean. I thought you were talking about going to your house. All right, all right. No problem. We can go. It's going to be dark soon anyway."

Anaya removed Snoopy's leash from Adanya's hand. "Come on, Snoopy. We're going home. I have a new bed, and I have Shrek 3D," she said to the dog who walked slightly ahead of her.

Adanya moved slowly because she was still pleasantly surprised to hear from Bleak. "u no what they say about all work." She hit the send button.

"Makes lots of money?" he texted back.

"that 2 but no time 2 spend it."

"Ur mom there 4 the night?"

"Ooooooh, what should I say?"

"hey, u still there?" he texted again, probably because she hadn't replied to his previous text.

Adanya was caught up with Anaya and Snoopy who were making the turn toward her building. Adanya was often in awe of her mother's uncanny abilities to recall places, memorize numbers, and the full lyrics to hundreds of gospel tunes.

"Why are you slow, Pretty Adanya?"

"I'm coming. I was sending a message on my phone. That's all," Adanya answered and approached the door to her flat. She retrieved her key and opened the door. As they went inside, Adanya's phone beeped again.

"Is somebody testing you?" asked Anaya.

Adanya smiled. "It's called texting and how do you know about texting anyway?."

"I know how to use a cell phone," answered Anaya. "Mommy lets me talk on hers sometimes."

"That's good. I tell you what, take off Snoopy's leash for me and hang it up. Then why don't you get a bath and we can get ready to watch our movies. Would you like that?"

"Yes. I want to see my movie."

"I'll go to my room and get ready, and you have your clothes in your bedroom. There are clean towels in the bathroom."

"Thank you," answered Anaya in her always polite manner.

Anaya disappeared into her room. Adanya walked toward her bedroom while she speed called Nanette and told her everything that Bleak had texted. "What should I tell him?" she asked Nanette.

"See, I told you that you should have been listening to my advice all along. But nooo, you were always so wrapped up in your daddy. Now you don't even know what to say to a man who obviously finds you appealing or something."

"Look, I don't have time for the I-told-you-so. I have Anaya here and we're supposed to be watching movies tonight. I don't know what to tell him."

"Listen, you said that he asked if your mother was going to be there for the night, right?"

"Right."

"Just tell him the truth. Tell him that she's there for the night. If you want to see him, this would be the perfect time. I mean, think about it. You'll have Anaya there with you, so you wouldn't feel so uncomfortable."

"Yeah," Adanya paused. "But he doesn't know about Anaya."

"Doesn't know what about Anaya? Are you talking about her being autistic?"

"Uh, yes. I don't want her to feel awkward. I don't know how well she'll take to him. As for Bleak, I don't want to put him on the spot either."

"Just go with the flow. Invite the man over. It'll be a purely innocent night of watching a movie. Put on some popcorn, fix something to drink, and sit back and enjoy the company. What movies do you have?"

Adanya chuckled before she answered, "Shrek 3D and The Preacher's Kid."

Nanette laughed into the phone. "Can't get more innocent than that. Go for it, girl."

"Yea, you're right. But I'm still a little on edge."

"About what?"

"Why would he consider coming to my house when he's never met my mother?"

"Duh, I don't see anything wrong with it. Frankly, I think it's a good sign if he agrees to come over. That says something positive about the guy."

"Okay, let me go. I'm going to text him back."

"Okay, good. We'll talk tomorrow."

Adanya ended the call and proceeded to text Bleak. "goin 2 watch couple DVDS w mom. Free 2 join us"

No answer. Adanya stripped down out of her clothes and walked into her bathroom. She started the shower. By the time she was ready to step into the shower stall, she still had not heard back from Bleak. Guess he decided he doesn't want to be bothered. Adanya pretended like it didn't bother her one way or another. In a way it didn't, because as long as she had her mother with her, she knew she was in for a special night. She felt her body being massaged by the jetted shower heads. The heated water relaxed her body.

"Anaya," she called out after she finished her shower.

"Yes."

"What are you doing?" Adanya asked as she finished drying off. She dressed in a lightweight pair of low rider slacks and a waist length, short-sleeved, tangerine shirt.

"I'm in the tub."

"Okay, I was just checking." Adanya looked at her phone. The message light was blinking and her heart started racing.

"Ur call. Do not want 2 intrude on time with ur mom," he had texted.

Adanya had a change of thought. She couldn't invite Bleak to come over when she hadn't explained to him that her mother did not know that she was her mother. It would be too confusing. No, she had to wait. This was her time to spend alone with Anaya. There would be other times she could spend with him, if she decided to.

Adanya exhaled. She was glad that she had thought about the repercussions of what could have happened, had Bleak came over not knowing the truth about Anaya.

She texted, "rain check" Part of her felt disappointed that she wouldn't see him tonight. The other part was relieved.

"understand hav good time w ur mom. gnite."

Adanya read the last text message and heard Anaya exiting the bathroom. "Do you need anything, Anaya?"

"No, my bag is in my new bedroom. Mommy helped me pack my things."

"Well, I'll get the popcorn started and we'll have us some fresh, homemade lemonade. When you finish, come to the den."

"Okay."

Adanya heard Anaya close the door to her bedroom. She took the time to call Nanette and tell her what happened, or rather what didn't happen.

"I think you were right. I really hadn't looked at it like that. I mean, who knows how it would have turned out if he walked in and said, 'Oh, so you're Adanya's mother?' Girl, that may have been hard to explain. But there'll be other times. You better believe that. If he texted you that many times and practically invited himself over, then I know you're going to be hearing from him again. And who says you have to wait for his call. Maybe you can invite him over during the week, or on a Sunday afternoon," suggested Nanette.

"You're right. It's no big deal anyway." Adanya pretended like she wasn't bothered. "Let me get this popcorn started. I'll talk to you tomorrow."

"Sure, I'll be around."

That evening mother and daughter cuddled on the sofa and watched their movies, ate popcorn, and gulped lemonade while Snoopy relaxed on his doggie bed.

◊

Morning ushered in a gorgeous, crisp, clear Saturday. Adanya was in her galley styled kitchen preparing homemade waffles, turkey sausage, and scrambled egg whites while she listened to Anaya singing in the bathroom. It felt good to hear the joyous sound of singing.

After they finished breakfast, they took Snoopy for a walk and then decided to take a ride downtown. Once they made it to downtown Memphis, Adanya found an available parking space and they traded the car for a ride on the trolley.

Adanya hadn't laughed so hard in a long time. The time with Anaya was priceless. Despite Anaya's challenges, Adanya felt exhilarated just by being around her.

Several hours passed, and it was time to take Anaya home. "Did you have a good time, Aunt Anaya?"

Anaya nodded. Her face was void of expression. She'd gone off into her own world, one where no one was allowed.

Adanya didn't press her. She focused her attention on the road ahead. The remainder of the drive echoed silence.

Adanya turned into her grandparents' driveway. Anaya, without saying a word, opened the car door just as soon as Adanya turned off the ignition.

Anaya ran up to the door and rang the doorbell. Before Adanya barely had time to get out of her car, Gram had opened the door. Anaya hugged her before dashing past her and disappearing inside the house.

"You're coming in, aren't you?" her grandmother asked.

"No, I'm beat. Me and Aunt...Anaya were on the go. She's tired too, I'm sure. She didn't say anything to me on the drive over here." Adanya frowned and stretched out her hands. "She went into her zone."

Gram nodded. "She'll be okay. She's home now. Don't worry about it, 'Danya. It's the nature of your mother's illness."

"Yes, I know that. I just hope that she doesn't get stuck in that zone."

12

"We sometimes encounter people, even perfect strangers, who begin to interest us at first sight, somehow suddenly, all at once, before a word has been spoken." F. Dostoevsky

Bleak completed one of several projects he had been working on the past several days. The pounding rain always made him a little lazy, so he neatly gathered up his materials and put them away.

He sat down in front of the picture window and started thinking about Adanya. He didn't quite know what to make of her. She intrigued him. He liked the way she talked, her smile, her intellect, not to mention she was gorgeous.

He was not the kind of guy that played the field or juggled women like some of his friends. He made it a practice to date one woman at a time. His stepfather told him that trying to juggle women would cause nothing but trouble and confusion, and playing the field only meant he'd be setting himself up to be kicked to the curve. Someone would get hurt in the long run. 'Being a man means being responsible,' he'd told Bleak many times. 'It means respecting yourself, as well as the other person.'"

His stepfather had been a part of his life for ten years, but his mother said she'd known him for thirteen years.

Now Bleak was twenty-five years old, doing his own thing, but still holding on to the principles his stepfather taught him.

Bleak's biological father had been in and out of the penitentiary for as long as Bleak could remember. This last prison sentence he received was for ten to twenty-five years. He wrote his daddy occasionally, and at least twice a year Bleak forced himself to make the trek to Texas State Penitentiary, nicknamed "Walls Unit," to visit him. He hated to go behind the steel walls, but he wanted to be the best son he could be, and treat his father the way God treated him - with forgiveness.

When his mother first introduced Bleak to his stepfather, he was apprehensive about his mother dating a black man, but she reminded him that God is no respecter of persons. Plus, the fact that his stepfather seemed to act like the sun and moon rose and set on his mother, made Bleak accept the man quite easily.

Bleak switched his thoughts away from his family and flipped them back on Adanya. He studied his phone carefully, and Adanya's name was at the top of his Contacts list.

He dialed her number, not knowing what he was going to say if she answered.

Adanya answered. "Hello,"

"Hi, are you and Snoopy okay over there?"

"Yep, why do you ask?"

"This storm doesn't seem like it's about to let up."

"I know. Thanks for thinking about us." A loud crack of thunder and a giant flash of lightning startled Adanya. She screamed into the phone.

"Hey, you okay?" he asked again.

"That sounded like something was struck by lightning." Instantly, she was surrounded by darkness. "Hey, did your lights just go out?"

"Yeah, they did." Another round of thunder roared. "I guess I won't hold you. I was just checking on you. If it's all right with you, I'll hit you up after this storm lets up."

"Ahhh," she screamed when yet another bolt of lightning streaked across her patio door. "Bleak, I hate to sound like a kid, but I hate storms. They make me scared, and uneasy. I hope the lights come back on soon."

"You want me to come over?" He detected her hesitation and was sure she was going to turn him down.

"Ughh, it's bad out there. You'll get drenched."

"I've got something for that. Just answer me; do you want me to come over?"

Thunder continued to pound the air, knocking on the earth like it was trying to force itself into a bolted door. Adanya screamed again.

"Yes," she cried into the phone.

Bleak put on his polo boots, and went to the coat closet and searched for his all-over rain suit. He hurriedly put it on, grabbed his cell phone, his keys, and ran out into the fierce thunderstorm. He jumped over forming pools of water, and raindrops pounded him like bullets.

He barely had a chance to knock when the door flew open. Adanya reached out and practically pulled him inside. "Come on. Get out of that storm."

The wind was powerful. Trees swayed and debris sailed through the air like feathers through the wind.

"Man, I got here just in time. Looks like it's about to be a tornado out there. That wind almost knocked me down, and that rain is no joke either." Bleak started removing his rain ensemble.

"Stay put," Adanya told him. "Take off your shoes; I'll put your rain gear in the bathroom."

"Thanks."

Adanya took hold of the soaking wet items and went to put them in the guest bathroom. "Make yourself at home if you can find your way around here. I just lit some candles," she said, talking to him from the bathroom.

"I'll wait up here."

"Okay. It'll just take a minute."

Bleak watched as seconds later she stepped back into the hallway. He could make out her slender silhouette, and to him she looked radiant as the candles flickered like lightning bugs.

"Have you always been afraid of storms?" he asked as she took hold of his hand and led him into the living room. He didn't say anything, but it took him by surprise. Her hand was soft and he pushed back the desire to caress it.

"Yes, I guess you can say that. But I was living at home with my parents, so I felt safe. This is the first time I've lived alone, other than when I was in college, but even then I had a roommate. This time, I'm really, really living by myself, and I guess it's going to take some getting used to." She followed the light from the candles, and led him to the sofa. "Have a seat," she offered. He did.

"I'll stay as long as you want me to. But you know, I was shocked that you let me come."

"Oh, well," Adanya looked away. "I guess I should have been more cautious. I really don't know you all that well."

"Come on, now," Bleak stated. "I didn't mean it like that. What I'm saying is that you seem to be a very private woman, one that doesn't let just anybody into her space. So I guess you can say that I feel, well I feel special." He laughed lightly.

"Oh, is that right?"

He could see that she was smiling, and he smiled back. "I

take it we're not strangers anymore?"

"I certainly hope not. I wouldn't dare allow a stranger into my humble abode," she chuckled and then jumped when a huge tree branch hit against her patio.

Bleak, on instinct grabbed hold of her and held her in his arms. He could feel her trembling, so he gently began to massage her hands as he held on to her.

She didn't resist, but rather clung to him even tighter. One round after another, the thunder and lightning played tag and the wind howled like an angry wolf. The lights in the flat began to flicker.

"You think they're getting ready to come back on?" Adanya asked. "I don't know. Maybe," Bleak answered without letting her go.

"But it's going to be fine. I won't leave you. I'll stay right here."

Adanya looked up at him.

He returned her gaze. "Let's talk," he said.

"About what?"

"Each other. I want to know more about you. Where did you go to college? Are you from here? Are your parents still living? How many brothers and sisters do you have? Where's the lucky guy? Why isn't he here with you?"

"You sure want to know a lot. But since you want to know everything, why don't I just tell you my entire history," she said mockingly.

"That's cool."

Adanya giggled. "I'll tell you my secrets if you tell me yours."

"Deal."

For the next hour, between the thunder and the lightning, the howling wind, and the pounding rain, they talked.

"So, you have two little sisters? That must be neat," Adanya said.

"It is. I was so used to it being just me and my twin sister, but when my mother remarried and had more kids, it was great. She's happier than she's been in years," Bleak explained. "And I love being a big brother. My stepfather is way cool, and so right now I'd say I can't complain."

Adanya briefly thought about her dysfunctional   family. She couldn't believe that she'd told Bleak about everything that had happened. But he had a way of making her feel like she could tell him anything, and so she basically did.

"Have you thought about moving your mother in with you?" he asked.

"I have, but I don't think it would be a good idea."

"Why?"

"Because, like I told you, my mother has some serious special needs. She's used to her world being a certain way, and she's used to having things done in a certain way. Me," Adanya touched her chest, "well, I have my career, and I'm always on the go. And, plus, I don't want to do anything to confuse her."

"I admire you for that," he complimented.

"Don't admire me too much. I can't even find it in my heart to forgive my parents, so please; don't put me up on a pedestal."

"I didn't think that was what I was doing. And I still admire you. I mean, here you are, all your life you grew up thinking your aunt was your mother. And, then to find out about it the way that you did, well, it takes a strong person to deal with something like that." The lights popped back on.

"Yayyy," Adanya said and moved from against Bleak. "They're baaack."

Bleak got up from the sofa and walked over to the

living room window. "The rain is letting up some, but the wind is still strong. And I see lightning over toward the east. But I'd say it's calming down."

Adanya stretched and yawned. "I just hope it stops altogether, because if it doesn't, I'll be up all night."

Bleak turned and walked back toward her. "Then I'll just have to stay up all night with you." He locked into her soft brown eyes.

She turned away without responding. "Hey, why don't I pop us some popcorn. We can finish talking if you'd like."

"Only if you put on tons of butter."

"Butter for you it will be."

"What about you?"

"I don't like butter."

"You don't like butter? Girl, shame, shame, shame. How can you say you're from the south and you don't like butter?" he joked. "I see I am definitely going to have to hang around you more often."

"And." Adanya smiled. "Why is that? You want to learn how to eat more healthy?"

"No, I want to learn all about you, Miss Adanya Anniston. I want to know everything."

13

"When you're looking for someone, you're looking for some aspect of yourself, even if you don't know it ... What we're searching for is what we lack." Sam Shepard

"So you two are going out again? What is this? The third, fourth time?" asked Nanette.

"The fifth since you're counting," Adanya said and chuckled. "And I cannot wait."

"Good for you. I had a feeling that he was a cool dude."

"Hold up; it's nothing serious. We're just friends."

"You don't have to convince me. Maybe you have to convince yourself."

Adanya played around with the straw in her glass of lemonade. "He's just, well so different from anyone I've ever met. He listens to me and he doesn't judge me. I feel like I can just be myself around him."

"You are serious about him, aren't you? Tell me the truth. Come on out and say it, Adanya."

"Okay, so I'll admit it. I like him. I like him a lot."

Nanette laughed.

"What's so funny?"

"You," Nanette said between snickers. "I can honestly say that you are a trip, girl. It's your best friend over here.

You could have told me in the first place how you felt about dude."

"It's nothing to tell. Yes, I like him, but that's all to it."

Nanette flipped a hand up in the air, then tossed a chip in her mouth. "Whatever. So where are you going tonight?"

"To see that new play at Minglewood Hall."

"I heard that. Well, I hope you have a good time. And do everything I think about doing," Nanette laughed again.

"You are some best friend. If I followed your advice, I'd be in a world of trouble." Adanya laughed along with Nanette.

They ate the remainder of their lunch before returning to their respective jobs.

◊

Adanya finished her last lecture, and rushed out of the building with her purse and laptop tote in hand. The weather outside was perfect for a night out with Bleak.

They had talked every single day since the night he came over during the storm, and that had been almost a month ago. She'd seen him just as much, and couldn't wait to see him again tonight. There was something different about Bleak. At first, she was hesitant to get to know him, but he was easy to fall for.

He reminded her of her daddy in a lot of ways. Not the daddy that betrayed her, but the one she grew up loving more than anyone on the face of the earth. She still missed him, missed talking to him, missed spending time with him, but the other part of her, the new Adanya as she called herself was a big girl. A big girl who was out on her own, living her own life, and doing her own thing. With each day that passed, she learned how to cope with the decision she'd made to strike her parents out of her life.

On the way home, she stopped at Macy's to buy herself a brand new outfit. She was a clothesaholic, and so she never got her fill of buying something new. She browsed the clothes racks for an hour or more before she chose a simple printed, center-pleat, shift dress. It took far less time to find a pair of stylish shoes to match.

Adanya paid for her purchases and headed home. The familiar tone notifying her that she had a text message sounded while she was driving. Knowing she shouldn't be driving and texting, she ignored what was right, and grabbed her phone from the console and flipped to the text screen.

"Can't wait 2 c u."

Adanya smiled after reading Bleak's message. She started pecking the keys on her phone when a car horn blared, forcing her to focus her attention back on driving. "Whew, that was close. Got to be more careful."

As she drove inside her complex, she took the route leading to Bleak's building. On occasion, he parked outside of his garage. Adanya hoped she would be able to tell if he was at home or not. She couldn't. His garage door was closed, and his car was nowhere to be seen, so she drove home.

Once she parked in front of her place, she texted him back, "Me 2."

◊

Evening couldn't arrive fast enough for Adanya. After she bathed and dressed, she still had some time before Bleak was supposed to arrive, so she called Anaya who always seemed happy to hear from her. Adanya talked to her mother asking her about her day and what she'd been doing since the last time they'd hung out a week ago. She promised Anaya that she would let her spend the night with her again real soon.

The doorbell rung and halted the conversation with Anaya. "Aunt Anaya, I've got to go," she explained as she walked toward the door. "I'll call you tomorrow."

"Okay, Pretty Adanya," Anaya said and the phone went abruptly silent. Anaya never waited to listen to whether the other person on the phone had parting words or not. Once she was finished talking, that was it.

Adanya stopped briefly in front of the leaner mirror in her dining room area to survey herself one more time. Satisfied with what she saw, she scurried to the door, peeped through the peep hole, and then opened it to a fine, sexy looking Bleak standing on the other side.

"Hi, come on in," she invited.

He took a step into the apartment, and kissed her on the cheek, causing her to blush as she stepped aside to allow him full entrance into her place.

"Don't you look pretty," he complimented.

"You clean up pretty nicely yourself, but I've told you that before haven't I?"

"Guess you have. Hey, you ready to get out of here?" He glanced at the watch on his wrist. "You know how terrible parking can be in Midtown, especially when they're showing a popular play like the one tonight."

"I'm ready. Just let me get my purse and keys."

"Cool."

The play was hilarious and Adanya had a great time. It felt good to be dating someone. At first she didn't want to admit that she and Bleak were actually a couple, but the more time she spent with him the more serious her feelings grew.

"The play was good wasn't it," she remarked as Bleak

drove toward their next destination. They were going to walk along the river and then have dinner at the upper scale eatery, Paulette's.

Bleak seemed to know exactly what she liked and satisfied her taste very well, just like her father. Sometimes the way he walked, and the way he looked at her reminded her of Kenneth Anniston, and it caused her to miss the relationship she once had with him. But it was time to keep moving forward. As for now, her daddy was a part of her past.

"So," Bleak said looking over at her. "You know I'm feeling you. I'm feeling you a lot, Adanya." He picked up his glass of cola. "Let's toast."

Adanya looked at him with caution, but raised her glass at the same time. "What are we toasting to?"

"The future and whatever it holds for you and me." Their glasses met in the air.

Adanya nodded in agreement and smiled. "I like that," she said right before she took a sip of her tea.

"I like you. I told you, I'm feeling you, Adanya. I want to keep this thing moving forward. What do you say about that?"

She looked away. "Hey, don't do that."

"Do what?"

"Don't check out on me." He reached across the table and took hold of her hand. "Look, whether you admit it or not, I know you're liking me like I'm liking you. I'm not trying to pressure you into anything. I just want to do like we're doing now. Spend time together. You know, hang out and all. I like having you in my life."

"Is that what this is? I'm in your life?"

"What would you call it then?"

"Umm," she hesitated before continuing. "I don't know. I

guess I never really thought about it. You know, Bleak I just don't want to get in too deep."

"Why? What's wrong with getting in deep, if that's what you call this."

"I don't call what we're doing now as getting in too deep. I'm just saying that I don't want to rush into anything. I know couples, well some of my friends who think they have the perfect match in a person only to have their hearts broken. And I, for one do not—"

"Hey, let me stop you right there. I'm not out to break hearts because I don't want my heart broken either. I believe what goes around comes around. All I'm asking is that we spend more time together, you know like a couple. I promise I won't hurt you. That's not my nature, Adanya."

Adanya wanted more too. She liked the idea of being Bleak's girl but at the same time, she recalled the words of her father, *Be cautious, tread carefully when it comes to men. They'll tell you everything you want to hear, but won't mean a third of it.*

She hoped Bleak wasn't like that. She wanted to believe that what he said he was sincere about, but she didn't want to chance it being crushed over some guy. She weighed her next words carefully.

"Look, let's just take it one day at a time. How about that?"

"That's all I ask." Bleak massaged her hand and Adanya felt her body react to his touch.

She cleared her throat before she changed the subject. "How's your grouper?"

Bleak smiled. "Good. How's your salmon?"

"Delicious," she said and put a forkful in her mouth. "I love dining here. My daddy and I used to come here whenever we came downtown. Their food is always good."

"Speaking of your father, have you talked to him?"

Adanya shook her head. "Nope."

"When are you going to forgive your parents, Adanya?"

"I don't think that's any of your business."

"I'm not trying to be up in your business. I was just asking. And if you didn't want me to say anything about the situation between you and your parents, then why did you bother telling me what went down with you guys?"

"I don't know why I told you. I ask myself that same question from time to time. I guess at the time I needed to vent. I mean, my best friend knows about it, but we don't have that much time to talk about it. She has a steady boyfriend and all, so you know how that goes."

"So, what you're telling me is that you used my listening ear as a crutch huh," he chuckled. "Okay, I'll let you use me."

Adanya smiled. "It's not like that, and you know it. And look, I don't mean to come across as mean. It's just that it's still a sensitive subject for me."

"Hey, I hear you, and I understand. So forget about it. Let's finish up this meal, and then I hope you'll come hang out at my place awhile." He looked directly into her eyes.

"Your place?"

"Yes. I'm always coming over to yours, so can't you do the honors and come to mine?"

She nodded slowly. "I guess."

"That's my girl," Bleak stood up and leaned in and kissed Adanya on her lips.

She welcomed his soft lips as they brushed hers. A tiny moan escaped from her throat and she eased back away from him. She looked around like perhaps she thought all eyes were on her.

Bleak didn't say anything. He sat back in his chair and

took the last couple of bites of his food.

"So, are you about ready?" Adanya asked some moments later. "I'm stuffed."

"No dessert?"

"No way. I'm way too full."

"Okay, whatever the lady says." He beckoned for the server to bring the check, paid their bill and then proceeded to stand up.

Adanya pushed back in her chair and Bleak quickly took hold of her hand and interlocked it with his as they exited the restaurant.

"I've had a great time," she said as they drove down Front Street in the direction of I40.

"Me too, but it's not over. Remember, you promised you'd come over to my place."

Adanya exhaled. She was about to respond but Bleak's phone started ringing.

"Excuse me," he said and answered it. "What? Is she all right? Where are you?"

Adanya listened and watched. Bleak was growing visibly upset.

"I'm on my way."

"What's going on?" she asked as soon as he ended the call.

"That was my mother. She and one of my little sisters were in a car accident." Bleak sounded frightened.

"Are they all right?"

"My mother said she's banged up, but my little sister, Caitlin, they're admitting her. I've sorry to have to do this, but I've got to take you with me to the hospital," Bleak said and immediately turned and headed toward Adams Street and LeBonheur Children's Hospital. "I don't have time to take you home."

"No, I understand. I'm fine. Just get to the hospital. Did she say if there was anyone else with them?"

"No, only that my stepfather and my other little sister are on the way to the hospital ."

"Well, calm down and just concentrate on getting there. Pray, Bleak. Pray," Adanya told him although she hadn't had a one on one with God in a long time.

Bleak sped up Adams Avenue then turned on to Dunlap. He parked in the first vacant space in the hospital parking garage. Jumping out of the car, the two of them hurried toward the elevator.

"Is she in a room?" asked Adanya as Bleak paced the small space of the elevator.

"I think they're still in ER. I think that's what she said," he answered nervously. Again, like her daddy often did when he was upset, Bleak rubbed the back of his neck. "I'll find out when we get there. They should be able to tell us something at Information."

"Yes, you're right." Adanya took hold of Bleak's hand in an effort to comfort him. "Bleak, you have to calm down. Everything is going to be fine."

Lord, he looked upward. *Take care of my little sister. Please, Lord, let her be okay.* "Can you tell me where I can find Caitlin Phillips." His voice trembled, as he spoke to the woman at the Information Desk. "She was in a car accident. My mother told me they brought her here."

The receptionist searched the database. "She was admitted and transferred to Critical Care. Take the elevators to the right and go up to fourth floor. Follow the yellow color coded floor signs to the CCU," she instructed.

Bleak ran to the elevator with Adanya still holding on to his hand. He pushed the button and like before, he paced back and forth on the elevator until the doors opened to the fourth floor. He followed the color coded floor as instructed until they arrived at the CCU Waiting area. Another receptionist was stationed right at the entrance of the waiting area.

"May I help you?" she asked.

"Yes, I...I want to see my sister. The woman downstairs said she was in CCU."

"What's your sister's name?" she asked politely.

"Caitlin Phillips."

The receptionist looked at her screen, then pointed to an area on the left, behind where Bleak and Adanya stood. "Her family should be over there."

"Thank you," Adanya said on behalf of Bleak.

He released his hand from hers and walked swiftly in the direction the receptionist told him.

Adanya followed close behind. She saw a woman who she assumed was Bleak's mother, leap up from a chair and come running toward them.

"Bleak, baby...oh, honey," the woman cried. A man suddenly appeared and stood next to her, with a little girl in tow.

"Momma, how is Caitlin? What are the doctors saying?"

"They're doing tests on her, son," the man answered instead, while he locked eyes with Adanya.

Adanya's mouth dropped open, and at the same time, she stumbled backward.

14

Those who are faithless know the pleasures of love; it is the faithful who know love's tragedies. -- Oscar Wilde

"Pumpkin, are you all right?" Her father led her to a nearby chair.

Adanya looked around. Bleak, along with the woman she assumed was his mother, and a little girl who looked to be no more than two, three at the most, were gathered around her. She noticed several people in the waiting room were staring in her direction.

"You...Her...She..." she continued to try to get the words out. Was she dreaming? Had she somehow gotten sucked into some awful nightmare and didn't know it? Did she really hear her father calling Bleak his son? "What are you doing here? She finally managed to ask.

Bleak spoke up before Kenneth. He looked totally confused. "What's going on? You know her?"

"It's a long story. But yes, I know her."

"You know me? It's a long story? Is that all you have to say?' Adanya's voice rose.

"Not here, not now, Adanya," Kenneth pleaded.

"Bleak, it's him."

"Who? What are you talking about?" Bleak looked around, obviously confused.

"My father. The man who rrr...—"

"I said, not here, Adanya," Kenneth yelled. "My little girl is in there." He pointed toward the exit, "And I don't know how she's doing. I don't need this right now."

"John, what's going on?" The frightened looking blond haired woman finally spoke up with tears crested in the corner of her eyes.

"John? I don't understand. Why is she calling you by your middle name?" Adanya pressured.

"Honey, who is she? What is this about?" The woman looked just as disturbed as she sounded.

Kenneth turned to the distraught woman. "This, she's my...she's my daughter." His eyes were flat and fixed on Adanya as he spoke to the woman.

The woman's hand flew up to her mouth.

"Your daughter?" Bleak said and looked at Kenneth and then back at Adanya. "But...you're married to my mother. What's going on here?" Bleak asked as his fury began to mount.

Adanya's tears poured. In the back of her mind she could hear Bleak's mother bawling. She heard her daddy talking to her, trying to calm her down. Without saying so much as another word to anyone, Kenneth wrapped his arm around the woman's shoulder and led her, and the little girl, out of the waiting room.

Bleak chased behind them mouthing words at her father that Adanya never thought she'd hear come out of his mouth. He was too mild mannered and respected his faith too much to say a curse word. But tonight the Bleak she saw was behaving like a raging bull. He ran up behind Kenneth and grabbed hold of his shoulder.

Kenneth turned around and Bleak got up in his face screaming and yelling. A nearby security guard ran up and demanded that they leave.

Adanya was left sitting alone and confused in the waiting room. She'd been sitting so long that she finally came to the conclusion that Bleak wouldn't be back.

She fumbled nervously inside her purse until she felt her phone. Removing it, she dialed Nanette.

"Nanette," she cried into the phone.

"Girl, what's wrong? You sound like you're crying."

"I need you to come and get me."

"What happened?"

"Please, just come and get me." Adanya sobbed.

"Where are you?"

"LeBonheur."

"LeBonheur as in the Children's Hospital?"

"Yes."

"What are you doing there?"

"I can't explain right now. Just come. Please. Come now."

"I'm on my way."

Adanya ended the call and put the phone back in her purse.

"Ma'am, are you all right? Is there anything I can do for you?"

Adanya looked up following the sound of the male voice. "No, I'm…fine. Thank you," she managed to say.

"Are you sure? I couldn't help but witness some of what happened. I was sitting right over there." He pointed to a nearby sofa. "Do you need something? Can I call somebody for you?"

"No," she said again. "But thank you. Someone is on the way to get me." Adanya stood up while she wiped the tears and snot away from her face with the back of her hand.

"Hold up," he said. Adanya stopped and watched as the stranger walked to the receptionist area and came back with some tissue.

"Here." He passed the tissues to her.

"Thank you so much." She sniffled and wiped her face and hands. "You're welcome. If you sure you're okay, I'll leave you alone."

"Yes, I'm good." She looked around like she was expecting to see Bleak, or her father. Nobody she knew was around, so she walked swiftly out of the waiting area and didn't stop until she was downstairs. She went to the front of the hospital and waited, hoping and praying that Nanette would be there soon.

As soon as Adanya spotted her car, she took off running toward it. Nanette pulled up and didn't have time to turn off the ignition because Adanya jumped in the car straight away.

"Girl, what's going on?"

"Oh, Nanette it's terrible."

"Where is Bleak?"

"I…guess he's still in there. I don't know," Adanya said between all the sobbing. "Just get me away from here."

Nanette yelled. "Look, I'm not leaving until you tell me what happened. Did he hurt you?" She was worried and confused. What could have happened that had Adanya so distraught?

"I'll tell you, but get me away from here first. If you won't do it, I swear," Adanya opened the door, "I'll walk, call a cab…anything," she demanded.

Nanette reached out and grabbed Adanya's arm and held on to her. "Close the door," she ordered.

Nanette sped down Dunlap and headed toward the interstate. For a couple of minutes they travelled in silence, except for the constant sound of Adanya crying.

"Are you sure you want me to take you home? You can come over to my place if you think that'll make you feel better."

"Yeah, let's go to your place. I think that will be best."

The twenty minute drive gave Adanya time to think. But the more she thought about what had just happened, the more mixed up she became.

"She called him John. She called my daddy by his middle name?"

"Who? What are you talking about?" Nanette asked as she surpassed the seventy mile per hour speed limit.

"Bleak. That woman."

"Adanya, you're not making any sense. Did you say Bleak was with another woman?"

"His mother."

"What about his mother?"

"His mother, Nanette. His mother called my daddy by his middle name."

Nanette shifted her gaze on Adanya. "What does Bleak's mother and your daddy have to do with this? You're not making sense."

Adanya inhaled, then exhaled. She chewed on her bottom lip and toyed with her hands. Again she inhaled and then slowly but deeply exhaled. "His, Bleak's sister and mother were in a car accident. She called and told Bleak to come to the hospital."

"Okay," said Nanette. "Just take your time."

"She, well, she…no, he," she babbled, "when we got there we had to go to CCU. That's what they told him. We, oh, Nanette it's so horrible." Adanya begin to lose control again.

"Oh my gosh, did something bad happen to his sister? Is she alive?"

"She's alive, but she was injured bad enough to be in Critical Care. But, we walked into the waiting room, and some woman, I guess Bleak's mother. She ran up to him when she saw him."

"Yes, go on," Nanette urged as she exited the interstate and drove toward the street that would lead to her apartment.

"She ran up to him and then next thing I know is, I don't even know if I saw him first or heard him, or what, but—"

"Hold up." Nanette pulled into her driveway. "Come on, let's get you inside. Then you can let it all out." Nanette opened the car door, hopped out, and dashed over to the passenger's side before Adanya could completely get out of the car. She yanked the door all the way open and allowed Adanya to get out.

Adanya moved like she was in shock. Each step was slow paced and her head was bowed down.

Nanette guided her to the door of her apartment, unlocked it, and ushered her friend inside.

"Sit down. I'm going to get you something to drink."

"I don't want anything. I'm okay. I'm here now. I'll be fine."

"Okay, sit down." Nanette followed Adanya as she walked over to the sofa and sat down. She buried her head in her hands.

"Now what about this woman? Bleak's mother. Did she say anything out of line to you?"

Adanya shook her head. "No, it wasn't her. She's probably just as messed up as I am. I don't know where they went."

"Where who went?"

Adanya lifted her head. Her eyes had already begun to swell. "A man walked up and called Bleak his son."

"And what was wrong with that? You told me he had a stepfather."

"It was my daddy, Nanette. The man was my daddy." Adanya broke down again.

"Your daddy? Mr. Anniston? But how could he, why would he be calling Bleak his son? I don't understand."

"Neither do I. I think he's living a double life."

"A double life?"

"Yes, and Bleak, he, his mother, all of us, his little sister…"

"But I thought you said his sister was in CCU."

"He has two little sisters. And now, oh my God."

"What is it?"

"Bleak told me that his mother had two kids by his stepfather. And if they're my father's children then you know what that means." Adanya's pupils grew larger by the second.

"They're your sisters too," Nanette finished.

"Exactly." Adanya's phone started ringing. She fished for the phone inside her purse. By the time she found it, it had stopped ringing. She looked at her Call Log.

"Who was it?"

"Bleak," Adanya responded. Her text message tone chimed. "It's him." She read the text message out loud. "Where r u? Call me, pleaz. We need 2 talk."

"Call him," insisted Nanette.

"I don't know if I can talk to him right now."

"Call him. You need to see what's going on."

Adanya quickly dialed the number before she had time to change her mind again.

Bleak answered almost immediately. "Where are you? I've been all over this hospital looking for you," he said with severity.

"Nanette. picked me up. Bleak, what's going on? My daddy? I don't understand any of this."

"I know," he said sounding dejected and lost. "I'm just as confused as you. But it's not good. That's all I can say. My mother is messed up about this whole thing. And my sister, my little sister has multiple fractures. A fractured pelvis, femur, and ankle." He cried.

"Oh, Bleak, I'm so sorry. She is going to be all right though, isn't she? What are the doctors saying?" Adanya asked as she momentarily laid aside her own problems.

"Yeah, eventually, but she's probably going to walk with a limp the rest of her life, and her pelvis is going to have to be fused too. She's got a long road to recovery. And having that...that, well I can't call him all the things I want to, but now things are really messed up. And I'm sorry. I'm sorry for everything you went through tonight. I had no intention of leaving you alone in that waiting room, but I got so upset, so angry with John."

"John? Humph. Is that what you know him as? John?" Adanya asked and looked over at Nanette.

"Yes, John Phillips, but who is he really?"

"His full name is Kenneth John Phillip Anniston. They gave him two middle names when he was born. John, after my grandmother's deceased brother, and Phillip after my paternal great granddaddy. Guess he took it upon himself to add the 's' to Phillip; gave himself a totally separate personality. I don't know. I'm confused. I'm telling you, this is so like a movie. I feel like I'm living out my life on the big screen."

"Tell me about it. I wanted to break his back, but I had to keep control for my mother's sake."

"Is he still at the hospital?"

"Naw, he's gone. My mother forced him to leave. Plus, I'm

sure he knew he better not hang around, because I don't know how much longer I would have been able to control myself."

"And your mother and baby sister?"

"My mother had to pull herself together for my sister's sake. She's in the room with her now. My stepdaddy," he hesitated. "John, took my baby sister with him. I'm going to be here for a while. But I need to see you too. I can't believe this," he said in a choked voice. "I can't believe any of this."

"Neither can I. Hold up, Bleak." Adanya pulled the phone away from her ear to see who was calling on the other line. It was him. Her father. She ignored his call. "Bleak, that was him calling on the other end."

"Are you going to talk to him?" Bleak asked.

"I can't talk to him. I don't know him anymore. I don't know who he is." She began to cry into the phone again. Nanette eased over next to her and put her arm around her shoulder.

"Adanya, baby, stop crying. I wish I could be there with you."

"No, Bleak. You're where you're supposed to be, with your mother and sister. They need you. I'll be okay. I'm going to be here with Nanette until I sort things out in my head. But you're right about one thing."

"What is that?"

"You and me...we need to talk. I need to know everything you can tell me about the man who's torn my life apart for a second time."

"And you deserve to know everything. I'll call you later. Try to get some rest, if that's possible."

"And you take care of your mother. I can't imagine what she's feeling."

"Yeah, she's pretty distraught. The doctor wanted her to go home after he came and talked to us and saw how messed up she was. He thought it was because of my sister, and of course that's a huge part of it, but he doesn't know about John. I don't know what to say to her, Adanya. Shoooot, I don't even know what to say to you."

"There's nothing for you to say. None of this is your fault. You're just as much a victim as me and your mother. And my mother, well, I mean Annalisse; when she learns the truth about her husband, think about what it's going to do to her. This man has managed to destroy everyone around him. I don't understand, Lord. I just don't understand."

"Me neither, but look, I'll talk to you as soon as I can. I need to get back to my mom. Hang in there, baby."

"I'll try."

15

"The hardest thing to govern is the heart." Elizabeth I

Kenneth Anniston didn't know what to do. How had things spiraled out of control the way they had? All the years he'd been with both Annalisse and Carla and he'd always managed to keep his two lives separate. He loved both women. He didn't care how much people said, 'You can't love two people at the same time.' That was a lie, and he was living proof of it.

He and Annalisse had been through some rough and tough times, but through it all they stood by one another. Their marriage was solid. And even though Annalisse had never been able to give him a child, he felt blessed to have had Adanya.

Granted, the way she was conceived was horrific. There was barely a day that passed when he didn't think back to that night some twenty-three years ago. He had honestly mistaken Anaya for Annalisse. If he hadn't been so drunk out of his mind, then his life, and Annalisse's life would be totally different. But that difference would have meant they would not have had Adanya, and Adanya was everything to him.

She had ways just like him. She was his pumpkin, the one who he adored. And Annalisse, well their relationship had been made stronger because of it, in Kenneth's opinion.

He hadn't meant to hurt anyone, but now in a matter of months his entire world was crumbling rapidly. All the monetary wealth and success he'd acquired couldn't change what was happening to him. And he thought his relationship with God was strong. He was a faithful churchgoers with both of his families. He paid his tithes, he prayed and sometimes fasted. He gave to those less fortunate, and still God let this happen?

He drove around town until he found himself on the street to his office. He turned into the parking lot of his office building and parked. The lot was empty except for the security team.

He got out of his car and headed toward the office building. Removing the keys to the building, he unlocked the double locks and was met by Dino, his lead security guy.

"Good evening, Mr. Anniston. What brings you here this time of night? Everything all right, sir?"

"Hey, Dino." Kenneth shook his head. "Man, everything isn't all right. It's a mess."

"Can I do anything to help? You wanna talk about it?" Dino offered his boss.

All the years Dino had worked for Kenneth Anniston, he'd always found him to be a pretty fair boss. He believed in treating his employees with the utmost respect, compensated them well, and he also believed in elevating them.

Dino was a prime example. He'd been with Anniston Digital Technology for going on eight years, starting off as a part-time temp from one of the staffing companies in the city. From working as a temporary security guard, he got on permanent and the rest was history. He had excellent work ethics and learned everything he could about his position in security. Dino considered himself more than the average Joe-blow security guy. He took ultimate pride in his job responsibilities, and he had been rewarded quite well in position and compensation for his loyalty to the company. He was the head of Security, and he loved his job.

"I'm going to be okay. I'm going to my office and try to settle my mind."

"Sure you don't want to talk about it?" Dino prodded.

"No, but you can pray for me and my family."

"Yeah, of course, Mr. Anniston. I will."

"Anyway, why are you here tonight?" Kenneth asked. "The rest of the team is in place, right?"

"Oh, yes sir, but you know how I do it. I'm not above coming out here at night to support my team. I told them I was going to come order pizza for the night team. They do a great job, and I wanted to show 'em I appreciate 'em; that's all."

"You're a good guy, Dino. I'm going on up. I'll talk to you later."

"Take care, Mr. Anniston. I'll be leaving shortly, but I'll tell the team you're here so they won't get alarmed when they see lights on in your office."

"Thanks, Dino," Kenneth said and walked toward the elevator with hunched shoulders and a downtrodden spirit.

He opened the door to his office and went and sat on the same sofa where just a few months earlier he had listened to Adanya's sobs. He stared blankly out the enormous window and began to think.

What was Adanya doing with his stepson? How did she even know Bleak? He thought about the night at the game when he saw Bleak approach her. He had purposely walked off to avoid Bleak seeing him and Adanya. Was that the first night Bleak met her, or had they already known each other? Had Bleak discovered that Adanya was his child? Were the two of them involved? The onslaught of questions kept racing through his mind, so much so that Kenneth couldn't wrap his thoughts around the events that had transpired. He didn't know what to think.

It was his personal mission to keep his life with Annalisse and his life with Carla apart. Bleak being a white boy, gave Kenneth an added sense of security because at least he wouldn't have to be concerned with Adanya ever meeting up with his other family, or so he thought. But as fate would have it, everything had backfired. And all the years he'd spent ingraining into Adanya's head about the importance of dating within her race had gone out the window. What could she have been thinking? Kenneth wrestled with thoughts of what might have gone wrong.

He met Carla some thirteen years ago at one of the technology conventions he used to frequent in the beginning stages of building his business. Back then she worked as an administrative assistant to the vice president of one of the companies that he later bought out, and now owned and operated.

When he saw her, he was immediately attracted to her. He was a happily married man, he'd told himself at that time. But in his eyes, there was nothing wrong with being attracted to another woman, as long as he didn't act on his feelings.

Carla was not only attractive, he later found out that she was smart, intelligent, and there was a certain something about her that made Kenneth want to get to know her.

The second evening of what would be a weeklong convention, Kenneth had spotted her downstairs in the hotel restaurant and bar dining alone. He and some colleagues were in the restaurant discussing sports and politics while eating and having a few drinks. Kenneth tried to keep his eyes from roving to the table where she sat, but it was hard for him to do. He got up and excused himself from the table and went to the bar and ordered a glass of white wine and had it sent to her table. He also told the server that he would take care of her check. Kenneth rejoined his colleagues, but barely took his eyes off Carla.

Carla looked around after the server delivered her glass of wine and that's when Kenneth met her look with a smile. She nodded, and then without touching the glass of wine, she got up and proceeded to leave the restaurant.

He got up and excused himself again and left his colleagues looking bewildered.

"Excuse me," he said to the tall, slender, blonde who reminded him of a fashion runway model.

Carla was aloof at first and refused to give him the time of day. He didn't know if it was because he was a black man or not, but he didn't care. The more she evaded him, the more he pursued her. She continued to brush him off during the course of the convention, and Kenneth decided to let it go. Months passed and she was quickly forgotten, until he saw her again. This time, it was in Seattle, Washington which at the time was quickly rising to the forefront as one of the nations' top digital cities.

Their chance encounter this time was more open and friendly. He saw her browsing at one of the hundreds of vending booths that lined the meeting hall where the digital convention was being held. He walked up on her, politely introduced himself as John Phillips and used the age old line, "Have we met before?"

Unknown to his immediate family, Kenneth often used his two middle names as a business pseudonym. He had chosen to do so as a d/b/a so the full knowledge of his business and now secret life would go undetected by Annalisse. He convinced himself that a d/b/a was the right thing to do just in case things ever fell apart between him and Annalisse. He didn't want everything he'd worked hard for over the years to be taken from him like he'd witnessed some of his constituents.

As for Carla, she never had a reason to suspect anything differently. And when it came to conducting business, it hadn't posed a problem because his financial and business attorneys managed to keep his affairs in proper order. He felt the name John Phillip, with an s, sounded more businesslike.

Anniston Digital Technology, Inc. had turned out to be a highly successful company, but it was never listed under the name of Kenneth Anniston. Unknown to Annalisse, everything Kenneth owned and operated, other than their shared property and assets was under the name of John Phillips. Now, years later his reasons for using John Phillips had backfired.

He continued to reminisce about when he first met Carla. That day in Seattle, Carla mesmerized him with her magnetic smile. This time around, for reasons unknown to him, Carla agreed to have lunch with him. While dining with her, he realized just how much he was attracted to her. Yes, he was a married man with a child, but he hadn't set out to have an affair on Annalisse. It just happened. That's what he told himself.

He had no real reason for lying to Carla either, telling her that he was divorced with no children. When she told him she was going through a divorce herself, and had two young children, instead of pulling back and respecting his own fully intact marriage, Kenneth went after Carla at full force.

By the time they ended lunch, he had her phone number

and she had agreed to have dinner with him later that evening. The rest was history because as often as possible, he flew to Seattle, Washington to be with Carla.

When he found himself falling in love with her, he couldn't entertain the idea of leaving Annalisse and Adanya, but he knew he couldn't let Carla walk out of his life either. He was not only in love with her, he had grown attached to her then teenaged son, Bleak, and his twin sister, Bianca.

Kenneth used the Bible to justify his actions. Mighty men of God in the Bible had hundreds of wives and concubines. He didn't believe he served a God who would God chastise him for having two. That would be absurd. When had things changed anyway from the way men lived in the Bible? If it was all right back then, surely God wouldn't frown on it now. The laws of the land didn't make sense to Kenneth. A man could have his cake and eat it too, and he was going to prove it.

The day he proposed to Carla, he had clearly gone overboard. He didn't stop to weigh the consequences of his actions. All he knew was that he didn't want anyone else to have her. He wanted Carla Blessinger all to himself and for himself. He proposed to her and she accepted.

In the beginning of his marriage to Carla, he commuted between Memphis and Seattle, spending sometimes two weeks at a time with Carla before returning home to Annalisse and Adanya. But when Carla became pregnant with their first child, Caitlin, Kenneth made a decision to relocate them to Tennessee. He purchased a house on the outskirts of Memphis in Eads, Tennessee. That way, he was assured that his two lives and two wives wouldn't collide.

Carla was naïve herself in many ways because she never questioned the times John was gone for days, sometimes weeks at a time. He had always been a frequent traveler due to the nature of his business. And when she became pregnant with Caitlin, she surrounded herself with being a good mother, but relished the times when John was at home. He had been a good father and a loving husband. Miraculously, Kenneth juggled both women without either of them finding out about the other. He'd always somehow managed to keep both households together. He believed the saying, 'You can't make two people happy at the same time' did not apply to him because he was doing it and had been doing it since marrying Carla ten years prior. Kenneth had gone so far as leasing office space in close proximity to where he and Carla and their kids lived. The name of that business was J. Phillips Technology Group.

He'd established that company for as long as the two of them had been married. And Carla, well Carla was clueless about Anniston Digital Technology just like Annalisse was clueless about J. Phillips Technology Group.

Bleak never had a reason to question his stepfather's motives because he always saw his mother with a smile on her face. John treated her like royalty, in Bleak's eyes, and even when he left for college and returned to Memphis, he saw how happy his mother remained. He'd treated him like a son, put him, and Bianca, through college, and did all the things he used to long for his biological father to do.

Kenneth pondered over what he was going to do. He didn't want to lose Carla or his kids. He didn't want to lose Annalisse, and Adanya, well he'd lost Adanya months ago, and now he knew that there was probably no chance of them ever reconciling. Their father daughter relationship was dead. Only God would be able to change that. His marriage to Annalisse was cooked meat too, that is if Adanya decided to spill the beans and tell Annalisse about his other life.

For the first time in his life, Kenneth Anniston

contemplated ending it all. Maybe he should just take his own life, call it quits. God would forgive him. And both families would be well taken care of. He'd taken out enough insurance policies so they would never have anything to worry about if something happened to him.

Both hands extended toward the ceiling. "God, help me. Take care of my little girl. Bless my family, both of them, Lord."

16

"When the mind is in a state of uncertainty the smallest
impulse directs it to either side." Terence

Adanya agreed to meet Bleak at her apartment the
following afternoon. She'd had the whole night to think
about what had happened, and the more she weighed out
the situation, the more troubled she became. Maybe Bleak
knew who she was all along. She thought back to when he
first approached her at the deli. That could have all been an
act.

"Nanette, what if Bleak knew I was his stepfather's
daughter and just wanted to use me?"

"What would make you think something like that?"

"Think about it. Out of all the women in the deli that day,
especially the white girls, he came over to our table and
introduced himself to me," Adanya reasoned and pointed at
herself.

"So, I don't see anything wrong with that. There are a lot
of white boys who go for black girls and vice versa."

"Yea, true, but it's still strange. I mean, this guy comes
out of nowhere. Neither one of us has ever seen him before.
Think about it."

Nanette frowned. "Umm, well I don't know. Sounds a
little far- fetched. But I guess it isn't impossible. But still,

Bleak doesn't seem like he's the kind of guy who would purposely deceive you."

"Exactly. Which makes it even more likely that he did. He hides behind all his God this, God that talk. Acts like the perfect gentleman. Not once has he tried to go to bed with me. Shucks, he's never even tried to kiss me, I mean kiss me, kiss me. You know what I mean."

"You do have a point. I mean, any other guy would have tried a million ways to get you into bed. And they most definitely would have sought some tongue action from you. I just thought he was a real gentleman. You do still have some men out there like that."

"Yeah, but have you ever run across one?"

Nanette laughed but didn't mean to. She didn't want Adanya to feel like she was making light of her situation because she wasn't.

"Suppose you're right? But how can you find out if he did or didn't?"

"He wants to see me tomorrow."

"Are you going to see him?"

"Yeah. And I'm going to let him know that I know he's been in on this the whole time. I'll see from his reaction if my suspicion is right."

"Oooo,kay. I hope you know what you're talking about. 'Cause I still don't think he's that kind of dude. Why would he take a chance of his mother and his siblings being hurt? If he knew your daddy wasn't who he said he was, seems like he would have confronted him one on one, not go in search of his daughter by another momma."

"Maybe he did confront him. We don't know what went down before I met Bleak. I mean, people are crazy these days. They hide behind their religion, they hide behind their jobs, their families, any and everything. Folks are scandalous."

"Guess you have a point. Well, what time are you going to meet him?

"Three. After he comes from the hospital."

"And what about your daddy? Are you going to talk to him? And poor Mrs. Anniston. What do you think she's going to do when she finds out? Of if she finds out, I should say."

"Oh, she's going to find out all right. You better believe that."

"How can you be so sure?"

"Because I'm going to make sure that she does. He's lied one too many times. Now I feel a little sorry for her. She was young and stupid back in the day, so maybe I can try to forgive her, but him, after this, never. Seeing this charade he's playing now makes me believe that he knew exactly what he was doing when he raped Anaya. Annalisse was young and in love and she wanted to believe that the sun rose and shined on him. And Bleak's mother is probably just like her–blinded by love."

Nanette shook her head in disgust. "That's terrible what he did. But all men are not like him, Adanya. And if your father really did take advantage of your aunt, then he is one sick puppy. I feel sorry for him because God don't like ugly. He will reap what he sows."

"Definitely. And his reaping is about to begin if I have anything to do with it," Adanya added.

◊

Adanya lounged around the house but her mind was still working overtime. She wondered what her daddy was doing and why he hadn't bothered trying to contact her again

Her phone started ringing. "Speak of the devil," she said to Snoopy. "Hello," she said with force.

"Adanya, please don't hang up."

"What do you want?"

"Pumpkin, I need to see you. We need to talk."

"Who are you to call me and demand that I talk to you. And what do we have to talk about anyway? I see you for what you are, a liar, and a manipulator."

"Listen, if you'll just give me a chance to explain, you would understand—"

"Understand? Oh, I don't need to hear anything you have to say. It's already clear to me that you've been living two lives. Does Annalisse know?"

Silence.

"Oh, so now you're all quiet, huh? I guess that means she has no idea that you're a phony."

"No, she doesn't know, and I hope you won't tell her. Just give me a chance to talk to her first.." His voice sounded deflated.

"So, this is what this call is really about?"

"What are you talking about?"

"You want to make sure I don't go running to Annalisse. You don't want me to tell her about John Phillips. You are something else. Did Bleak's mother know about me and Annalisse?"

"No. And how do you know Bleak anyway?"

"Wouldn't you like to know? Well, too bad. If he didn't tell you, then you won't get anything out of me. The best thing you can do for me is never to contact me again. Not ever," she screamed into the receiver before she ended the call.

Inhale. Exhale. Inhale. Exhale. Adanya tried to settle her nerves by taking deep breaths. She nervously paced around the apartment.

Picking up the phone, she dialed her mother's number.

"Thank you, Lord. Adanya I'm so glad to hear from you, baby," Annalisse said before Adanya could get a word in edge wise. "Baby, I've been praying that you would call. I have so much to say to you. But first, tell me, how you're doing?"

"Mom, Annalisse, slow down. I'm doing fine."

"Baby, where are you? Where do you live? Your Aunt Anaya tried to tell me but…"

Adanya sliced into her mother's conversation. "She is not my aunt. You are."

Silence.

Annalisse stuttered like she was taken off guard by Adanya's remark. "Can I see you? I miss you."

"That's why I was calling. We need to talk."

"I agree. Tell me when and where."

"Now."

"Ohhh, well."

"So, you can't?" Adanya retorted.

"No, no, I can. Do you want me to come where you are?"

Adanya paused before answering. She had to think what would be the best place for them to meet? Did she really want Annalisse to know where she lived?

"Is Daddy there?"

"No, he called and said he'd be late. He's meeting with some new clients."

I just bet he is. Probably at the hospital, or somewhere pleading with Bleak's mother, filling her head with more of his lies. Poor woman. "I'll be there in about half an hour."

"Okay, baby. I'll see you shortly."

"Goodbye," Adanya said and ended the call.

Without missing a beat, she gathered her purse, keys,

and phone and dashed out the door, jumped in her car and shot out of the parking lot in record time. In less than half an hour she was knocking on the door at the house she used to call home.

When Annalisse opened the door, Adanya was shocked. The woman standing before her looked like she'd aged by at least ten years. There were bags underneath her eyes, and she looked like she'd lost at least fifteen or twenty pounds. She had never been a big woman, and now she looked sickly. It frightened Adanya but she kept her mouth closed.

"Adanya," Annalisse shouted and grabbed hold of her. "Baby, I've missed you so much," she cried.

Adanya didn't return the hug or share Annalisse's sentiments. She stood rigid while Annalisse continued to hold on to her like she would never let her go.

When the woman stepped back, Adanya politely asked, "Do you mind if I come inside?"

"What kind of question is that? Honey, this is your home. It will always be your home. You know that."

Adanya stepped inside. Her eyes immediately zeroed in on the familiar surroundings of the huge house. Everything looked larger. It was almost like going into one of those Vesta Home Show houses that showcase huge, luxurious, newly built homes.

"Come on, let's go into the kitchen. I fixed us a couple of sandwiches and some tea."

Adanya raised her hand, "I don't want anything to eat. I won't be here long."

Annalisse didn't respond. She walked toward the kitchen and Adanya followed. "Well, sit down" Adanya did.

"Are you sure you don't want me to get you something?"

"No." Adanya shook her head. "Tell me, how much do

you know about my father?"

"What kind of question is that?"

"I mean, how much do you know about him? Like, how can you be sure that he's really meeting a client tonight? How do you know he's not, well that he's really who he says that he is."

"Adanya, please I don't know what this is about, but your father is a good man. She said as she turned her head from side to side. "Your father's hard work and smarts got us all this. We have a good life. He raised you to know God, and he's always done everything he can to make a good life for you and me. So what's this all about?"

"Uh, hah," Adanya said. "Oh, Annalisse. I hate to do this. I really do, but I have to tell you about the real Kenneth John Phillip Anniston."

"Honey, when are you going to forgive your father, and me? We made a horrible, horrible mistake. That I know. But please don't make us pay for it the rest of our lives. And please, don't be angry at your father. He loves you. I love you." Her voice sounded tired.

"You think he loves me as much as he loves my two little sisters? Do you think he loves you as much as he loves his other wife?"

Biting her lip, Annalisse's face became clouded with uneasiness. "What are you talking about? Sisters? You don't have any sisters? And wife? Adanya, I know we've messed up, your father and I, but that's still no reason for you to come up in here and tell lies about him."

"Lies," Adanya jumped up from her chair, struggling with her conscience about whether she should go on with telling Annalisse the real deal about her so good and perfect husband. Her conscience lost. "All of it is a lie, Annalisse. My father has another family," she shouted and screamed.

Annalisse jumped up this time, curses spewing from her mouth. She took hold of Adanya and began shaking her violently. "Stop it, stop your lies," she yelled. "Stop it, stop it, stop it." Her face had turned into a glowering mask of rage.

"It's the truth," Adanya screamed back. "I saw her. She's a white woman, and they have two little girls. I saw her with my own eyes. I saw him with her," Adanya said throwing words at Annalisse like daggers. "You don't believe me, then call him. Call him up right now. Ask him where he is, who he's with."

"I will do no such thing," she said, as tears formed in her clouded eyes. "What's wrong with you, Adanya?"

"Then let me do the honors." There was no turning back for Adanya. Annalisse's refusal to believe her, set her heart ablaze. She was sick and tired of being sick and tired. Tired of the lies. Tired of the deceit. She fumbled around inside her purse until she felt her phone and pulled it out. With shaking hands, she called him. No answer.

"See, I told you, he's in a meeting."

Adanya looked at Annalisse and her anger began to turn into pity for the woman who'd raised her, taken care of her and yes, loved her. She didn't want to see Annalisse hurt, but she had to tell her the kind of person her father really was. Annalisse deserved to know. She wouldn't do Annalisse like they'd done her. She wouldn't keep the truth from her.

The phone rang. Adanya looked at the screen. "It's him calling back. I'm going to put him on speaker."

Annalisse appeared dazed.

"Don't say a word," Adanya told her. "Hello."

"Pumpkin. I'm sorry. I didn't get the phone in time. I... well I was visiting Caitlin."

"How is she? And how old is she anyway?" Adanya

peered over at Annalisse who grabbed hold of the kitchen chair like she needed it for support. Cold eyes stared at Adanya's phone.

"She's seven. And she's still in critical condition. They're keeping her heavily sedated. Thanks for asking. Listen, Pumpkin, about our earlier conversation."

"What about it?"

"I still need to talk to you. I'm asking you, no, I'm begging you not to say anything to Annalisse. Please, Pumpkin, let me do it." He continued to beg. "Right now I'm so messed up. My little girl is laying up in a hospital bed and I don't know how long it's going to be before she's back to being a bright, healthy, happy, little girl. And Carla won't let me see Caitlin unless she's not with her. I haven't seen or talked to Bleak . I don't know where they have Cady."

"Ohhhh, poor you. You want me to feel sorry for you? How long were you going to let this go on? Were you ever going to tell me, or my sisters the truth? Or would they have to learn the truth about you like I did? Over some phone conversation or something? What about Carla, your other wife. What kind of woman is she to marry a man who already has a family."

"Don't blame her. Carla was just as much in the dark as you and Annalisse."

"And don't give me the chivalry act."

"I got caught up. It's a long story, but I can't talk about it now. I don't have that much time left to spend with Caitlin. And she needs me. She needs to know her daddy's here." His voice sounded broken. It was like he was choking on his own words. But Adanya refused to allow herself to feel anything but contempt for him.

Annalisse had a fiery, angry look. A look like Adanya had never seen. It was frightening.

"So that's how you explain it, huh? Why don't you try saying that again."

"Saying what again?" Kenneth asked.

Adanya nodded and Annalisse released a loud, curdling scream of rage filled curse words into the air.

"Annalisse," Kenneth cried out. "No, baby. No, Annalisse. Why, how could you do this, Adanya? His lash was venomous. "How could you? You're going to pay for what you've done."

Annalisse snatched the phone out of Adanya's hand. She continued yelling obscenities at him, while her hands stabbed aimlessly in the air.

Adanya stepped back out of the range of Annalisse. She'd never witnessed her mother so angry. Blood filled her temples as she stiffened her body like she was going into a diabetic shock.

"Mother," she called out to Annalisse, hoping she would be able to stop her from destroying everything around her.

Kenneth continued wailing in the background.

"Mother," Adanya yelled again. She took a step forward and with caution she walked toward her. Annalisse's eyes were fiery red, snot dripped down her face and past her mouth. Adanya managed to pry the phone from her hands.

"See what you've done," she said when she got the phone back. "Are you satisfied?" She hit the flat of her hand against wall, then ended the call.

"How could he do this? Why?" Annalisse fell to her knees and wept.

Adanya stood motionless. She couldn't hold back her tears. It pained her to see the hurt her father had caused. Maybe she shouldn't have told her. Maybe she should have kept it all a secret. But then she would be no better than her father. No better than they were when they lied to her. No,

Annalisse deserved to know the truth. Better hurt now than years down the line.

She bent down next to her. "Mother, I'm so sorry."

Annalisse looked up and stared at Adanya like she was demon possessed. She started chuckling like a mad woman.

"You're not sorry. You're glad all this happened."

"What?" Adanya stood upright. "Glad? How can you say that?"

"Because you are. You wanted to hurt me. If you wanted to get back at me you succeeded. How long have you known about your father and his secret little family?"

"Me? What are you talking about?" Her breath quickened. "I just found out a couple of days ago. I'm just as shocked as you."

"So shocked that you couldn't wait to run over here and tell me, huh? So shocked that you used this to break me. Well, you won. I'm broken," Annalisse screamed as she held on to the chair and pulled herself up. Without warning, she started swinging at Adanya. She pounded her over and over again.

"Stop," Adanya screamed and took off running toward the front door.

Annalisse followed. "Get out. Get out. I don't know you. I don't know who you are. Get out of my houuuusse."

Adanya's faced streamed with stinging tears. She ran out the door without closing it, without looking back. She could barely open the car door, she was shaking so. Once inside, she hit the locks, afraid that Annalisse might come charging out at her again. She fumbled with getting the keys into the ignition for several seconds before she finally got the key in the hole and flipped the switch, backed up, and then sped off down the street almost blinded by the crocodile tears falling down her face.

"Oh, God. What have I done?"

The phone jarred her from her thoughts of what had just happened. "Hel..hello."

"Hey, you all right?" It was Bleak.

"Why?"

"What do you mean, why? Because you sound like you're out of it, that's why. Are you okay?"

"I'm fine and dandy. Perfect. Hunky-dory."

"Hold up, I didn't mean it like that. I know you're not fine. Neither am I. Thanks to your father, we're all messed up."

"No, it's your stepfather, your sisters' daddy, your momma's husband." Her temper rose with every response.

"Okay, I get it. And I'm just as angry as you. But right now I have my mother, sisters and you to worry about."

"Oh, so you want me to believe you're worried about me?" She sped on to the interstate. "How noble of you."

"You act like this is my fault. I'm not the one who lied. I'm not the imposter, Adanya."

"Are you sure about that?"

"What are you trying to say?" The force of his seething reply threw her a little off guard.

She paused. "I'm not trying to say anything. I said what I had to say. And the question remains. Are you sure you didn't know about any of this? Now I see why you were so eager to get to know me. Pretending like you just happened to walk up on me. You're just like him. I bet he taught you everything he knows. How to be a con artist just like him. How to go around masquerading, acting like you're somebody other than who you are."

Click.

"Hello? Hello?"

17

"Assumptions are the termites of relationships."
Henry Winkler

Bleak was fed up, furious, and frustrated. He couldn't believe Adanya actually blamed him for her father's double life. And to think that he purposely met her just to hurt her, was preposterous. He was not about to let her get away with falsely accusing him. Yeah, maybe he was supposed to turn the other cheek, but in this case before he turned it, he was going to confront her – face to face. He walked over to her flat. With every step he took he became more and more appalled that she would think he was anything like the man he once proudly called his stepfather. He was nothing like John Phillips, Kenneth Anniston, whoever he was.

Knock. Knock. Knock. Knock.

Bleak wasn't going to stop until she answered. He couldn't see inside her garage so maybe she wasn't home when he talked to her. He stood outside the front of her place thinking about all the things she'd said about him.

He could understand her being upset with John, but he wasn't John. Bleak was just as disturbed by the chain of events as the rest of them. And his mother, his poor mother was trying hard to be strong for Caitlin and Cady, while dealing with the anger and pain that John had inflicted on their lives. Maybe Adanya could care less about his mother's feelings, but he cared about them. He cared about his family just as much, if not more, than she cared about hers. Sure, in the end, he believed that God would turn things around for their good, but right now he didn't see how that was going to happen and wasn't sure when it would happen. But as bad as John had hurt their family, part of him was glad that everything had come out in the open.

God had a way of bringing anything done in the dark into the full light. And he'd certainly revealed the dark secrets of his stepfather. Bleak placed both hands in his pockets and walked in tiny circles in front of Adanya's door. He knocked again. This time he heard Snoopy barking.

She must not be in there. He turned to leave and that's when he saw her car coming toward him. "Man, is she going to run me down?" he yelled.

Adanya drove past him and just as the garage door opened, she drove inside.

Bleak jumped in front of the garage door as it began to close. "Adanya, we need to talk. And I'm not going anywhere until we do."

Adanya didn't say a word. The garage door completely shut.

Bleak huddled against her front door and started knocking again. This time he knocked even harder than the previous times. Snoopy barked even louder.

"You don't have to break my door down," Adanya yelled when she opened the door.

"I would have if you hadn't opened it." He didn't wait for an invitation to come inside. He bolted past Adanya, ignoring her cold, penetrating stare.

"No one invited you in," she snapped.

"Why do you think I had something to do with your father's little shenanigans?" His voice sounded harsh and his ocean colored eyes looked dark and haunting. "Answer me."

"If the shoe fits, wear it," she said, her temper rising again.

"You are so full of yourself. I see why you're alone and miserable."

"How dare you?"

"How dare I what?" he shot back. "Tell the truth? Well, how dare you judge me when you don't know anything about me. I'm not the one who hurt you, Adanya. I'm not the one who lied to you. I'm not your father." His handsome, chiseled face twisted in anger.

"Why did you come to my table all those months ago? Why did you insist on getting to know me? You must have known something. Don't you think it's more than a coincidence that my father just so happens to be your stepfather, Bleak? Come on, now. Let's be real about this."

"Be real? You want to be real? Real is looking in the mirror, and seeing the person you really are. I wonder if you'd be happy with yourself. Or maybe, just maybe you're more like your father than you think. Maybe you get off on seeing how much pain you can inflict on someone else."

Adanya slapped him before she could even think about it. She scared even herself. Never before had she hit anyone, especially in anger. She'd never had a fight with anyone all while growing up and now it took Bleak Blessinger to bring out the worst in her.

"I'm sorry," she countered as his hand flew up to his cheek and started rubbing it.

"See, you're more like him than you thought, huh, Adanya?"

"Leave, Bleak. Right now," she demanded.

"I won't leave," he said. "I'm not leaving until I tell you how I feel. You want to blame somebody for what your father did, well blame him. I'm not the bad guy here, Adanya. I saw you that day in the deli and it was like something, some irresistible force pulled me to you. I'd been in that deli a thousand times, and I've never been tempted to flirt with any female in that place. But for some reason, I looked in your direction and my eyes zeroed in on you. I thought you were the most stunning woman I'd ever seen. I had to take a chance. And so I did. You rejected me that day, but I prayed that I would see you again one day. And I did."

Adanya looked away in shame.

"No, don't turn away from me. Look at me, Adanya. Listen to me." His voice had softened. He extended his hand and placed it underneath her chin, lifting her head gently up to face him. "I hate what's happened. I don't know how to deal with it myself. I've been praying and praying. Praying for my little sister who's fighting to regain her strength, fighting to get well. I've been praying for my mother. It's breaking my heart to see her so hurt, Adanya. And then, I've been praying for you. Everything that's happened to you in the past with your parents, and now this. I can't begin to know what you're feeling or how you're feeling. I can only guess. And then I've been praying for us. I don't want what your father has done to tear us apart."

"Bleak, we can't be together any more. It won't work."

"We can get through this. Somehow we can, I know it, Adanya. And if we lean on one another, and God, we can make it. Remember what the scripture says, "Two people are better off than one, for they can help each other succeed. Help me, Adanya. And let me help you." His eyes had grown soft with sincerity.

Adanya felt guilty and ashamed of how she'd treated Bleak. She hadn't thought to put herself in his shoes. Bleak was right. It had been all about her. She had been selfish and heartless. Hot tears rolled down her cheeks and traces of her resentment began to vanish.

Bleak stepped in closer. Adanya did not move. He so wanted to break through the barrier she'd so expertly woven over her heart. Her father was a jerk, but she was just the opposite; she was a jewel in his eyes.

He embraced her. She gave in to the uncontrollable, compulsive sobs that shook her. He held on to her. His body ached for her. He kissed her hair, and felt her heart beat against his.

Adanya looked up, gazing into his piercing eyes. A shuddering, brief ripple passed through her. A knot formed in her throat. She tried to speak, wanted to speak, but no words came forth. She put her arms around his neck, and Bleak covered her mouth with his in a slow, deliberate, kiss.

Adanya was shocked at her eager response and acceptance of his kiss. Her father, her deceitful, lying, cheating father had cautioned her time and time again about how men wanted nothing but to get what they wanted from a woman. She felt she had truly become wiser over the last few months. Before Bleak Blessinger, she had never thought about giving herself to any man, but as his demanding lips caressed hers, she could think of nothing else she wanted more than to give herself totally and completely to him.

"We can't do this." He released her. "Not until things are settled in our families."

She suddenly felt ashamed, ashamed for her eager response to his touch, to his lips against hers. She remained quiet.

"Hey, it's okay," he said like he could read her mind. "I want you, Adanya. I want to build something with you. I know we have a lot of drama, to say the least, going on, but if we can make it through this, I believe things can work."

"Do you really, Bleak?"

"Yes. I do. Matter of fact, I'm banking on it." He kissed her chin this time, and Adanya quivered at the tenderness of his lips.

I believe too.

18

"It is better to dwell in the wilderness, than with a contentious and angry woman." Proverbs 21:19 The Bible

Kenneth Anniston didn't waste time. Barreling into his garage, he threw the car into park. He had to see the extent of damage Adanya had caused. And why? Why, was she out to ruin his life? Ruin what he'd taken all these years to build?

If God had forgiven him, why did she have to wreak havoc in his life? He had made a huge mistake ever thinking he could juggle two families at the same time. But it had been hard, no downright impossible for him to choose between Carla and Annalisse. Maybe the typical man would have just played around on the side with Carla, but he wasn't the typical male. He was in love with both Carla and Annalisse.

Now here he was, torn between two lovers and he didn't know what he was going to do. Carla had given him two precious, beautiful daughters. He couldn't turn his back on them or her. And as for Annalisse, she had stuck by him when he thought his whole world was about to crumble. Stuck by him when the unspeakable happened between him and Anaya. He owed her. She may not have birthed any children for him, and only God knew why because doctor after doctor told her there was no reason why she shouldn't be able to get pregnant. And still it wasn't too late for her to conceive, not really. She wasn't even forty years old and women her age became pregnant every day, maybe Annalisse would too. But that wasn't the issue right now. Right now he had to see if Adanya had permanently destroyed his marriage to Annalisse.

"Annalisse," he yelled as he ran inside the massive house. He took off in the direction of the winding stair case. "Annalisse," he yelled again, as he set foot on the stairs.

He hesitated when he saw a figure in the corner of his eye. He didn't have a chance to make it pass the third step.

"Ahhh." The back of his thigh felt like it was on fire. Everything began to move in slow motion. His lower leg was being ripped off, or did it just feel like that? Kenneth couldn't tell. His body fell backwards, his hands flew up, his mouth opened, but he heard nothing coming out of it.

Annalisse. He saw her. Her eyes narrowed while his widened with alarm. Did she hear him? It looked like she was screaming. He saw the gun in her hand. *Oh, God, she's going to kill me. Don't do it, Annalisse. Don't. Kill. Me.*

Blackness.

Annalisse stood over Kenneth with the gun pointing directly at him. His eyes fluttered. With shaking hands, she lowered the .357.

"Annalisse." Kenneth gasped for breath. "Call 911."

Annalisse was frozen. She wanted to move but couldn't. What had happened? Why was Kenneth lying in the floor? The dark, sticky looking, purple substance oozed from underneath the lower half of his body and on to her freshly stained concrete floors.

Annalisse tilted her head from side to side, ever so slowly. She studied the purple goo that now looked like it was a deep red. How would she clean it? Get up, Kenneth. Move out the way.

Annalisse ejected a blood curdling scream. "Oh, my God. What have I done? What have I done?" She started screaming like she'd suddenly come back to life, while running around in a circle, one hand still holding the heavy, black piece of metal. She looked at it and started screaming again.

"Annalisse. Listen." Kenneth's mouth then his entire face contorted as he struggled to locate the place he'd been shot.

She knelt down on her knees beside him. "Oh my, God. What have I done?"

"Call, call, 9-1-1," he stuttered just above a whisper, before he went unconscious.

Annalisse released the gun. The sound of it landing on the concrete floor gave her cause to jump. Her hand flew up to her chest.

"Kenneth," she called over and over again as she tugged on his shirt. Next, like she'd been popped with a needle, she jumped up and ran to the nearest phone, in the kitchen. With slippery, bloody fingers she dialed 9-1-1.

◊

Annalisse huddled in fear, shock, and remorse as she shook while dialing Kaye's number. She had been transported to Jail East and placed in an open room full of other women. It reminded Annalisse of a smaller version of the now defunct Mid-south coliseum. A huge TV was mounted high up on the wall. Several pay phones lined the walls too, and there were picnic type metal benches sporadically placed in the room. A metal door separated them from the rest of the world.

Annalisse gripped the phone in her left hand until her knuckles turned white. She punched the numbers on the oily, nasty, and smelly black jail phone quickly, like she was afraid someone might come along like they did in the movies and jack her for it.

Kaye barely had time to mouth the word, "Hello," before Annalisse started hollering into the phone. Her spit flew everywhere.

"Kaye, I shot him," Annalisse screamed into the phone. "I shot Kenneth. I need you to locate Adanya. Make sure she doesn't hear about this from anybody outside of our family."

"You did what? Girl, don't call me with your sick sense of humor, 'cause it isn't funny."

"I'm not joking. Oh, my God," Annalisse hollered again.

"You said you were going to leave him high and dry, not kill him," Kaye screamed into the phone. "My, Lord, what have you done?"

She kept her death like grip on the phone. "I'm at Jail East. They said they needed me to come down here to answer a few questions. But they fooled me," she cried. "They're talking about charging me with attempted murder."

"What have you done?" Kaye paused like she was afraid to hear the answer to the question she was about to ask her best friend. "Is he dead, Anna?"

"No, he's not dead. I said, attempted murder. But I didn't mean to do it, Kaye. Please, please call my father, and tell him to come down here. I need him to post bond for me. Hurry, Kaye. Just do it, please," Annalisse begged.

Kaye exhaled loudly into the phone just before it died.

◊

"She shot Daddy?" Adanya cried. "How is he? Where is he?" she asked without waiting for her grandma to tell her what had gone down. All she heard were the words 'shot, hospital, your mother, daddy', coming through her ears like missing pieces of a puzzle.

"I'm on my way." Adanya shut down the phone, while she looked frantically around for her purse and keys. When she found them, she ran to the garage and jumped inside her automobile. She started the engine, remotely opened the garage door, and backed out of the driveway.

It was after turning on to the main intersection that she realized she didn't stay on the phone long enough for her grandmother to tell her the hospital they'd taken her father to. She pushed the phone button on her steering wheel and vocally instructed it to "Call grandparents." What sounded like phone keys being pushed, flowed from the car's top-of-the-line sound system.

"Methodist University downtown," she heard her gram say immediately when she answered.

"I'm on my way." Adanya pushed the button and sped in the direction of I-240.

Adanya paced the hospital floor. Wringing her hands constantly, she twitched as she walked like a junkie in need of a fix. "Gram, this is all my fault."

"Baby, don't do this to yourself. This has nothing to do with you."

"Yes it does. I shouldn't have told Annalisse about his other life. I shouldn't have." Adanya cried into her hands.

"I know he's wrong on so many levels, and I feel her pain because well you already know, Gram. But to want my father dead? No way. That's taking things too far. If I had thought for a minute she would do something like this, I never ever would have said anything. Oh, God, please forgive me," she ranted.

"Honey, come sit down." Gram patted the empty seat next to where she sat. "Making a trail in that floor is not going to change things. And until you can feel someone else's hurt, you can't say how you'd react if the same thing happened to you. Annalisse was cut deep by your father. I mean, another family? That is not your fault, and my Annalisse deserved to know. What in the world was that man thinking?" Gram shook her head.

"Still, trying to kill him wasn't the answer," Adanya shot back without regarding her grandma's opinion. "I'm in pain too over what he did. Shuuu, I'm in pain over what both of them did to me, but I would never," Adanya gestured with both hands, "And I do mean never inflict bodily harm on them."

"Well, that's what you say, but Annalisse was pushed over the edge. She's been drowning herself in self-pity ever since you cut her out of your life. And then to learn that for what over twenty four, no thirty something years since they first met, that your father is a liar. She doesn't know who he is. God knows I don't either," her grandmother said. "I tell you, it's a shame. But I want him to be okay. I'm praying that he'll be just fine. God knows Annalisse wouldn't hurt a fly."

Adanya gave pause as she thought about what her gram was saying. "I do feel bad for her. I know she's hurt by all this. But I just wish she hadn't shot him."

For the first time, Adanya witnessed her grandma crying without it being related to praising God. Adanya walked over to her and sat in the chair next to her. Reaching around her gram's shoulder, she hugged the woman who appeared to have aged by years in a matter of a couple of hours.

"God, please let him be okay." Adanya leaned on her grandma.

Gram Kaplan held Adanya's hands and began to pray. "Lord God, restore Kenneth's health. Father, heal his wounds," she cried. "I know you can. Take care of my Annalisse. Guard her mind, Father God. Help her, Lord. I know you're able, Lord."

Both women cried into each other's bosoms.

Adanya lifted her head. "Did you call MaMaw and GrandPaw Anniston? They would be livid if they found out their son has been shot and no one bothered calling and telling them about it."

Gram Kaplan wiped away her tears with a wad of tissue that was encased in her right hand. "No. I was waiting to see how he was doing first. I guess I'll call them now." She sighed heavily. "Lord, I hate to tell them that Kenneth's been shot, and that it was Annalisse who shot him."

"I don't ever want to see her again, Gram. She's evil. She's a terrible person. She grew tired of me and she grew tired of him. That's why he went to the other woman. She's always been selfish, so wrapped up in herself. Now, she's gone too far. And she deserves to pay, Gram."

"You shut up talking like that," Gram yelled at Adanya and then looked around the tiny family waiting room area like she expected someone other than herself and Adanya to be in the room. "Shut up before you say a bunch of stuff you'll regret. Like I said, pray. That's the only way we're going to make it through this. It's the only way your daddy is going to make it through this, and it's the only way my child is going to make it through. Prayer and the grace of God." She shook her bowed down head again.

◊

It was nearing eight-thirty p.m. when Adanya's cell phone rang. "Bleak, my daddy's been shot," she rushed to tell him just as soon as she answered her phone. "We're at the hospital now, Methodist downtown."

"Shot? Who shot him?" Bleak's tone didn't reveal any hint of being upset. "Guess he must have messed over another unsuspecting, helpless, woman. I say he got what he deserved."

"At first I thought the same thing, but then I realized he's my father, Bleak. And no matter how angry or disappointed I am in him, he's still my dad. I love him, Bleak."

"Well, he's not mine. And now I have to break my mother's heart all over again by telling her that her husband has gone and got himself shot by some other irate female out there."

"That irate female happens to be Annalisse...my mother." Adanya could understand why Bleak felt the way that he did. His mother was having a hard time too. She had to also try to come to terms with her Caitlin being seriously injured and still in the hospital. Now this. Kenneth had been almost killed?

"Your mother?"

"Yes," Adanya sobbed.

"Where is she? Is she all right?"

"She's not hurt, physically, if that's what you mean. Mentally and emotionally, well, I'm not sure. Anyway, my gramps was on his way to Jail East the last time we spoke. He's going to see if they're going to let him bail her out."

"Oh. Man, everything is so messed up. How is he?"

"The doctor is supposed to be back to talk to us as soon as he gets out of surgery. She shot him twice."

"Twice? Wow, that's wild."

"Tell me about it. The doctor did say that one of the bullets traveled through his right thigh and out the back of his leg. The second one shattered his left ankle. They're going to try to save his leg. One of the bullets came awfully close to his jugular vein. Depending on what they find during surgery, and from x-rays and ultrasounds, and all of that, they'll be able to tell us more. But he could lose his leg, or he could never walk again. There are so many ways it can go according to the doctor."

"Who's with you?"

"Gram Kaplan."

"Nobody is up there but the two of you? No church members? No pastor? Nobody?"

"I haven't thought of calling anybody, and I don't think Gram has either. I guess I'll call the emergency line at the church and leave them a message."

"I'll be there as soon as I can, but I want you to know that I'm going to tell my mother about this. It's her husband too, you know."

"As much as I hate to be reminded that my father is a bigamist, I know you have to do what you have to do. Your mother deserves to know. She's the mother of his children too."

"Thanks, Adanya. How are you holding up?"

"Okay, I guess. Anyway, why don't you go on and call your mother. No, on second thought, go tell her in person. She's going to need your support."

"I know. And thanks, I'll probably see you out there. I'm figuring she's going to want to come to the hospital, although after the pain he's caused her, I don't see why she would want to. But knowing my mother like I do, I know when I tell her what's happened, she's going to forget all about what he's done. She's going to want to be by his side."

"She has to do what she feels she has to do. But I'm not leaving on her account. I'm telling you now."

"Did I say anything about you leaving? No, I didn't, so don't go there with me. She has every right to be at the hospital with him if that's what she wants to do. I can't stop her, and I won't even try to stop her. I'm just going to be there for my mother, just the same as you being at the hospital because it's your daddy laying up in there." Bleak sounded like his temper was rising but he was tired of Adanya's little innuendos and smart jabs she was taking against his mother. Maybe his mother had been naïve, stupid, not so smart or just plain crazy in love, but she was his mother and she was a good person. It was John Phillips, Kenneth Anniston, whoever he called himself, that should bear the weight of what had happened. Him and him alone.

Bleak found it difficult to feel sorry for the guy. He'd caused far too much damage and pain to his mother, his two little sisters, to Adanya's mother, and if he admitted it, to him as well. He'd come to love the man he'd known as John Phillips, like a father. The man had been nothing but good to him. He'd stepped up to the plate when his own father chose to take another path in life, one that didn't include Bleak. His father's life was a life lived on the run, involved in one crime after another.

Bleak drove to his mother's house. He wasn't surprised when he found her not there. "I forgot, you said you were going to be at the hospital with Caitlin this evening," he said aloud. He left his mother's house and drove to LeBonheur.

Bleak was awfully glad to see his sister sitting up in the bed with far less tubes stuck in her. Her eyes were glued on the television set when he walked in, but she managed a weak smile when she saw her big brother.

He asked his mother to step outside of Caitlin's room with him. When he told her about what had gone down with Kenneth, he was surprised at her response.

"I don't blame her. She had more guts than me. I could have easily been the one who shot him. Thank God I don't believe in guns in the house. And I didn't think John did either, but again, the man has so many secrets that you can't tell who the real John Phillips is."

"I know, Mom, I know. But at least you know that he's no good. No good for you, for Caitlin or Cady. He's lucky that God spared his life."

Carla looked at her son. Her eyes were puffy and bags had formed underneath them due to sleep deprivation. "I want to hate him, Bleak. I want to hate him so bad, but…well, I can't. I don't," she said in a broken voice. "I have to see him," she suddenly said as her voice rose. "Can you stay with your sister for a while? I want to go see him. I won't be long."

Bleak, as much as he hated to, waved his hands and told her, "Yeah, sure; go on. You know I don't mind staying up here. Caitlin will be fine."

"Thank you, son." She went back inside Caitlin's hospital room and came back out in the hallway with her purse. She kissed Bleak on his cheek "I'll be back as soon as I can."

Bleak nodded as he watched his mother walk away in the direction of the elevator. He recalled a passage of scripture he'd learned long ago while attending a Sunday School class. "The bread of deceit is sweet to a man; but afterwards his mouth shall be filled with gravel," he said loud enough for only him and God to hear, before he turned and walked into Caitlin's hospital room.

19

"How much more grievous are the consequences of anger than the causes of it." M. Aurelius

Gramps tried but getting Annalisse released from jail was not going to happen, so he called one of his friends who suggested he get her a good criminal attorney.

Mr. Kaplan adhered to his friend's advice, and after hearing a synopsis of what had happened, Attorney Joel Greenside agreed to take the case for a five figure retainer. Mr. Kaplan made arrangements to pay him the next day.

Attorney Greenside arrived at Jail East ready to fight for his new client. Within a few hours after the bond hearing, Annalisse was scheduled to be released. It took almost ten hours from the time they went to court until she walked out of the jail free on a $100,000 bond.

"Honey," Mr. Kaplan said, "everything will be fine." He patted Annalisse on her hand as he drove her home.

"Have you seen Kenneth? How is he?"

"Your mother and Adanya are at the hospital. He's going to be fine, but the verdict isn't in on the extent of long term or permanent damage.

Annalisse put her head in her hands. "Oh, Daddy, I'm so sorry for everything I was so angry."

She looked at her father. His eyes were fixed on the road ahead.

"We all do things we regret, and Kenneth, well he isn't exactly an altar boy. Sometimes people bring trouble on themselves. And with what I've just heard since this all happened, the man has been leading a dangerous lifestyle. Who would have thought that he could do such a thing." Mr. Kaplan shook his head and quickly looked over at his daughter. "I'm not saying that you were justified in shooting him, but I can certainly understand how you snapped."

"Don't try to make excuses for me. I was wrong, and now I'll probably have to spend years of my life behind bars. Daddy, what am I going to do?" Annalisse cried.

"Attorney Greenside says you have a good chance of getting off. And you've never so much as had an outstanding traffic ticket. Your record is squeaky clean. Given the circumstances under which this happened, he feels that he's going to be able to get you off on probation. Don't you remember him telling you that?"

Annalisse shook her head. "No, I guess I'm still in shock. I can't believe I shot Kenneth." Annalisse shook her head and buried her face in her hands. "And the judge; when I walked into that courtroom all shackled and handcuffed, I thought she was going to throw the book at me right then and there. Thank God, she seemed to be empathetic with my story."

"You just try not to worry, Annalisse. Go home, take a hot shower and get yourself some rest. I know you probably didn't sleep a wink at that jail."

"No, I didn't. But I have to go to the hospital. I need to see for myself that Kenneth is going to be okay."

"Annalisse, you can't do that. It'll only cause more problems, and you don't need that. Your mother will fill you in on everything once she gets home."

"Where's my cell phone?" she asked.

"It's probably in that bag of personal items they gave you when they released you."

"No, I don't remember seeing them put my phone in there."

"It has to be in there if you had it when they arrested you. And you should have signed off on your personal property when they released you."

"Yeah, you're right. Let me look." Annalisse retrieved the bag from the back seat. "It's in here."

"Who are you going to call?" he asked.

"Momma. I want to see if Adanya is still at the hospital with her. If she is, I hope she'll talk to me."

"Uhh, I don't know, sweetheart. That child still has some serious anger issues. Adding the fact that her father is laying up in a hospital bed, well, who knows what's on her mind."

Annalisse ignored her father's words and started hitting the number keys. "It went straight to voice mail." She sighed and looked out the window.

"You'll talk to her soon enough."

"Take me to the hospital."

"I can't do that."

"If you don't take me, I swear as soon as you let me out at home, I'm going to jump in my car and take myself down there."

"I'm telling you, it's not a good idea."

"Daddy, I'm begging you."

Mr. Kaplan relented after weighing his options. He decided that he'd much rather take Annalisse to the hospital where he could monitor her rather than her taking herself and then God knows what would happen. She would be like a loose cannon unless she had someone to help restrain her.

"Okay, but I'm telling you, Annalisse, you're going to see your mother, and Adanya, and then I'm getting you out of there. You are not going to see Kenneth. You understand?" His voice was firm and unmoving.

"Yes. I understand."

◊

Carla walked up to the ICU nurses' station. "I'm here to see my husband."

"And who is your husband, ma'am?" one of the nurse's at the desk asked.

"John Phillips."

Two other nurses plus the woman who addressed Carla all looked at each other. "We don't have a John Phillips. Are you sure he's in ICU?"

For a brief moment, Carla looked dazed. She shook her head. "Oh, uh I mean Kenneth Anniston."

The nurses looked at each other again, puzzled. "And who are you to him?" one of them asked.

"I just told you. I'm his wife," she snapped. "So, please just tell me where I can find him."

"He's down the hall, to the right. ICU 577."

"Thank you," she said and strode off. With each step she took, she nervously pondered what she would say to John. She hated to admit, even to herself, that she still loved him. No matter how upset she was with what he'd done, she could never do anything like Annalisse had done. Shoot him? Want to see him dead? Never. She arrived at his room, and from outside the glass walls she saw him lying in the bed with IV and tubing. She wanted to cry, but held back her tears.

She pushed back the glass door and entered the room. "John," she said in a whisper. "John?" she called his name a second time.

Slowly, he turned toward her. His eyes were barely open, but she could see a smile form on his face. It was a tiny one, but she was glad for that.

She walked up to his bed, leaned over it and kissed him gently on his lips. "How do you feel?"

"I can't believe you came. How is Caitlin?"

"Caitlin is slowly improving. Bleak is at the hospital with her. I told him I wouldn't be gone long. I wanted to check on you. John," she paused.

"I'm sorry, Carla," he said, halting her from saying anything else. "I didn't mean for any of this to happen. Believe me. I love you. I love the girls." A tear, then another one, followed by another one, started rolling down his cheeks.

Carla reached out and stroked his face, and gently wiped away each tear. She bent down and kissed him on his lips again, this one more lingering than the previous.

"I know you do. It might sound dumb on my part, but I really believe you love me."

He nodded. "I do, Carla. I love you with all my heart. And I'm sorry."

"Well, now is not the time to discuss it. I want to know what the doctors are saying."

Kenneth was quite groggy from having undergone surgery, but he managed to talk with forced effort. "My ankle is shattered and my thigh, my leg is numb." He slowly raised his head and opened his eyes as widely as he could manage but his head fell back against the pillow. He closed his eyes, unable to fight against the effects of the anesthesia and the morphine pump.

Carla placed her hand over her mouth and this time she was the one whose tears began to fall.

"What are you doing here?" the voice took Carla off guard. She looked toward the glass door. "Haven't you caused enough trouble?" Adanya yelled as she stepped all the way into the room. "You shouldn't be here."

She had told Bleak she understood if Carla wanted to come and see Kenneth, but now seeing her pushed Adanya over the edge.

"Don't, Adanya," Kenneth said from his drug induced state. His voice was extremely weak and his eyes fluttered. "She...mother... of...my...children."

"Oh, so that makes it all right?" It was apparent in the tone of her voice that she was not a happy camper. And she hadn't seemed to notice that her father was still under the influence of anesthesia. He'd only been out of surgery for a few hours. "You almost lost your life because of her."

"I should have killed you," another familiar voice said. Carla and Adanya looked and saw Annalisse standing just outside the door.

"Mother, what are you doing here?" Adanya asked with a startled look on her face.

"Nurse," Carla called as loudly as she could. "Somebody, get her out of here."

"So this is her. A white woman? This is the slut you've been seeing?" Annalisse snarled, dismissing Carla's pleas. "What kind of woman are you? What kind of woman sleeps with another woman's husband, has children with him, and pretends to be married to him? You're some piece of work. You're nothing but a tramp, a home wrecker," Annalisse cursed and yelled.

"How dare you show your face up here after you almost killed my husband," spat Carla. "Nurse." Nurse," she called again, then then walked boldly past a suddenly scared looking, but angry Annalisse.

"Don't bother. I'm leaving. You can have him." She huffed as she looked at Kenneth laying helpless on the hospital bed, tubes connected to his body. "And here I was feeling bad about almost killing you. You deserve whatever happens to you." She bolted out the door and down the corridor leading to the elevators.

Annalisse stopped shy of the elevator door and turned to face her daughter. Tears flowed from her red eyes.

Adanya ran up to her and embraced her. She wanted to be angry but for some reason, she could not. She held on to her mother and the both of them cried.

The sound of the elevator brought them apart. "Come on, let's get you out of here before security comes. You don't want to go back to jail."

They rushed on to the elevator. When the doors shut, Annalisse exhaled. "Thank you, baby. I don't know what I was thinking back there. Daddy brought me here so I could see you and momma. I promised him I wasn't going to try and see Kenneth, and look what I did. I could be put back in jail. What's wrong with me?" Annalisse folded both arms together.

"You're human, and you're hurt."

"Where is Momma?"

"In the waiting room. She's fine. She's been up here with me. But after seeing and hearing what just happened back there, I don't know why I even bothered staying around this place." The elevator door opened and the two women stepped out. Mr. Kaplan was standing in the corridor.

"Adanya, baby, how are you? How's your daddy? Where's Eva?"

"I'm fine, Gramps. And Gram is still upstairs in the

waiting room. Daddy, well I'm sure he's just great now that his other wife is up there."

Gramps looked shocked. "His other wife?" he said.

"Yes. Her name is Carla. Carla Phillips. Isn't that just dandy?" quipped Adanya. "I can't go back up there, Gramps. I don't want to see him anymore. Do you mind going up there and getting Gram? A couple of church members came not too long ago, and they're in the waiting room with her, but let her know that I won't be coming back. Ask her to bring my purse down with her."

"Sure. And Annalisse, you didn't do anything did you?" He looked at his daughter like he suspected that something had gone awry when she went upstairs.

"No, I didn't."

He nodded and walked on to the elevator when it opened to let other people get on and off.

When Adanya was alone again with Annalisse, she led her to a nearby row of chairs. "Let's sit down here until Gramps comes back."

"Sure. Look, baby, I'm so sorry for everything. I can't imagine all of what you're going through."

"I have to admit that I was angry when I heard that you'd shot my daddy. I know he was wrong for what he did, but you tried to kill him. You tried to kill my daddy. And that was wrong, mother. I mean, Annalisse."

"You were right the first time – I am your mother. I always will be. And yes, I was wrong, and now I will probably have to go to jail for what I've done. But you must believe me when I tell you that I didn't want things to be like this, Adanya. These last few months have been a complete nightmare. And now for me to be in the situation I'm in, and for well," Annalisse looked up toward the ceiling. "For Kenneth to be laid up in ICU because of me…it's unforgiveable."

"Stop it, it isn't unforgiveable. You know better than that. And I'm just as wrong. I hated you, and I hated daddy for what you did to me. How you destroyed my life. And then I hated you even more because you tried to take his life. After witnessing that scene upstairs with Carla, I see where my daddy's heart really lies. And it's not with me."

"And, it's certainly not with me either," added Annalisse. "It's with that white woman. Oh, my God, a white woman. Why did he have to cheat on me, and why, oh, Lord did it have to be with a white woman? I can't believe he did this." Annalisse started crying.

"Don't cry, he's not worth it. And as far as Carla being a white woman, it doesn't matter. That's not what's important."

Adanya thought of Bleak. What would Annalisse think about him if she met him? Annalisse would probably stroke out on the spot.

"I want him to be okay," Adanya said after she shook off the thoughts racing through her mind. "But I can't have him in my life. Not now. He's gone too far. Seeing her up there with him, well, it just made me realize that he's not the man I thought he was. I looked up to him, practically worshipped the ground he walked on."

"I know, honey," Annalisse sniffled, as she wrapped an arm around Adanya to comfort her.

Annalisse began to feel a sense of calm washing over her spirit. She hadn't been able to hold her daughter for months. And now, through a tragic set of circumstances, she was granted a second chance to prove to Adanya that she loved her. She didn't know what the future held for her, but right now, she reveled in the fact that maybe, just maybe, Adanya would forgive her for the mistakes of the past, and let her back into her life.

Adanya relaxed in her mother's arms. She didn't seem to notice that her mother wasn't exactly fresh and groomed, not after having spent the night in a jail cell. But Adanya didn't care. She felt like she was where she belonged, in the comforting arms of her mother. They had a lot to go through, a long way to go, and there was bound to be more pain ahead for their family, but Adanya had determined that some things would have to change. If she was going to be able to move forward with her future, she would have to release the pangs of her past. It would be up to God to deal with the actions of her father.

"Bleak," she said for no apparent reason, and her head popped up off her mother's shoulder.

"Who? Bleak? What is that?" asked Annalisse.

"It's not a what. He's a who," Adanya said and grinned.

"Well, who is he?"

"That's another long story. I'll tell you all about him after you promise me that you'll go home, get yourself cleaned up, and try to rest."

"Only if you promise to come to the house," Annalisse said, and looked over Adanya's shoulder as her parents walked toward them. Annalisse popped up from the chair and raced toward her mother.

"Momma."

Adanya walked up to them and stood next to Gramps.

"Okay," Gramps interrupted the emotional reunion after a few seconds. "Let's get you home, Annalisse; you too, Eva."

"I'm going to go home and then I'll come over to your house a later."

"You promise?" Annalisse queried.

"Yes, I promise. I'll see you shortly. Gram, Gramps," she kissed each of them, "I'll talk to you later. And Gram."

"Yes, baby," answered Gram.

"Thank you for staying here with me. I couldn't have gone through his without you by my side. I love you."

"I love you too, baby. You be careful going home. Okay?"

"I will." Adanya's phone rang.

"Hello," she said as she waved her hand at her family and proceeded to walk ahead of them toward the exit doors.

"You still at the hospital?" Bleak asked.

"I'm just leaving," Her reply was unpleasant.

"What's wrong with you?"

"Your mother."

"What about my mother?"

"She's here."

"Yea, I know. I told you she was probably going to come up there once she heard about him being shot. I'm at the hospital with my sister until she comes back."

"Well, before she tells you, let me be the first to let you know that I'm done."

"What do you mean, you're done?"

"Seeing the two of them together, I realize his blood may be running through my veins, but so what. What's blood got to do with it anyway? "

"Did you see my mother?"

"Yes, *and* she saw me. *And* she saw Annalisse."

"Your mother is out of jail?"

"Yes. Things got a little heated, but it's all good. I'm leaving the hospital now. So are my grandparents and my mother."

"Where is my mom?"

"I guess she's still upstairs drooling over that devil," Adanya spoke with sarcasm.

"Don't act like you're mad at me. My mother is a grown woman, and so is your father. It's not my fault, not your fault, not anybody's fault when it comes to them and the decisions they've made for their lives. I just don't want you tripping."

"Tripping? Like what?"

"I told you, Adanya. I want to build something with you. Don't let the actions of our parents tear us apart. Please."

Silence.

"We'll talk later, Bleak. I'm tired. I just want to go home and chill for a while."

"Can I come by when I get home? I need to see you."

"I don't know. I promised Annalisse that I would be over to her house. So I don't know about seeing you. It's probably not such a good idea for us to see each other right now anyway, given the circumstances."

"See, that's what I'm talking about. You're making me pay for what your daddy did."

"That's exactly what you're doing."

"Bleak, we're practically in the same family. And I don't feel comfortable knowing that my father and your mother are well, they're together. It's nasty. Just plain nasty."

"Come off it, Adanya. You act like you're some prude or something. Like you don't know about life. People do things, Adanya. Some of the things they do, we won't approve of, but then again some of the things you and I do other folks won't approve of either. That's called life and making choices. I can't help that I happen to fall for a girl who happens to be the daughter of my stepfather. There's nothing I can do about it. And there's nothing you can do about it. So, please, don't penalize me for their actions."

"Look, I've got to go. I can't talk about this right now. Good bye." Adanya hung up the phone, got in her car and drove toward home. She thought about everything Bleak had said. And he was right, but she couldn't see herself being with him, not now. His mother had the audacity to be up in the room all goo-goo-ga-gaing over her father. How could she? Didn't the woman have any respect for his real wife? How could she even want to be with a man who was cheating on her ever since they'd been together. If she was like that, maybe Bleak was weak too. And the last thing she wanted was some weak man who couldn't or wouldn't stand up for what was right. What was right in her book was for him to tell his mother to back away from her father. What was right was for him to stand up to her father too and let him know that he was no good for his mother, but did he do that? No, all he had to say was that they were two grown people. In Adanya's book, there was no way she could ever hope to be in a real relationship with Bleak. Not after this.

She pulled into her garage, got out and went inside. As soon as she stepped foot inside her place, Snoopy bum rushed her.

"Hey there, boy. Mommy's home," she told him while tickling him underneath his chin. "Come on, you wanna go out?" she said in a childlike voice.

She took Snoopy outside to relieve himself. Once back inside, Adanya peeled off her clothes, went and took a shower and put on some fresh clothes. She sauntered into the kitchen to prepare herself something to eat before she left for Annalisse's house. The sound of the doorbell jarred her from her meal preparation.

"I bet it's Bleak. Dang, why did he come over here when I told him I couldn't see him now?" She stood still for several seconds while pondering whether or not she was going to answer the door.

Knock. Knock. Knock.

"Adanya, I know you're in there. Open the door. We need to talk," he insisted.

Adanya remained stationary while Snoopy started barking and bouncing, and turning around and around.

"Shhh," she said and put a finger up to her lips but Snoopy continued to bark.

Knock. Knock. Knock.

Adanya made her way to the front door, pausing before she turned the door knob.

"Bleak—" She flashed him an evil look.

Without warning, he pushed the door fully open and just as swiftly closed it behind him. Pulling her into his arms, his lips sought hers and he explored the moistness of her mouth. His hands roamed her body like he was searching for hidden treasure.

Adanya had no desire to back away. There was a bond between them, one she couldn't fight, didn't want to fight. His mouth against hers made her tingle. Her heart fluttered, and she couldn't deny her desire for him.

Twisting in his arms, she tried to break free, but it only made him pull her closer. With little effort, he swooped her in his arms as she put her arms around his neck.

"I can't let you go," he whispered hoarsely, his hot breath against her ear as he carried her into the bedroom. "I want you, Adanya. I want you so badly."

Unable to resist, Adanya allowed him to ease her down onto the bed. His touch aroused her to the point where she screamed in pleasure.

"Bleak, stop," she cried out. "I can't do this. We can't do this. Not like this," she managed to say between outcries of pleasure.

He tumbled over onto the bed, fighting his own battle of personal restraint. He didn't want to do anything that she wasn't ready to do. His spiritual and moral convictions began to flood his mind, and he had to agree with Adanya.

He didn't want her to be another conquest. He'd had far too many of them in the past. He wanted something different. Wanted to live a more God like life. Adanya was the kind of woman that he could see himself marrying one day, and he didn't want to let one night of sexual wantonness ruin what could be a lifetime of pleasure for them if they took things slowly, and did things right.

"I'm sorry," he said as he pulled her next to him with one arm. "You're just so beautiful. And, I love you."

Adanya raised up to a sitting position. She looked back at Bleak. "You love me? How can you be so sure?"

"I think I know what love is, Adanya. And if you admit it, I think you love me too."

"Bleak, we haven't known each other a good six months. How can we say we love each other?"

"Who said falling in love had to be on a time table. I love you, plain and simple. I don't know when it happened, but I do know that what I feel is real."

She teared up, and Bleak sat up and gathered her again into his strong arms. "It's going to be all right," he whispered into her hair. "I won't hurt you. I promise. Just let me in, Adanya. Let me in your heart."

They curled up in the middle of her bed. She turned to look at him, facing the undeniable fact that Bleak was right. There was no denying her feelings for him any longer. She nestled comfortably underneath him, her head resting against his chest. Any thoughts of going to Annalisse's house were squelched. Adanya was where she wanted to be, and with who she wanted to be with. There was no turning back.

"My life has been one crazy thing after another." Adanya twisted in the bed and eased from underneath Bleak's embrace. "I don't know how much I can take."

Bleak sat up. "Come on now. Let's not go there. The

bottom line remains, God is in control, Adanya. And don't get me wrong, I know we all mess up, and a lot of the time it's our fault, but other times it's not. Everything that's happened to you is not your fault. It's not your fault that your parents chose to keep the secret from you about your birth. It's not your fault that your father, my stepfather, my mother's husband, my little sisters' father is a two timing, lying, bigamist. It's not your fault that your mother shot him." Bleak's mouth curled downward and a frown formed on his face.

"I know that, but it still doesn't make me feel better. I have two little sisters that I never knew I had. My mother may be facing years behind bars. My father, well as much as I hate what he's done, I still love him, and he might be a cripple for the rest of his life. And, you, well you're my stepbrother. It's just so much to take in."

"Yes, it is a lot. I think about my own mother. What she's going through. Maybe you hate her, but think about it, Adanya. She fell in love with a man who she thought was her dream man. And to be honest, I thought he was a good dude too. He always treated her like a queen. He was a good father to Caitlin and Cady, and a good stepfather to me. I have to give him his props. He was all right with me, until all this stuff happened."

Bleak gathered her in his arms again. "And look on the bright side of things. We met each other, and I may be your stepbrother, but that's the extent of our relationship. We don't share the same blood, so forget being my stepsister. I want you to be my woman," Bleak said and kissed her on the forehead.

Adanya flinched. "I need to go see Annalisse. I promised her that
I would be over there."

"Why tonight? It's getting late."

"It's only seven o'clock or so. And I don't plan on staying long. Hey, why don't you come with me? She needs to meet you anyway."

"I don't know if that's a good idea. I'm the son of her husband's other wife. I don't think she's going to be too cool with that."

"It's time to get everything out in the open. No more secrets. I'm tired of it all. If you're really serious about a relationship with me, then it's time to face the piper. And we're going to start by you meeting Annalisse."

20

"Lukewarm acceptance is more bewildering than outright rejection." M. L. King, Jr.

"You have some nerve, bringing this boy up in my house. And talking about the two of you are trying to have a relationship. You must be insane. What's wrong with you?"

Annalisse didn't think it was possible for her world, or her life to come crashing down like it had. And to have Adanya stand up in her house accompanied by some white boy, well not just any white boy, but Kenneth's stepson. What was Adanya thinking? Was this some kind of a cruel joke? When would it ever end?

Annalisse hissed and spat one round of cruel words toward Bleak after another. She even talked about his mother, belittled the fact that Kenneth was the father of Bleak's little sisters.

"Stop it," Adanya yelled. "I'm sick of this. When are you going to listen to me? It's not Bleak's fault. We met each other and neither of us knew about my daddy's other life. Bleak is a good man. And we care about one another."

"Humph. You have no idea if he's a good man or not

because you've never been in a relationship," Annalisse said with venom dripping in her every word. "And now you bring some white boy up in here talking about he's a good man. Girl, you need more than book sense up there." She pointed a finger at Adanya's head. "And how do you know he didn't know who you were. He's probably known all along. Probably knows about our whole family."

Bleak had turned what looked like two shades darker than his normally fair skinned complexion. He held back from talking, choosing rather to let mother and daughter fight the battle.

"I don't believe that. Bleak would do anything like that. Would you?" she turned and looked at him.

Bleak bit his bottom lip. "Are you kidding me? You know I wouldn't. I came on to you because you are a beautiful woman, Adanya. Not because I was trying to hook up with my stepdaddy's daughter. What would I get out of that? But if you want to blame me for all this, then go ahead. I'm tired of defending myself. But God knows the truth."

"Hah. Don't bring God up in this. I see right through you. You're not right. But one thing is for sure, God will bring it out in the light. Just like this came out about your mother and my husband, then the real deal is going to come out about you," she shouted. Turning back and focusing on Adanya she added, "Why would you bring this punk up in here anyway? I don't want to hear anything he has to say."

"I brought him here because I didn't want to be like my loser daddy. I didn't want to keep any secrets from you, like the two of you did me. But I see that you can't look past Bleak's skin color, or the fact that he's Carla's son. When are you and daddy going to act like grownups, and stop blaming everybody else for your mistakes?"

"Listen to yourself. Look at who's standing next to you, then think about what his mother did to this family."

"His mother? I don't think Daddy's exactly squeaky clean in all of this. If it wasn't for him, then none of this would have happened. And you." Adanya pointed. "Barely have one foot out of a jail cell, and you're blaming Bleak's mother?"

Annalisse looked stunned.

"We're leaving."

"Good. Go right ahead." She shooed Adanya off. "I can't make sense of any of this mess. It's too much. Just way too much," Annalisse said angrily.

"Come on, Bleak. I can't do this anymore either. I want to go home."

Bleak grabbed her hand and led her toward the door. He opened the car door for her and waited on her to get inside. "Are you all right?"

Adanya shook her head. "I don't know what to do. What else can happen to me?" She bowed her head.

"Pray, baby. God is the only one who can get you through this. He's the only one who can get any of us through this. But there's something I want you to know," he said as they drove toward home. "My mother is just a much a victim as you are. First of all, she would never knowingly date, let alone marry a man who already had a wife and child. That's not in her nature, or character. Like you, my mother is a loving, kind, and decent human being. She's a great mother, and she's been nothing but good to your father. If she had known, or even suspected, that he had someone else, she would have divorced him in a heartbeat, and this I know."

"I'm sorry. I shouldn't be judgmental. I didn't mean to come off the way I did about her. I don't even know the woman."

"You don't, but you do know me. But if you're going

to keep on coming down on my mother, acting like she's the one to blame for all of this, then I'm telling you now, Adanya, I won't deal with it. I love you, but I won't put up with the way you're downing my mother. I have two little sisters who need me. And if you don't trust me, if you want to take out your frustrations on me and my family, then all I can do is bounce."

"Do what you have to," she said, her mouth suddenly tight, and a frown came over her face.

The rest of the drive was made in silence. As soon as they arrived in front of Adanya's flat, Bleak opened the passenger's door, got out, and immediately began walking toward his building.

"So, that's it? You're just going to walk off without saying anything?" Adanya stood outside of her car.

"It could have been nice," he said as he walked away without looking back.

Tears welled up in Adanya's eyes. She turned and walked toward her flat, unlocked the door and let herself inside.

Snoopy met her at the door, ready to go out to relieve himself. Without saying a word, she went to the hall closet, retrieved his leash, put it on, and walked him outside. Tears overflowed, her heart pounded against her chest, and unexplainable grief overpowered her spirit.

If Bleak wanted to walk out on her, so be it. She couldn't, wouldn't waste her time or effort on chasing after a man. That was one piece of advice from her father that she would take heed to. Bleak isn't the man for me anyway, she told herself as she walked Snoopy around the doggie area of the complex.

When she returned to her flat, she went to the fridge to see what she could find to snack on. She settled on making a peanut butter and jelly sandwich on whole wheat toast. Her message tone beeped. She'd received a text.

"Hey whats goin on. haven't heard from u n 2 days"

She'd forgotten that she hadn't talked to Nanette. She had to fill her in on what had happened. Instead of texting her back, she called.

"Are you kidding me?" Nanette remarked after listening to everything Adanya told her. "Is your dad going to be okay? Do you think your mother is going to have to go to prison?"

"I don't know." Adanya sat on the couch, with Snoopy curled up next to her. "At this point, I don't know anything. Girl, it's like I'm living in somebody else's world."

"I don't know what to say."

"You don't know what to say? I don't know what to say myself."

"What about Bleak? I know he's got to be messed up about everything too. I hope you two are leaning on one another. I mean, I'm your best friend, and you know I'm always going to have your back. But you and Bleak, well you two can have something special, I think. If you can move past the fact that your daddy is his stepfather, then who knows where your relationship can lead."

"It's not possible."

"Why?"

"I can't do it, Nanette. His mother? My father? No way. And think about it. Even if I wanted to stick around to see how things turned out, I don't think I could do it."

"What? Do you think it'll be too awkward seeing your daddy and Bleak's mother together? Is that it?"

"I guess, if she stays with him that is. But I don't see how any sane woman would stay with a man like him." Adanya folded her feet underneath her bottom, pushing

Snoopy off of her at the same time. "And you're right, how could I face seeing my daddy with Bleak's mother? And my sisters? I have two sisters, and I still can't believe it, Nanette. This is so soap opera, so Lifetime."

Nanette sighed into the phone. "Well, I'm just glad you found out all of this now. I want you and Bleak to work things out, and be together. But I sort of understand where you're coming from. I know you like him, but still, it would be awkward. I mean, running into your daddy with Bleak's mother, that is if she decides she's going to stay with him. It's going to be tough enough if you plan on getting to know your sisters. So, whatever you do, just know that I'm here for you."

"You are such a good friend. I love you, Nanette."

"I love you too. Look, you just chill out the rest of the night," Nanette suggested. "I'm going to lay this body down too. I'm tired. It's been a long day."

"I heard that. Thanks for listening. I'll talk to you later."

"Okay, bye."

"Night, Nanette." Adanya got up, slipped on her shoes, grabbed her purse and keys and left the house. She drove straight to the hospital to confront her father. Maybe by now the anesthesia had worn off.

When Adanya arrived to ICU, the nurse told her that her father had been moved to a regular room. Adanya hoped that it meant her father was going to have a relatively fast recuperation. She caught the elevator down to the second floor, and walked the corridors until she arrived at Room 227. She tapped on the door.

"Come in." His voice sounded stronger.

Slowly, she pushed the door open and walked in the room with exact caution, like a lion on the prowl.

Kenneth saw her and smiled.

Adanya stood at the foot of his bed. "Daddy, why did you have to ruin everything?"

Kenneth stretched out his hand. "Come over here, Pumpkin." Adanya didn't move.

"No. I'm here because I need you to tell me the truth for once. Please." She wiped a tear from her face.

"What can I say except I messed up." His voice remained low, but he spoke clearly and deliberately. "I didn't mean to hurt anyone."

"You keep saying that, but you hurt everyone. I don't understand. You have another wife? Children? A whole other life?"

"I got caught up. I didn't mean for any of this to happen. It just did. I know it sounds like a cop out, but I don't know what else to say."

"Do you love her?"

"Who? Carla? Or your mother?" Adanya shrugged. "Both."

Kenneth nodded. "I love Annalisse. I've loved her since we were kids. I've told you that many times."

"And Carla?"

Kenneth smiled. "Yes. She's the mother of my children. She makes me smile. She makes me feel good about being the person that I am. When I look in the eyes of those two little girls, it's an amazing feeling. She's a great mom. Just like Annalisse."

"Come on, Daddy. How can you? I am so not ready for this. And it's obvious that Annalisse isn't either, or you wouldn't be laying up here in a hospital bed with two gunshot wounds."

"I know. And I deserve to be here. I hate what I did to Annalisse. I hate what I've done to you, to Carla, to my little girls, to Bleak. To all of you. And speaking of Bleak."

"What about him?"

"You never told me what was going on between the two of you."

"I don't think I have to explain anything to you. But I will say this, that Bleak is no longer a concern of mine."

"He's a good guy. And I hope, no, I pray that you won't judge him because of me."

"Like I said, I don't have to explain anything to you about Bleak and me. What I do in my private life is my business, not yours. You've done enough damage. But I do want to know one more thing."

"What's that?"

"Are you pressing charges against Annalisse?"

Slowly, he shook his head from side to side. "Of course not. But from what the police tell me, it's not up to me. The state is the one who determines her charge. I feel bad that I pushed her over the edge." Kenneth looked off toward the window.

"So she may be going to prison because of you? That's what you're saying?" Adanya remarked.

"I'm afraid so."

"And what about you? Are you going to jail for being a bigamist?"

"Ummm." Kenneth cleared his throat. "My lawyer told me that in Tennessee it's considered a misdemeanor. I could be facing up to a year in jail, a fine or probation. Maybe all three."

"A misdemeanor?" Adanya frowned. "You've destroyed the lives of two families and all you face is a tap on the wrist, if that?" Adanya giggled nervously while shaking her head. "I've heard enough. I'm leaving."

"Adanya," ple—"

"Mr. Anniston," the short, robust doctor said as he

walked into the hospital room. Adanya remained stationery.

"Yes, doctor. I'm glad you're here. How am I?" Kenneth asked as the doctor walked up and stood directly next to Kenneth's bed. He looked over at Adanya and nodded.

"That's my beautiful daughter, Doc."

The doctor and Adanya nodded at each other.

"Mr. Anniston, your blood pressure is a little high, so we're keeping an eye on that. Could be due to the traumatic injury."

"What about my leg? Am I going to be able to walk again?"

"The good news is that you will be able to walk again, but you are going to have to go through extensive rehab. You have rods in your ankle. And you'll have to wear an orthotic device on your leg for well, maybe a lifetime. I'm not sure. We'll have to see how you progress. You will have quite a noticeable limp. You're more than likely going to have some problems, chronic pain in your thigh, maybe your entire right leg for the remainder of your life."

Adanya turned away, hoping to avoid the panged look on her father's face. But he was alive. No matter how angry, how hurt she was, she was glad that Annalisse hadn't killed him. She breathed a soft sigh of relief before she focused back on what the doctor was saying.

"You're fortunate, Mr. Anniston. You could have very easily lost your leg. And I know this is difficult for you, but the fact remains is that things could have been a whole lot worse. You could be dead."

"Yeah. God is merciful. When can I get out of here?"

"You'll be here until we can get you up and walking around some. Someone will be in here tomorrow to cast you for a brace. I've ordered physical therapy too. So you're probably be here for another week, maybe more. You have pain medication available to you. Any more questions?" he asked and then looked at Adanya.

"No, thanks again," Kenneth said.

"Then, I'll see you tomorrow. Have a good night." He turned and walked out of the room.

"I have to go," Adanya spoke up.

"Wait, will you come back?"

"I don't know."

"I just pray that one day you'll find it in your heart to forgive me. Adanya, I want Caitlin and Cady to know you. I want them to know what a wonderful, big sister they have."

Adanya shot him a disturbing look then proceeded to speak. "You are wrong on so many levels. What you've done is unacceptable. He'll deal with you, and that's good enough for me. Adanya walked toward the door.

Pumpkin, don't leave like this."

She opened the door and walked out.

21

"Whether you spend your days in sorrow or in joy, time will still continue to tick away. The longer you take to move on, the less time you'll have to spend being happy." Kevin Ngo

For the past nine weeks, Adanya had managed to stay clear of Bleak. She hadn't returned to see her father or her mother. She called the nurses' station almost every day to check on Kenneth up until she was told three weeks ago that he'd been discharged.

She learned through her grandparents that Annalisse was scheduled to go to court soon, and that her mother's lawyer was optimistic about the judge giving her probation rather than sending her to jail.

"want 2 go out 2 eat?" Nanette texted.

"Yea. Will call when I get home. Need 2 change out of these clothes. lst" Adanya texted back.

"TGIF, c u in a few"

"Yea . K" Adanya drove to the mailbox after she arrived inside the gated complex. From her mailbox station she had a clear view of Bleak's building. Not once during the past weeks had she seen him. Part of her felt relieved, while there was another part of her that missed him terribly. But it could never work she told herself every time she thought of him.

She saw the U-Haul truck in the parking space next to his

building, but Adanya wasn't prepared to see Bleak and a couple of guys coming out of his flat carrying a leather sofa. She stood frozen, and eased behind the mailbox building out of his possible view. The three men went back inside, only to come back out again, this time with a flat screen television. Another guy single handedly carried a large table. He's moving?

She remained out of sight behind the building for another ten minutes, watching as they went in and back out of Bleak's flat. Finally, she saw him climb inside the driver's side of the U-Haul. She stood back even farther as he passed by the mailbox station.

Adanya remained at the station until she saw the U-Haul depart from the complex. Quickly, she got in her car and drove home.

"I think he's moved."

"Where do you think he moved to? Out of town?" asked Nanette while she took a forkful of food and placed inside her mouth.

"I don't know. I haven't heard from him, you know."

"Whose fault is that?"

"I'm not saying it's anybody's fault. I'm just saying that I haven't heard from him. I guess he's doing what he feels he has to do." Adanya shrugged.

"This is me you're talking to, Adanya. I know this is bothering you. Don't play."

"I didn't say that it wasn't bothering me, but at the same time, what can I do about it? There was nothing between us anyway."

"And again, whose fault is that? You could have given the guy a break."

"Nanette, you are so wishy-washy. One minute you say you understand why I felt the way I did about Bleak. I mean, there was no way, no matter how much I might have wanted it, that we could have had a drama free relationship. Not with my daddy, his momma, my momma, ugh, it goes on and on."

"I'm not wishy-washy. I just know you were really feeling him. That hard outer shell you had was beginning to fall away, and then like that," she snapped her fingers, "it was all over."

"And that's my fault?"

"It's nobody's fault. It's called life." Nanette swallowed some of her soda.

"I hope everything works out for him wherever he is. He was a nice guy. I'll admit that I had feelings for him. But you know me, Nanette. I can't take the drama. I hate conflict."

"I know. But I loved seeing you happy. Someone else will come along."

"I don't want anyone else to come along. And, as far as Bleak, he's in the past."

"Yeah, gone but not forgotten," Nanette said.

"Whatever," remarked Adanya. "Anyway, time heals all wounds."

"Umm, Keep telling yourself that, you might just start believing it.

22

"You are responsible for your life. You can't keep blaming somebody else for your dysfunction. Life is really about moving on." Oprah Winfrey

The one year mark was approaching since the beginning of her heartache, and Adanya still refused to see or talk to her parents. Her free time was divided between spending time with Anaya, or chilling at home.

Adanya stepped into a pair of pumps. She went to the den, and picked up her Bible from off the center table. Nanette was supposed to call and let her know what time she was going to pick her up for church. She wished she hadn't agreed to go with her, but she no longer attended her home church because she didn't want to chance running into Annalisse. Annalisse had been spared prison, and granted three years of probation, along with being ordered to complete a twelve week anger management and domestic violence class. She was still considered a felon, but Annalisse didn't let that bother her. She was thankful that she was a free woman. Church service was more like a confirmation for Adanya. Nanette's pastor preached an on fire, soul convicting, sermon about redemption and forgiving. Adanya felt like the pastor had specifically prepared it for her. Now only if her family had heard it.

The Sunday before Valentine's Day and what better topic to preach about than loving, forgiving others, and loving people as they are. Adanya squirmed slightly in her seat. The Word of God was definitely stronger than a two-edged sword, and she felt like she was experiencing the prick of the sword first hand.

"What have you done that's keeping you from receiving the full blessings of God? What has the enemy placed on your back and forced you to carry for years because you felt shame and afraid? What have you done that you think is simply unforgiveable?"

The pastor kept preaching. People started standing. Others started shouting. Adanya and Nanette sat quietly, but an elderly lady nearby more than made up for their silence.

The woman stood up and waved her white handkerchief in the air. "Hallelujah. Thank you, Jesus. Thank you, Lord," she continued to shout. Tears streamed down her smooth, olive toned face. Her hands spread out and she kept praising God. Adanya looked around and no one seemed to be disturbed or agitated by the woman.

"What has been done so badly to you that you're too mad to forgive?" Pastor asked the congregation. "The word of God commands us to forgive, and to forgive endlessly. Who are we to hold grudges and to stick our noses up and tear families apart over something that has happened? What you need to do is pray. God can turn any bad situation around and make it work for your good." Adanya was pulled to his voice, and the words he spoke seemed to penetrate her heart bit by bit.

"Any circumstance, not some circumstances, but anything and everything that Satan has planned against you to make you fall, stumble, trip and die, God already has it covered. God doesn't quit on the job. You sitting out there dressed all up on the outside, and dirty as dirty can be on the inside because you call yourself mad about something; or you can't get over what your momma and daddy did when you were little, or so and so did this to me fifty years ago! Stop holding on to that mess."

"Glory to God," the woman shouted. "Speak today. Have your way," she said."

After the sermon, the pastor opened the doors of the church and extended an invitation to come to Christ to be saved. After several people came forth, he invited anyone who wanted to come to the altar for prayer, to do so.

"You know, my brothers and sisters, it's that time of year where people celebrate and show each other how much they love one another. I'm asking you to come to the altar today. Ask God to restore His love, a love like His in your heart."

Adanya became lost in a world of her own. The past year had really been difficult. She'd entertained the idea of leaving Memphis altogether. Since Bleak was out of the picture and her family had been further torn apart, she didn't see a reason to stay.

◊

"Pretty Adanya, I love you," Anaya told her while sitting across from her in the restaurant.

Adanya and Nanette had swung by to pick up Anaya after they got out of church. Anaya seemed to bring out the best in Adanya. She could make Adanya laugh when she felt like crying, or smile when she felt like frowning.

Anaya took a bite out of her hamburger, and the three of them laughed and talked while they ate. It wasn't until they were almost finished with their desserts that Adanya spotted Bleak entering the restaurant with a strikingly attractive, blonde female clinging on to him like plastic wrap.

"What are you looking at?" asked Nanette and looked over her shoulder. "Ohhh, snap," she said. "Who is that with him?"

"How do I know? And anyway, who cares?"

Nanette turned and looked directly at Adanya. "Girl, please. You know you're just a little bit curious. I know I am. But I can't say I blame him."

"What?" Adanya's voice rose, but then she quickly quieted down when she remembered she was in a public establishment.

"You heard me. You let him walk out of your life. Yeah, it would have been awkward for the two of you to be together, but that would have passed. Everyone would have gotten used to it."

"I don't want everybody to have to get used to it. That's not what bothered me. What bothered me is me, myself," she whispered to Nanette. "I've told you that. No way could I be around Bleak's mother. I just can't do it. And I couldn't expect him to just desert his mother, his little sisters, all for me."

"But you could have—"

"His sisters are my sisters, and you're going to tell me that it wouldn't be a mess to deal with and explain to them? They're innocent in all of this. They wouldn't understand about me and Bleak. I couldn't do that to them, and I won't do it to myself."

"It's your decision, but if you really mean what you say, then why are you looking like you could choke her out." Nanette asked and briefly took another look over her shoulder to see if Bleak and the female were still in view. They weren't.

"What you doing?" asked Anaya.

"Oh, nothing, Aunt Anaya. Nanette and I are just talking." Adanya turned her attention back to her food.

"Where did they go?" Adanya whispered to Nanette while scanning the restaurant. "Wait, I see them."

"Where?" asked Nanette.

"Look over your left shoulder, then slowly allow your eyes to follow that row of tables next to the window. They're in a booth toward the end."

Nanette looked. "I see them."

"Who? Can I see?" Anaya asked.

"Honey, it's no one. Just a friend, but she's gone now. How's that chocolate lava cake?" she asked Anaya hoping to shift Anaya's thinking.

"It tastes mmmhum good."

"Good. I like mine too." Adanya took a bite of her peach cobbler.

"I'm not trying to come down on you, Adanya. I just want you to be happy. And I thought you and Bleak could have had something. That's all."

"Yeah, I know. And I'm sorry for losing my cool. I'm just so frustrated."

"Hello, Adanya. Hi, Nanette." Adanya couldn't move after hearing Bleak's familiar voice. She hadn't seen him coming. *Why didn't I get up and leave when I saw him coming in here?*

Hi, Bleak," Nanette said first.

"Hi, Bleak," Anaya repeated like she knew him.

"Hello, Bleak," Adanya said last while looking past him and eyeing the woman holding on to his arm.

"It's good seeing you," Bleak said with his eyes penned on

Adanya. "Hello, Miss, uh," he said, shifting his gaze toward Anaya.

"Anaya," replied Adanya.

Bleak's eyebrows rose. "Hello, Anaya."

Anaya laughed. "You're funny."

Bleak introduced the woman holding on to him. "This is Mallorie." Mallorie clung even tighter to his arm.

"Nice to meet you," Adanya mumbled.

"Hello, Mallorie," said Nanette.

"You have gold hair," said Anaya.

Mallorie laughed. "Yes, I do. Nice to meet y'all too," she said in an exceptionally strong southern accent.

"It's been a while since I've seen you. How are you?"

Adanya nodded. "I'm good."

"Glad to hear that."

Awkward silence.

"Well, I just wanted to say hello. Take care. Come on, Mallorie, let's get back to our table so we can order our food."

"Sure." She turned to walk away, without releasing her hold on him.

"Nice seeing you, Bleak," Nanette said before looking at Adanya.

"Yeah, and take care," Adanya followed.

Bleak and Mallorie left. Immediately, Adanya placed a hand over her chest and exhaled.

"You okay?"

"Yeah, but I'm ready to leave." She looked at Anaya. "Anaya, it's time to go."

"Okay, I'm ready," Anaya took the final spoonful of cake and placed it inside her mouth.

No matter how hard she tried to read, she couldn't concentrate. All she could think about was Bleak. Seeing him had awoke feelings she still held for him. But there was nothing she could do to change everything that had transpired.

How could she ever feel totally and completely comfortable with Bleak? *I have to let the past go. I can't move into my tomorrow until I let it go. God, help me through all this. Show me what your will is for me, because I don't know which direction to go. I'm confused. I need a word from you.*

Ding. Her phone beeped. "It was good seeing you today. Still beautiful." The text was from Bleak.

Should I answer or just ignore it? She read the text again then she typed, "u 2. Good 2 see u moved on w ur life."

Ding. "B blessed."

Be blessed? Is that all you have to say? She threw her phone down next to her on the sofa. *Get it together. You're the one who said you couldn't handle being in a relationship with him, so let him go. Move on in your life. He obviously has,* she inwardly chastised herself.

"You know what, Snoopy, maybe we do need a change of scenery. Would you like that, boy?" she said to the dog as he whined at her feet. "But that would mean moving away from Anaya. But what does she know? Out of sight, out of mind for her. Right? Let's see what else this big old world has to offer. You game?"

This time Snoopy barked like he was in agreement. Adanya smiled and pat his head. "Yeah, maybe a change is exactly what we need."

23

We must be willing to let go of the life we have planned, so as to accept the life that is waiting for us." J. Campbell

Adanya walked inside the doorway of Elizabeth City State University. It was her first week in her new position as professor of communications.

The position in Adanya's eyes was nothing short of a burst of God's favor over her life because it seemed to have come out of nowhere. The university itself was ranked second in US News and World Report's 2012 Edition of Best Colleges, and number fourteen among the nation's Historically Black Colleges and Universities. Adanya felt fortunate to be part of the Language, Literature, and Communications Department.

One of the professors at Rhodes had casually mentioned the vacancy position during a meeting one evening. Adanya had heard of the prestigious university, but never dreamed, thought, or desired to teach there, let alone move to North Carolina. But after doing some research on the university and what they offered, Adanya became intrigued by the prospect of the chance to take her life to another level.

Nothing was changing in Memphis, and she had resigned herself to believe that nothing would, at least not anything positive. So she bit the bullet, applied for the position, was

interviewed on three separate occasions, toured North
Carolina, and now here she was – in a new city, with a
new apartment, a nice salary, and the chance for a new start in
her life.

Three weeks before she moved, her grandparents told
her that Annalisse' divorce from Kenneth was finalized.
Her father was living with Carla and their kids.

Adanya missed Anaya most of all. The fact that Anaya
was her mother, Adanya had plans to make her a priority in
her life. But she hadn't expected to make a major move. She
promised Anaya, and Mr. and Mrs. Kaplan that she would
visit Anaya as much as possible, and that she would even send
for her to visit North Carolina, if they would permit it.

Adanya talked to Nanette everyday either on the phone, on
one of the social media sites, or text.

◊

"In today's lecture on literary criticism I will share with
you three major subjects for discussion. First we will look at
trends in African American literature. Next…."she continued.

She was in her element, doing what she loved. Standing
in front of her class, she was adorned in a slate blue dress
pleated from the waist down, with a V-style neckline. The
dress complimented her figure and her profession.

The move to North Carolina had been a bold one. Adanya
didn't know anyone other than the staff she'd met during
her interview sessions. There was one lady, Belinda Garrett
that Adanya especially connected with. Like her, Belinda
was single. She was a few years older than Adanya, also
relatively new to North Carolina, and loved hanging out. She
helped Adanya unpack and get settled into her new
apartment when she first arrived in the city. Belinda also

adored animals. She had two dogs and three cats, and Snoopy seemed to enjoy meeting some canine and feline friends of his own. At the end of the school day, Adanya had plans to go with Belinda to a restaurant called Caribbean Cuisine. Belinda had told her that it was known to serve some of the best jerk chicken around the city. She had been in the city less than a month, but already Adanya felt that her life was on a far better track. She felt like she was breathing new air into it. As she walked to the faculty parking area, she actually smiled. Looking upward, the sky was clear. The fall weather in North Carolina was perfect.

A few steps from her car, she stumbled, fell to her knees, and in the process dropped her laptop case and her car keys. "Oaahhh." She tried getting up but was halted by a piercing pain coming from her left ankle.

"Hold up, let me help you," the deep baritone voice offered. Before Adanya could look up to see who the voice belonged to, she felt a strong, sturdy hand grab hold of her hand. His other hand wrapped around her waist as he helped her to her feet.

"Thank you," she said as she looked into charcoal colored eyes. He smelled good and definitely looked good and had concern written all over his face.

"Are you all right? I saw when you went down." He looked around the perimeter of where they stood. "What made you fall?"

"I...I don't know. I just stumbled over something. Probably my own feet." She started laughing.

"Well, we can't have that now, can we?" He turned her loose and Adanya took a step closer to her car.

"Ahhh," she winced in pain.

The stranger grabbed her. "Whoa, looks like you may have twisted your ankle. Is that your car?" He pointed to the vehicle in front of them.

"Yes."

"Are you going to be able to drive? Do I need to help you back inside? Or can I call someone for you?"

"No, I'm fine. Thank you." She looked at him again and then turned and walked to her car.

"Oh, here are your keys."

"Thank you." Adanya hit the remote to unlock the car. She opened the door and sat down inside.

"Are you sure you're okay?"

"Yes, I'm fine. I just feel like an idiot. It's so embarrassing."

"No need to be. I'm just glad I was here to help. By the way, I'm Johnathan."

"I'm Adanya."

"Nice to meet you, Adanya."

She smiled. "I don't know about that. I mean I wish it could have been under other circumstances."

He smiled. His tone was jovial. "I haven't seen you around. Are you new to ECSU?"

"Yes. I'm in Literature and Communications. You teach here?"

"Yes. Aviation and Science Program."

"Impressive," she said and smiled. Her smile turned into a frown when she tried moving both feet inside the car.

"Sounds like you might need to take a trip to the ER."

"I don't think so. I'll go straight home, ice it, and prop it up. I can't afford to miss work already. This is my first week."

"Well, welcome to the home of the Vikings. Look, why don't you let me call someone for you. Or, if you'd like I can drive you home. I don't mind, and I promise I won't bite."

Adanya shook her head in jest. "Really, I'll be okay. But

thank you, Johnathan."

"Will you at least take down my number and call me when you make it home."

Adanya hesitated, but then dismissed any reservations she had about him. After all, he was in the private faculty parking lot, and he looked innocent, and on top of that he was totally nothing but nice to her.

"Sure. What is it?"

Johnathan gave her the number. Adanya added it to her phone contacts.

"Promise to call or text me," he said.

"I will." She reached for the door, but Johnathan took hold of the outside door handle.

"I've got it," he said and closed the door. He stood back from the car and watched as Adanya drove off.

True to her word, after calling and telling Belinda about her fall, Adanya called Johnathan. After several rings, his phone rolled over to his voice mail. Her first thought was not to leave a message, but then she changed her mind.

"Hi, Johnathan. It's Adanya Anniston. You know the lady you saw practically kissing the pavement earlier." She laughed into the phone, amazed at herself. "I told you that I would call."

Her phone buzzed as a call came in. *It's him.* She hit the swap icon on her phone. "Hello."

"Hi, there. You make it home okay?"

"Yes, I was just leaving you a message."

"I was on another call when yours came in. Sorry about that."

"Oh, no problem. I was just calling you because I promised I would."

"I'm glad you made it home safely."

"Thank you."

"How's the ankle?"

"Too early to tell. I just made it in the house so I haven't had time to work on it. But I will."

Snoopy started barking. "Hold up, Snoopy."

"English bulldog?"

"Excuse me," said Adanya.

"Sounds like an English bulldog."

"He is. How can you tell?"

"I love dogs. Their barks fascinate me. If you ever notice, each breed has a distinct type of bark."

Adanya hobbled toward the door, opened it, and let Snoopy out on the patio area of the one bedroom bungalow-style apartment. She'd have to go out and clean up behind him later, but right now all she wanted to do was get some relief from her aching ankle.

"So, you're telling me that you can tell what breed a dog is without seeing it just by listening to their bark?" Adanya was amused. Already she found Johnathan to be not only handsome, but entertaining as well.

"Not all the time, but I'm pretty good at it. But, let's not talk about that now. I want you to do whatever you have to do to feel better because I'd really like to see you again."

Adanya didn't know what to say or how to respond. She didn't know if this man was married, had a girlfriend or boyfriend for that matter. For all she knew, he could be a bigamist like her daddy. It was just hard for her to trust a man again. She thought about her daddy, and it made her sad.

"Hey, look don't get all quiet on me. I just want to have a chance to sit and talk to you under different circumstances. You know, when you feel better. Tell you all about ESCU."

"Okay. Why not."

"Good. Now get some rest. And if you don't mind, I'd

like to call you again."

"That's fine. And thanks again, Johnathan."

"No problem. I'll talk to you later, Adanya."

"Sure, goodbye.

Adanya nursed her ankle the remainder of the evening. By the time she got in bed for the night, there was still some swelling, but after calling her gram and explaining to her what happened, she took three aspirin and mixed them in with some green alcohol. She shook the concoction until she was satisfied that the aspirins had fully dissolved. Following her grandmother's instructions, Adanya rubbed her ankle and leg down with the mixture. Afterward, she got two pillows and placed them at the foot of her bed and propped her leg up on them. Much to her surprise, and just like her gram told her it would, it had started to feel much better.

Her phone rang. It was Belinda. "Hey, girl."

"Hey, Belinda."

"How's your ankle?"

"I have it propped up on some pillows. I rubbed it down in alcohol and aspirin, so it's actually feeling better."

"Alcohol and aspirin?"

"My gram's remedy. And it seems to be working."

"Cool. Do you need anything?"

"Naw, I'm fine."

"Did you eat? I can bring you something if you'd like."

"No, I don't want you to do that. I ate a sandwich and some chips. That was plenty for me, but I appreciate it."

"Okay, just checking with you. Are you going to try to come to work tomorrow?"

"Girl, yes. I just started. I do not plan on missing when this is my first week."

"You can't help it if you fell. You have to take care of you, girl."

"I know, but I think I'll be better in the morning."

"Do you need me to pick you up?"

"Now, that's an offer I might accept. I don't know how much weight I'll be able to put on my foot in the morning."

"I have a pair of old crutches over here from a couple of years ago."

"Oh, what happened to you?"

"I tore my ACL. I had to have surgery and I was on crutches for a minute. I never got rid of them."

"That's right on time. Bring them with you in the morning."

"Okay, I will. Well, I'm going to get ready for bed. I'll call you in the morning when I'm on my way."

"Okay, Belinda. And thanks too."

"It's nothing. I'll see you in the morning."

Adanya twisted and turned for the first half of the night. Her ankle had started to throb. She rubbed it down again and soon was able to doze off.

North Carolina may not be so bad. Everyone seemed to be nice and meeting Belinda made Adanya feel like she wasn't alone in the strange city. Also Johnathan seemed especially nice too.

Adanya smiled when an image of Johnathan flashed in her mind. She couldn't wait to call Nanette and tell her about his chivalry.

24

"Getting over a painful experience is much like crossing monkey bars. You have to let go at some point in order to move forward." Unknown

The following weeks began to get somewhat better. She enjoyed her new position. She'd talked to Johnathan several times since she first met him. Her ankle had healed, and she had the pleasure of being shown around the city by Belinda.

She accepted an invitation from Belinda to go to church the upcoming Sunday. She was looking forward to it. It had been months since she'd been inside a church, and she missed it.

Tonight, however, she was having dinner with Johnathan. Since their chance encounter, the two of them had been talking quite frequently on the phone, and on campus. The more she talked to him, the more at ease she became around him. He was nothing like Bleak or her father. Johnathan was his own man, with a different personality, a different swagger.

He was polite but at the same time, he didn't hesitate to speak his mind. He was well respected on the college campus and had received many awards for his outstanding service to in his field. Johnathan was a few years her senior, but that suited Adanya just fine. He owned his home, and had several other properties he rented out to mostly college students. During one of their phone conversations he told her that he was not involved with anyone, had no children, and had never been married. Adanya was further impressed that they shared the same Christian belief.

Johnathan attended a small church in North Carolina that he had belonged to since he was a young boy. Both of his parents, and two of his seven siblings, remained members of the church. He was close to his family, another plus for him in Adanya's eyes. Hearing him talk about his siblings made her want to get to know her little sisters. Maybe one day she would after her life got back in order.

Adanya told Belinda about Johnathan, and much to her surprise, Belinda knew him. After having been reassured by Belinda that he was a cool guy, Adanya was looking forward to getting to know even more about him. This would be their first time going out on an official date, and Adanya was slightly nervous.

◊

Sunday arrived and Adanya listened to her GPS as it directed her to Belinda's church. After parking, she walked to the front of the church where she waited on Belinda. She didn't have to wait long. Belinda came and escorted her into the massive sanctuary.

Adanya enjoyed the fellowship. The pastor delivered a dynamic message. He reminded Adanya of the pastor in Houston, Texas, Joel Osteen. His message was clear, easy to understand, and addressed everyday issues.

After church, she and Belinda went out to eat. It was

over lunch that Adanya found herself telling Belinda about her family situation. "That's messed up," Belinda told her after listening to the whole spiel. "But you know what?"

"What?"

"They're still your family. They may have hurt you, but I'm sure they love you. Don't you love them?"

"Sure, I do. They're my family; I just can't deal with all the mess."

"We all have some kind of mess, Adanya. I'm not condoning any of the things you say your father did or what your mother did. But what I am saying is that life is too short to live it being mad, angry and having an unforgiving spirit."

"But I do forgive them."

"If you have, why haven't you talked to them? Why haven't you reached out to at least try to get to know your little sisters? I'm sure having a big sister would be fun for them. But you'll never know because you've chosen to punish them."

"I'm not punishing them."

"You sure aren't trying to have them in your life. We all have done something we're ashamed of, Adanya. I'm sure you can agree with that."

Adanya nodded. She thought about how she started abusing alcohol when she found out Annalisse wasn't her real mother. She thought about how she acted like she was an executioner and a judge when it came to her parents.

"Look, all I'm saying is you should pray, and I mean really go before God and ask His direction. If something happened to your parents, or even little sisters, while you were harboring all that bitterness in your heart, then you would be devastated."

"Maybe I do need to get things in order with them. It's just so hard, but I guess it's even harder not talking to them, and not being around them. I miss them. I really, really do."

"Then, I say, when you get home this afternoon, call them. Check up on them. Sometimes you have to be the bigger person."

"I might."

"Okay, now that we've got that out of the way, tell me how things are going between you and Johnathan." Belinda smiled and then placed some of her food in her mouth.

Adanya drank some of her tea before she answered. "Good. Slow."

"Uhhh, good and slow?"

Adanya smiled. "Not that kind of good and slow," she giggled. "Good like I like him. Slow in like we're just friends. I don't want to get involved with anyone right now."

"Is it because of the guy back home? Your stepbrother?"

"No, not really. I mean, I liked Bleak, but it wouldn't have worked. It would have been too awkward."

"I understand. So, why do you need to take it slow with Johnathan then?"

"I'm in a new city, with a new job, meeting new people. I don't want to get hung up on the first guy that steps my way. I want to enjoy life. And when, or if the right man comes along one day, and after I work on myself, then maybe I'll entertain getting serious with someone. But until then, I like things just the way they are."

Belinda shrugged. "Nothing wrong with that.

◊

Later that evening, after she made it back home, Adanya decided to follow Belinda's advice. Annalisse was the first person she called. She was glad she did, because Annalisse was ecstatic when she heard Adanya's voice.

During the two hours they talked Adanya felt like heavy weights were being lifted off her shoulders.

Next, with much more difficulty, she called her father.

"Pumpkin, God knows I'm sorry for hurting you, and Annalisse. But believe me when I tell you that I love you. You're my firstborn. You'll always be my special lady."

"You said that you worked everything out between you and God. Guess that's good enough for me. I want you to be part of my life again. I want to get to know my sisters."

Adanya could hear Kenneth sobbing, and she released her tears as well.

"You have made my day, my week, my year," he cried into the phone. "This is an answered prayer. I love you so much, Pumpkin. Please believe me."

"I do, Daddy."

Before she ended the call, she asked to say hello to Caitlin and Cady. Adanya couldn't help laughing as each of the girls talked over the other one. They told her that they wanted to see her. Adanya was overjoyed, and for the first time in a while she felt happy.

◊

Thanksgiving was approaching, and Adanya decided to go home to spend time with Anaya, see her father, meet her sisters, and try to let the past remain in the past.

Her first stop after arriving in Memphis was Nanette's apartment. It was still her safe haven. The wounds caused by the pain of her past lingered. Would there ever come a time when it wouldn't hurt? She shook the confusing thoughts and refaced on why she was in Memphis. This visit, she prayed, would prove to be a journey of healing for all of them.

Nanette and Adanya sat on the sofa talking. "Are you going to see your daddy?"

"Yes. If I say that I forgive my parents, then I have to act like it. You know some folks say they can forgive but they'll never forget."

"Yeah, I hear that a lot."

"Well, think about that. Is that really true forgiveness? I mean, when God forgives us, He forgets."

Nanette nodded. "You're right."

"He says, as far as the east is from the west, that's how far He removes our sin from us, so who am I not to at least try to forgive and move forward."

"I think it takes a lot out of a person to hold on to unforgiveness and anger."

"This is why I have to do my part to make things better. If I can do that, then I believe I can return to North Carolina a better person."

"So what's next?"

"I'm going to see him, and meet my little sisters."

"Are you going to get in touch with Bleak too?"

"Nope. I think I better let that stay where it is – in the past."

"I just knew you and Bleak would become a couple. Guess some things aren't meant."

"Guess not. Anyway, I'm going to get ready to go see my daddy." Adanya gathered her purse, stood up and walked toward the door.

Nanette remained seated. "You need me to ride out with you? Eads is quite a ways you know, and I can be there with you for moral support."

"Thanks, but I need to do this on my own. I'll keep you posted."

"Okay, I'll be here."

Adanya turned around just as Nanette got up and started toward her. The two embraced.

"I don't know what I'd do without you. You really are my best friend."

"I better be." Nanette laughed.

"I'll see you later." Adanya went back to the door, opened it and without looking back, headed to her car, got inside, and drove off.

◊

Adanya put in the address and followed the instructions of her phone's navigation system. She turned on her father's street an hour after departing Nanette's apartment. Her throat muscles tightened as she looked at the luxurious homes lining the streets. They made the one she'd grown up in look miniscule. Adanya felt her anger and resentment mounting as the navigation system said, "Your destination is on the right."

The English style Tudor was back off the street. The closer she drove toward the home, the more she could see just how massive it actually was. She swallowed, and told herself, *don't go there. Let it go. You're past this, Adanya.*

She drove and parked in the circular driveway behind a pearl white Jaguar. *Bet that's Carla's Jag.* Again, she swallowed, turned off the ignition, and proceeded to get out of her car and walk up the long walkway until she found herself planted in front of the equally massive door. She pushed the doorbell, and sucked in her breath and slowly released it.

She heard her father from the other side saying, "I'll get it." She braced herself, took one last sigh, and waited.

"Pumpkin," he said when he saw her standing in front of him. "I'm so glad you came."

Her father was in a wheelchair, his legs held in place

by wide, black Velcro straps. He hadn't said anything about being in a wheelchair, no one had.

"Come on, in." He pushed the button on the electric chair, rolled to the door and closed it. He then turned and led her into the foyer.

The sounds of children's chatter caused her to become a little nervous. At the same time her daddy slowly took hold of her hands, lifted them to his mouth, and gently kissed them.

"Caitlin, Cady, this is Adanya, your big sister," he announced before she had a chance to make one more step into the house.

"Hi, there." Adanya smiled at the two little blond curly haired girls, who had strong features of the father the three of them shared.

With a pronounced limp, residuals of the car accident, Caitlin walked toward Adanya.

"I'm Caitlin.."

"Nice to meet you, Caitlin. I'm Adanya."

She pointed at her younger sister who stared intensely at Adanya like she was trying to size her up. "This is Cady."

"Hello, Cady."

"Hello," the little girl replied.

Adanya followed behind the wheelchair. *This is what your infidelity cost you, Daddy. What a price to pay.*

They entered into a hearth room that looked like it been pulled straight from a magazine. Adanya was used to having lived a rather expensive lifestyle, but this place was nothing like she would have imagined. Her father had definitely gone over and beyond for his so called other family, but Adanya kept talking to herself, trying to maintain self-control. She was here to meet her sisters and come to some resolution with her father – that was it.

"Sit down anywhere you like," Kenneth offered. "Carla will be back in a few minutes. She's running some errands."

"Thank you." She sat down in the plush sofa chair.

"Are you moving here with us?"

Adanya smiled and shook her heard. "No, honey. I came here because I wanted to meet you and Cady."

"Oh."

Cady waited on her daddy to get settled, then she climbed up on his lap. Adanya smiled as she watched the little girl. She used to do the same thing when she was her age.

"I know it took a lot of courage for you to come," Kenneth said. "But just being here, seeing you again makes me the happiest man alive. I have all three of my girls under one roof. This is going to be some Thanksgiving." He smiled and Adanya nodded.

"Baby, did you get everything taken care of?" Adanya followed his eyes and his voice and saw Carla's entrance.

"Yes I did. I have everything I need to assure we have a good Thanksgiving dinner. Hello, Adanya." She walked over to Adanya and offered her hand to shake.

Adanya accepted and smiled slightly. "Hello, Carla."

"We are so glad to have you. Did John offer you anything to drink or eat?"

Adanya shook her head, still feeling somewhat weird hearing her father being called by his middle name. "Uh, no, but I'm fine. Thank you."

"Are you sure? Because I can get you something. It's no bother."

"That's right, Pumpkin. Would you like a sandwich, something sweet, something to drink, anything?" Kenneth offered.

"No, really I'm fine." Adanya felt awkward. She wanted to jump up and run out of there as fast as she could, but she knew that would not be the thing to do.

"Look, Daddy, Carla, I can't stay long. I just wanted to come by, meet my sisters, and well try to make a fresh start with you, Daddy."

"I know this isn't easy for you. God knows I haven't exactly made it easy, have I?" He held on to Cady as she pushed herself farther on to his lap before she laid back and stuck her thumb inside her mouth.

Adanya looked at him, and suddenly felt pity for him. She studied his face and he looked worried.

"It is hard, Daddy. It's real hard, but God has been dealing with me lately, and I knew it was time to face my fears, so I'm here."

"Excuse me, but would you like some alone time with your father?" Carla asked.

"No, that won't be necessary."

"No, really, I don't mind. Me and the girls need to get changed for dinner anyway. We'd love for you to join us."

"No," Adanya quickly said. "I can't. I have some other stops to make. But before you leave, I want to say something to you, Carla."

Kenneth looked uneasy. Carla stiffened.

"I want to tell you that I'm sorry for the way I treated you in the past. I had no right to take things out on you. Will you forgive me?"

"Of course, but I know you've gone through a lot. None of this is easy, not for any of us. So much has happened, but I love your father, Adanya. No matter what he's done, I love him, and I can't see myself living without him. He's a good man, and a good father." She looked over at Caitlin who was sitting quietly on the sofa opposite Adanya, then at Cady who remained nestled in her father's lap.

"I'm sure he is. Daddy, how are you? Does your leg give

you many problems?"

"Let's just say I'm learning to cope a little better every day. I'm just glad to be alive. I know what happened was my fault. I caused a lot of pain to the very ones I professed to love, and again I want you to know how sorry I am." He wiped his eyes like he was trying to keep tears from pushing forth.

"I'm sorry too. I love you, Daddy. And like Carla said, and I have to agree with her, you are a good father. You always were. I can't deny that. I just wanted to come by here because it's leading up to Thanksgiving, and I don't want another day to go by without first of all letting God know how grateful I am, and then to tell you that no matter what has transpired between you and me, that I still love you."

Carla, as if unspoken words had been exchanged between them, walked over and removed Cady, who had fallen asleep on her father's lap. She squirmed when Carla lifted her, but did not wake up.

"I knew she was going to do that. She always falls asleep when she sits in his lap." Carla spoke in a whisper. "If you'll excuse me, I'm going to go lay her down."

"Sure," replied Adanya.

"Come on, Caitlin, sweetheart."

"But I want to stay here with my sister," she whined. Carla looked over at her husband, and he nodded.

"Please, don't make her leave. This is the first time I've seen them."

"Okay, if you say so," he answered.

Carla smiled. "I want you to know you're welcome here anytime, Adanya."

"Thank you." Adanya replied and Carla disappeared up the hallway.

"Have you seen or talked to your mother?"

"Yes."

"That's good. Real good."

"Do you want to see my room and my dolls?" Caitlin suddenly asked.

"Honey, not today," Kenneth said.

"I don't mind," Adanya answered.

"Okay, it's up to you."

"Come on, I want to show you all my Barbie dolls and my Karito dolls. I have a lot of them." Caitlin sprung up off the couch.

"Have fun," remarked Kenneth. "I'll be out in the garden when you come back downstairs."

"Okay," Adanya replied.

Caitlin grabbed Adanya's hand and led her up the stairs and to her room.. For the next few minutes, Adanya listened to Caitlin tell her the names of what seemed like about twenty or more dolls. The Barbie dolls were in all colors with gorgeous doll outfits and the diverse line of Karito dolls included Wan Ling, a panda lover from China, to Lulu, a soccer star and co-host on a children's TV show to Zoe, a bohemian songwriter from New York.

On her way back down the stairs, Adanya stood momentarily frozen when she heard Bleak's familiar voice.

"What's wrong?" Caitlin asked.

"Uh, nothing."

Adanya took the last step and there, in front of her stood Bleak. He looked just as handsome as ever, and Adanya felt like she'd lost her breath for a moment.

"Hi," he said, looking just as stunned. "What are you doing here?"

"Hi, Brother," Caitlin said, and as quick as her body would carry her she rushed over to Bleak who swooped her up in his arms, and kissed her on her cheek before putting her down.

"Hello, Caitlin," the blond haired woman said. It was the same female who had been in the restaurant that day with Bleak.

"Hi, Mallorie. Guess what? Daddy bought me a new Karito doll," Caitlin said. "You want to see her?"

"I sure do." Mallorie flashed a beautiful, flawless smile.

"Babe," Bleak said. "Hold up. Let me introduce you to, to uh, my step sister." He looked just as dumb as he sounded.

This was the part of the trip she hoped she could avoid. She didn't want to see him. She just wanted to meet her sisters, spend a little time with them and her father, and then leave. But if she was going to completely heal, and completely let go of the past, she knew she had to release the love she felt for Bleak, and allow it to slowly develop into what she hoped one day could be a solid friendship.

"I think we've already met, honey. Remember, the restaurant. I know it's been a minute, but I never forget a face. Am I right?" Mallorie asked, and eyed Adanya with caution.

"Uh, yes, I believe you're right. I forgot about that."

"Adanya," Bleak stuttered slightly. "Mallorie and I are engaged. We're getting married next June."

Mallorie immediately lifted her left hand and showcased the nice sized diamond on her ring finger.

"Oh," Adanya managed to say. "Congratulations."

"Thank you. Nice seeing you again. Come on, Caitlin. Let's go see your new doll." Mallorie kissed Bleak on the lips before she took hold of Caitlin's hand and led her back up the stairs toward her bedroom.

"Why are you here?"

"I came to see my father, and to meet my sisters of course."

"Oh, is that right?"

"Yes, that's right. I see you and he have made amends too."

"Yes. I had to forgive Him if I expect God to forgive me."

"Look," she said to him as her heart continued to play somersaults with her tummy. "It was good to see you again. I hope you and Mallorie are happy. Now, if you don't mind, I'm going to find my father and say goodbye."

"He's outside in the front garden."

"Thanks." Adanya walked around and past him.

"Adanya?"

She stopped at the sound of his commanding voice. "Yes."

"Have a good life."

Adanya looked but did not respond. Instead she turned back around and walked out the door.

She saw her father sitting in the beautifully designed garden. "I'm getting ready to leave."

He looked. "Already?"

"Yes, I have to."

"Is it because of Bleak and Mallorie? Be truthful with me, Pumpkin. You know I know you probably better than anyone. And I can tell that you're upset."

"I'm not upset. Bleak was a good friend while it lasted, that's it; nothing more."

"I wish you would stay a little longer. We've barely had time to talk."

"I know, but I really do need to get going. We'll talk again soon. I'll stop by before I go back to North Carolina."

"Is that a promise"

Adanya nodded, turned, and walked off to her car.

He's going to marry her. Why should I care? Why does it hurt? Adanya drove in silence, no radio, no CD playing.

Only silence accompanied her on the way back to Nanette's apartment. Silence and thoughts of what she and Bleak might have had. But her life had been transformed and it was time to let fresh memories come into her life.

Her phone rang. "Hello."

"How are things in M-town?" Adanya smiled when she heard Johnathan's voice.

"Great. Everything is going according to plan."

Adanya liked Johnathan. He made it easier to forget Bleak. She was determined not to put her heart on lock down. She had been praying about Johnathan, and was ready to let God do whatever He saw fit to do in her life. If they were meant to have anything together, then she was not going to be the one to put a damper on things.

"I just called to hear your voice. I miss you."

"It's good to be missed. I miss you too. I can't wait to get back."

"See you in a few days. Take care of yourself, and Happy Thanksgiving."

"Happy Thanksgiving to you too, Johnathan."

She smiled again as she ended their call, while at the same time thoughts of Bleak and his impending marriage quickly disappeared.

◊

The Kaplan family gathered for Thanksgiving dinner at Annalisse's house.

Annalisse was rebuilding her life, and seemed to be adapting well to being single. In the divorce, she had walked away with a substantial lump sum settlement, the house minus mortgage payments, her car, alimony for seven years, and 49% stock in Anniston Digital Technology.

She became heavily involved in the company, which

presented some extra perks for Annalisse.

Adanya was glad to see how well Annalisse looked.

"Adanya, you remember Mr. Hunt, don't you; VP of Marketing at Anniston?" The expression Annalisse wore revealed a relaxed, rejuvenated, revitalized woman. The way she looked at Mr. Hunt, it was easy to conclude that they were probably involved.

Adanya looked at the well-dressed man and immediately felt at ease when she remembered how nice he had always been to her. When she was a little girl, he would give her candy whenever her father brought her to his office. He sported a bald head, almond colored skin, and had a certain ruggedness about himself.

"Yes, I remember. Hello, Mr. Hunt." Adanya smiled. *Good for you, Annalisse.*

"It's good to see you, Adanya. Happy Thanksgiving."

"Happy Thanksgiving to you too, sir."

As they sat at the dining room table and prepared to dive into the delicious meal, Adanya cleared her throat and stood up next to her chair.

"Before we eat, I'd like to say something."

"Sure, go ahead," Annalisse said

"God has been dealing with me for a while. I know I haven't been the best person to get along with, but I want to be better and do better. I've listened to everything each of you had to say about what happened in the past. Adanya placed her hand on Anaya's shoulder. I even talked to Aunt Anaya. She made me see life so clearly, through the eyes of innocence and a childlike faith. She showed me what love truly means. Love is unconditional. I do believe that you all did the best that you knew how to do at the time that you did it. I believe everything happened the way that it did for a reason. One of those reasons is so that I could be born and experience how blessed, and how loved I am by you all."

Adanya started to cry. "Mother." She looked directly at Annalisse. "Please forgive me. I was wrong to treat you the way I did. You have been by my side all of my life. You have loved me and cared for me. You taught me about the love of God. You have shown me how to be a lady. And I'm so thankful for you."

Breaking her eye connection with Annalisse, she looked at Joe Hunt then back at Annalisse. "I'm glad to see that you're getting on with your life. I hope happiness follow you everywhere you go, Mother."

Annalisse smiled, nodded, and wiped tears from her eyes.

"Each of you provided me with a life that has overflowed with blessings." She turned toward her grandparents. "Gram. Gramps, thank you for your guidance and for never giving up on me."

Lastly, Adanya looked at Anaya who had never stopped eating. "Aunt Anaya, I love you so much."

"I love you too, Pretty Adanya."

"I feel like this is the beginning of better and brighter things for the future of our family. I once asked my dad, 'What's blood got to do with it? Well, I finally understand that the blood of this family is what connects us; joins us together as one. Through all of this, I have come to realize that blood, our spiritual blood, has everything to do with it. "

THE END

Words From The Author

How important is family? How much are you willing to forgive your family when they wrong you? Today there are many dysfunctional families. As I think about that word, dysfunctional, I wonder if there are any families that are NOT dysfunctional. I have come to the conclusion that all families have some type of dysfunction. If they did not, that would mean that they are perfect, and as you know there is none perfect, not one. If there is no one that is perfect, then how can families be perfect? The answer: they can't.

But, you know what? Knowing that every family is dysfunctional in some shape, form, or fashion only means that we cannot get around God. We need God in every area of our lives. It makes no difference whether we need him as an individual, or as a collective body, the fact remains we need Him.

Without God, the family will fall apart. Much of that is happening today because society as a whole wants to strip God out of everything, and from everywhere. Society wants to put Him away and keep Him away. Nowadays it isn't the proper thing to do to mention God. Our children and grandchildren are limited as to what they can publicly do when it comes to their Christian faith.

That is why it is important that we not allow society, government, or any organized religion to destroy the family. Yes, families may be dysfunctional, but they do not have to be destroyed. We have a savior who though we are weak, though we make mistakes, though we hurt each other sometimes in our family structure, we can maintain the family as long as we keep God first.

Learn forgiveness when family members wrong you.

Learn how to seek God's face for strength and direction when you feel that there is nothing that can be done to salvage your family.

Look in the mirror. See what role you have played, or are playing in the disintegration of your family. Learn and remember that love is the key. Forgiveness is necessary. Relying on God is a must if you want your family to stand under the pressures of a world that is quickly going on a downward spiral.

Look up to the hills from whence cometh your help. Know that all of your help comes from God. He is the ruler and He can heal the broken areas of our lives. He can heal families. He can save children, and deliver parents. He can do any and everything, but we must rely on him.

Adanya experienced some harsh things in her life because of the decisions her family made. They made many mistakes, but the bottom line remains: family is still family. She had to learn that even the worst mistakes are worthy of forgiving. She had to learn to look within herself, and recognize her own shortcomings, her own faults, her own weaknesses.

Family is important. Whether your family is dysfunctional, dissected, damaged, or destroyed, God is able to restore, reunite, resurrect, and revitalize it.

Discussion Questions

1.How did Anaya have the mental capacity to give Adanya a name that fits in with the family name structure?

2. Was the family right to keep the truth from Adanya? Why or why not?

3. If you believe Adanya should have been told the truth, at what age or time would it have been appropriate to tell her?

4. Do you know anyone who is autistic? If so, how does autism affect them?

5. What role did Maurice and Eva Kaplan play in the family?

6. Would you say that Adanya grew up in a 'good' family? What makes a good family?

7. Do you know of someone who has led or is leading a double life? What affects can it have or does it have on the family?

8. Do you believe Bleak knew who Adanya was when he first approached her?

9.Do you believe Bleak and Adanya could have had a relationship despite their family connection?

10. Discuss the relationship Adanya had with her father? Are daughters closer to their fathers than sons? Why or why

not?

11. How did Annalisse feel about Adanya?

12. Do you believe the fact that this was an upper middle class family affected the family dynamics?

13. If this was an average family, would the secret about Adanya have been kept hush-hush or would it have been out in the open from the very beginning?

14. How do you feel about Carla's relationship with John Phillips?

15. Was Carla wrong, dumb, stupid, or just plain in love for the way she reacted about her husband?

16. Could you forgive someone like John Phillips? Why or why not? (Male or female)

17. What does family mean to you?

18. Is there ever a time when you should cut your family off? Why or why not?

19. Were Bleak and Adanya in love?

20. Should Annalisse have done some time for her crime?

21. What is the significance of the title of this story as it relates to the characters and the overall story line?

A Personal Invitation from the Author

If you have not made a decision to accept Jesus Christ as your personal Lord and Savior, God himself extends this invitation to you.

If you have not trusted Him and believed Him to be the giver of eternal life, you can do so right now. We do not know the second, the minute, the hour, the moment, or day that God will come to claim us. Will you be ready?

The Word of God says:
"If you confess with your mouth, 'Jesus is Lord,' and believe in your heart that God raised him from the dead, you will be saved. For it is with your heart that you believe and are justified, and it is with your mouth that you confess and are SAVED" (Romans 10:9-10 NIV).

To arrange signings, book events,
or speaking engagements with the author,
contact books@shelialipsey.com

To send your personal comments to the author please contact:
books@shelialipsey.com

Connect Via Social Media http://twitter.com/shelialipsey
Shelia E. Lipsey Readers on Facebook Urban Christian
Authors Group on Facebook Web site –www.shelialipsey.com
www.perfectstoriesaboutimperfectpeople.com
www.UCHisglorybookclub.net

Thank you for supporting my literary career!

Remember to
Live Your Dreams Now!

Shelia E. Lipsey, God's Amazing Girl

CPSIA information can be obtained at www.ICGtesting.com
Printed in the USA
LVOW06s0048041213

363802LV00001B/122/P